STARCROSS

STARCROSS

OR

THE COMING OF THE MOOBS!

OR

OUR ADVENTURES IN THE FOURTH DIMENSION!

A Stirring Tale of British Vim upon the Seas of Space and Time!

As Narrated by ART MUMBY, Esq.
(& Miss Myrtle Mumby)
to Their Amanuensis, MR PHILIP REEVE,
& Illuminated Throughout by DAVID WYATT

GOD SAVE THE QUEEN!

PRESENTED FOR THE EDIFICATION OF A GRATEFUL PUBLIC BY
BLOOMSBURY PUBLISHING PLC
SOHO SQUARE, LONDON, EARTH.
2007.

First published in Great Britain in 2007 by Bloomsbury Publishing Plc
36 Soho Square, London, W1D 3QY

A CIP catalogue record of this book is available from the British Library

ISBN 978 0 7475 8913 6

The paper this book is printed on is certified by the © Forest Stewardship Council 1996 A.C. (FSC).
It is ancient-forest friendly. The printer holds FSC chain of custody SGS-COC-2061.

FSC
Mixed Sources
Product group from well-managed
forests and other controlled sources
Cert no. SGS-COC-2061
www.fsc.org
© 1996 Forest Stewardship Council

Typeset by Dorchester Typesetting Group Ltd
Printed in Great Britain by Clays Ltd, St Ives Plc

1 3 5 7 9 10 8 6 4 2

www.larklight.co.uk
www.bloomsbury.com

For the reader's safety, this volume has been baked in a Snagsby & Co. Patent Book Oven,
and is certified free from Unearthly Animalculae, Harmful Spores and the dreaded Sequel Bloat.

For Sarah & Sam — P.R.
For Natalie — D.W.

CONTENTS

*The grand hotel at Starcross sleeps peacefully tonight
beneath a sky dusty with stars.*

Prologue

The grand hotel at Starcross sleeps peacefully tonight beneath a sky dusty with stars. Starlight slants down upon the sandstone bluffs which rise behind it, and silvers its ornate roofs and myriad windows. Starlight glitters upon the sea which fills the broad bay before it, a velvet blackness flecked with shimmering scales. And starlight falls upon the wary faces of the pair who suddenly fling wide the glass doors marked 'Reception' and come running down the steps on to the promenade. A handsome, bearded gentleman and a young lady of elfin beauty. We must forgive the gentleman if he lets the door slam behind him. And if his fair companion mutters something not *quite* ladylike beneath her breath as she descends, perhaps it may be excused. For they are Sir Richard and Mrs Ulla Burton, agents of Her Majesty's Secret Service, and they are running for their lives.

They reach the balustrade
at the promenade's edge
together, and vault over it.
The gravity is suddenly gentler
here, away from the influence
of the hotel's generators, and
Sir Richard and his pretty wife
drift down in a dreamlike way and
land with two soft scrunches in
the sand. Ahead of them the white
waves curl and crisp upon the shore,
and a row of candy-striped bathing
machines stands silent and dark along
the strand. Sir Richard runs to the closest,
but Ulla hisses, 'No, dearest – that is the
first place they will look!' She points instead to
where a little rowing boat has been drawn up on
the sand, and together they hasten over and start to
shove it forward into the white foam of the breaking waves.

And then, without warning, they feel a falling sensation,
a sense of dizziness that makes Sir Richard clutch a hand to
his brow, and Ulla reach out and hold him to steady herself.
It is quickly past. But when they look up, the sea is gone.

The rowing boat sits beached on the sands of a bone-dry desert which stretches away to a hard horizon, not ten miles distant. Beyond that, the sky is cluttered with small, lumpish, unwelcoming, stony worlds.

Behind him, Sir Richard hears the sand crunch. Sun-bleached canvas flaps softly in the night wind as something emerges from the shadow of the bathing machines. It is a red-and-white striped booth – an automated Punch & Judy show of the type that you may have seen upon the promenades of Bognor or Brighton. Inside the opening a fearsome, hook-nosed puppet suddenly rears up, seeming to focus on Ulla and Sir Richard with its painted eyes.

'*Hello, boys and girls!*' it squawks.

Sir Richard pulls out his service revolver and empties all six chambers through the front of the booth. Black holes spot the striped canvas like ink blots, and the impact of the bullets sends the whole contraption shuddering backwards. But as the echoes of the shots fade and the cloud of powder smoke thins, the booth begins to creep implacably towards him again.

'*That's the way to do it!*' crows Mr Punch.

From within her clothes Ulla whips out a slender, sickle-shaped throwing knife and sends it whirling towards the booth, neatly slicing off the puppet's leering head before flying back into her waiting hand.

Yet still the devilish machine advances!

The Burtons start to run towards a ramp which will return them to the promenade. But already another of the sinister sideshows is descending to cut off their escape. They turn again, and strike out across the dry sand, where the sea rolled until so recently. A hundred yards away a knoll which was an island when the sea was there offers some hope of shelter, or at least a patch of high ground which they may defend against the automata!

The wheels of the two Punch & Judy shows squeak as they swing round and begin to trundle after the fugitives. Ghastly, mechanised voices demand, '*Who's got the sausages?*'

The former island is steep sided; it is a scramble to get up on to its crown, which is planted with ornamental clumps of Martian horsetails and tickler vines. A clump of ogleweed turns curiously to watch Sir Richard and his wife as they clamber on to the summit. Below them the first of the Punch & Judy booths extends steel arms and starts to drag itself up after them.

They stand, and turn, and find more enemies awaiting them. Six figures, not all of them human. The starlight spilling through the leaves lends an oily sheen to their tall, black silk hats and imparts a ghostly glow to their white gloves and starched white shirt fronts. In the shadows of their hat brims gleam the circular eye-pieces of hideous, wheezing, elephant-trunked masks: patent respirators of the

type worn by men who have business in the atmospheres of gas-moons like Spiv and Phizzgig.

'Dick Burton!' says one of these grim apparitions, stepping in front of the others. 'And dear Mrs Burton, too. Surely you're not leaving us already?'

Ulla draws her knife again, but the Punch & Judy show has scrambled up unnoticed behind her. Steel arms lunge out from beneath its canvas cowl and pinion her, twisting her arm until the blade falls uselessly in the gravel. 'Richard!' she gasps. 'Run! Flee while you still can, and warn them . . .'

But it is already too late. Sir Richard is in the clutches of the second of these sinister booths. The infernal machines turn them to face their captors. The leader of the masked men advances warily, reaching into a pocket as he comes.

'You unspeakable fiend!' growls Sir Richard. 'Unhand my wife, or –'

'Or *what*, Burton?' Laughter bubbles behind the respirator. 'Don't you understand? You have lost! I shall have my way here, and there is nothing your department can do to stop me!'

Out of his pocket comes a small brass atomiser, such as fashionable ladies use to spray on scent. He holds it near Sir Richard's face and squeezes the rubber bulb, just once, quite firmly. Sir Richard sneezes, engulfed for a moment in a cloud of silver particles, which fades almost instantly. Swiftly the masked man turns and does the same to Ulla.

Sir Richard stares at the atomiser. 'What have you – done . . . ?'

Already his voice is growing slow and slurred. His eyes dull. His struggles cease. In the starlight, his skin is taking on a silvery look.

'Release them,' says the man in the silk hat.

The Punch & Judy booths back away. Ulla reaches out groggily to take Sir Richard's hand. Together they stumble off the path, trying to make their escape through the shrubs which cluster in the flower bed there. After a few steps Sir Richard stops and stands still. He raises his arms.

'Richard!' cries Ulla weakly, clinging to him, but he cannot hear her. She, too, is changing, taking on that dazed, glazed silveryness. Their toes force a way out through the leather of their boots and curl down into the soil. Their fingers bud. Ulla lets out a last sigh, like the sighing of wind through leaves. She is a tree, wrapped about the trunk of the slightly larger tree that was her husband.

The men in silk hats carefully cut away the scraps of clothing which are snagged on the roots and branches of the new trees, and walk away. For a while, all is silent, save for the uneasy muttering of a nearby bed of mumbleweed. Then, quite suddenly, the sounds of the sea return.

Chapter One

In Which We Deplore the Din of Decorators and
Receive a Most Intriguing Invitation.

W hat a fuss! What storms of dust! What
cannonades of hammering and what snarling
of wood-saws! What quantities of sawdust and
shavings heaping up upon the stairs and filling the very air,
making the poor hoverhogs sneeze and cough! What
endless, topsy-turvy rearrangements of the household
furniture! What confusion!

In short, we had the decorators in. Larklight, our dear old house, which has hung in its lonely orbit north of the Moon for goodness knows how long, gathering space dust and barnacles and generally declining into a picturesque decay, was being renovated from top to bottom.* Mother had come home from her long captivity among the First Ones' webs quite determined to see the old place dragged into the Nineteenth Century at last, and Father, once he had overcome his surprise at learning that she was actually a four-and-a-half-thousand-million-year-old entity from another star, was only too happy to spend some of his income from the Royal Xenological Institute satisfying her feminine desire for new rugs and the latest wallpapers.

* Even though it has neither, technically.

Yet I do not think that even Mother, with all her other-worldly knowledge and vast experience, had quite reckoned on how much disruption would be involved: workmen in the parlour, sawdust in the tea, the thud of hammers and the growl of drills drowning out my sister Myrtle's piano practice . . .* And it had been going on for absolute ages. When Mother secured the services of Mr Chippy Spry, General Builder & Specialist in Orbital Property Maintenance, he had assured her that his work would be done by mid-July. But September came, and still there was no sign that his carpenters and paper-hangers would ever be done.

I well remember one morning in particular. We had all taken refuge in Mother's conservatory, and were gathered

* So, you see, it was not *all* bad.

around a little table there among her pots of space flowers. Father was perusing a recent copy of the London *Times*, Myrtle was declining French verbs in her notebook with a wistful air, Mother was opening a pile of letters lately forwarded from the Lunar Post Office at Port George, and I was puzzling without much success over some problems in Long Division which she had set me. I believe that she had been rather startled to find that I had reached the grand old age of almost twelve without any sort of formal education, and had determined to Take Me In Hand. (Though what use Long Division might be to me in later life I could not then guess, and cannot now. My heart was set upon becoming an explorer, and I should much rather have spent my mornings learning Martian Ideograms or studying charts of the Trans-Jovian Aether.)*

Yes, we made a pretty scene as we sat there, an English family united. Yet even there we could not quite escape Mr

---

* Mother was concerned about Myrtle's education, too, for it seemed to have been confined to piano playing and deportment. She kept asking anxiously whether Myrtle would not like to study for some Career or Profession, for, as she said, 'This is the Nineteenth Century, Myrtle, dear, and many avenues of life which were once purely the preserve of men are now wide open to members of the fairer sex.' Had not Mother's dear friend, Miss Marian Evans, lately been

Spry's siege. For some of Mother's flowers had picked up a popular music hall song from one of his carpenters, and kept singing it over and over in their ethereal little voices. It was called 'My Flat Cat', and it went:

> *Oh what a pity,*
> *My poor Kitty,*
> *Peg him on the washing line to dangle!*
> *Pa's new auto-maid,*
> *Our clumsy clockwork laundry-aid,*
> *Put poor Kitty through the mangle!*

It was rather a jolly song, and I tapped my foot in time to the refrain as I struggled with the knotty problem of forty-four thousand and two divided by seventeen.

appointed editor of the *Westminster Review*? But Myrtle insisted that a lady does not seek anything so common as Paid Employment, and continued playing her horrible piano, and embroidering improving samplers. However, she did agree to learn a little French, for, as she said, 'then I may write my diary in French, and if *A Certain Person* is ever tempted to steal bits of it again, he will be most aggrieved to find he cannot read it!'

Now poor Kitty looks highly unconventional:
Six foot wide but only two-dimensional . . .

But my sister, Myrtle, has no time whatever for what she calls 'vulgar music'. As the flowers began again at the beginning of the first verse she wailed, 'Oh, Blast and Drat you!' and hurled her notebook at them, scattering petals everywhere. The flowers turned away, humming softly in a wounded manner, and Mother, Father and I exchanged a Look.

We all knew, you see, that it was not the song flowers which had put Myrtle in such a tearing rage. We knew that the real fault lay with Jack Havock. She had developed a sentimental attachment to that young space pirate during our adventures together the previous year, and to my utter astonishment Jack had appeared to return her feelings. But once he left

Larklight aboard his newly repaired aether-ship, *Sophronia*, we heard no more of him. Myrtle had been writing poems ever since, and striking soulful poses on all the balconies in the manner popularised by Mariana in the Moated Grange. About once a week she sent Jack a long, heartfelt letter, to which he did not reply.

My own suspicion was that as soon as he was back upon the aether seas Jack had realised what an absolute blight she was and what a narrow escape he had had, and resolved to have nothing more to do with her. But Mother always tried to comfort Myrtle, reminding her that Jack now sailed under the orders of Her Majesty's Secret Service, and might e'en now be undercover in some far-off corner of the sky, where the mails are slow and unreliable. Even if he had received her letters, he might be much too busy to pen a reply.

'Their singing *is* somewhat distracting, isn't it?' she said gently, as hoverhogs scooted about, gobbling up the drifting petals, and Father delved behind the watering can for Myrtle's notebook. 'Perhaps you should ask Mr Spry's men to move your piano up here, so that you may teach the flowers some new songs.'

'Oh, please, no!' I groaned, imagining them all warbling

out-of-tune versions of 'Birdsong at Eventide' and other selections from *A Young Gentlewoman's Pianoforte Primer*. But Mother gave me a warning glance, and Myrtle gave me a warning kick on the shin with her surprisingly hefty boot, so I did not warm to my theme.

'Now, what have we here?' Mother asked, turning back to her pile of letters. 'This one looks rather important. Do you think it is from some newspaper, requesting a True Account of Larklight's journey to London?'

'Oh, I do hope not!' cried Myrtle.*

But when Mother slit open the stiff, white envelope, what fell out was not a missive from the yellow press, but a letter written on crisp, monogrammed stationery, along with a printed advertisement. Myrtle and I each made a grab for the latter, and I won. It turned out to be a flyer advertising a new hotel in the asteroid belt, and I reproduce it here.

---

* Ever since that day in May when our house had miraculously been transported into the skies above the capital, hopeful journalists and newspaper proprietors had been pestering Mother, no doubt sensing some mystery about her. Myrtle lived in fear that they would find out the truth. 'I shall never be received in society if it becomes known that my mother is four and a half thousand million years old!' she told me once.

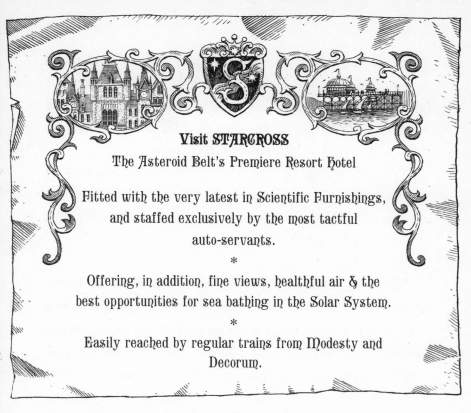

Visit STARCROSS
The Asteroid Belt's Premiere Resort Hotel

Fitted with the very latest in Scientific Furnishings,
and staffed exclusively by the most tactful
auto-servants.

*

Offering, in addition, fine views, healthful air & the
best opportunities for sea bathing in the Solar System.

*

Easily reached by regular trains from Modesty and
Decorum.

'Sea bathing?' I cried, in disbelief. In preparation for my future career as an explorer I make a keen study of the *Boy's Own Journal* and other organs of note, and I was almost certain that there was no sea to speak of in the asteroid belt.

'Let me see that,' said Myrtle, wrenching the paper from my grasp (and crumpling it rather badly in the process, as you can see).

'How sweet!' said Mother, who had been too engrossed in her letter to notice this little display of filial love and affection. She held the letter and read aloud what was written there.

My Dear Mr and Mrs Mumby,

I wonder if you remember me. My name is Mortimer Titfer, and I had the pleasure of meeting you and your darling children while you were in London in the spring, after those regrettable occurrences at Hyde Park.

('I confess, I cannot call the gentleman to mind,' admitted Mother.

'We met so many people at that time,' Father agreed.

'If he thinks Art is a darling,' said Myrtle tartly, 'it makes one wonder whether he really met us at all. Perhaps he has mistaken us for some other Mumbys.')

The letter went on:

I was speaking of you only the other day to my dear friend Sir Waverley Rain, and was distressed to learn that you are currently afflicted by builders. Therefore I thought that I might

*take the liberty of writing to invite you to visit me at Starcross.
It is a modest asteroid, which was a mining concern until it was
abandoned in the reign of the late king. I have, however, made
some improvements, and the hotel there offers the most genteel
accommodation, and some of the finest sea bathing to be had
anywhere in British Space. I should be honoured if you would
consider using the place as a refuge or 'home-from-home' while
the horny-handed sons of toil improve your own house.*

*Your Obedient Servant,
Mortimer Titfer, Esq.*

'What a sweetly kind offer!' said my mother.

'Yes, but who is this Titfer?' asked Father. 'I do not
recognise the name.'

'He says he is a friend of Sir Waverley's,' Mother
reminded him, 'and that is good enough for me. For though
Sir Waverley is somewhat reclusive, he is a very sweet
gentleman when one gets to know him. Take, for an
instance, the way that he took it upon himself to help us
strip out Larklight's old Shaper engine and cart it off to be
melted down, without charging us for carriage or any other
thing. I would imagine that this Titfer is a business

acquaintance of his, and clearly shares his kind and thoughtful nature. Now that I come to think of it I believe I *do* recall being introduced to someone of the sort at that reception we attended in Kensington . . .'

'So may we go?' I asked. For it is not every day that a chap gets offered the chance to go swimming on an asteroid, and I was all agog to know if Mother and Father would accept this invitation.

'It is most kind,' Father agreed, peering over Mother's shoulder at the letter. 'Alas! *I* cannot go. I have to travel down to London next week, there to present a report on my investigations into *Tegenaria saturnia* to the Fellows of the Royal Xenological Institute. But there is no reason why *you* should not go, Emily, my dear, and take Art and Myrtle with you.'

'Oh, I could not think of leaving you behind, Edward,' cried my mother, though I could tell that she was thinking how nice a holiday would be.

'I should love to see the asteroids,' I ventured, as wistfully as I could. 'We soared through the belt at such speed when I was travelling aboard the *Sophronia* that I had barely time to catch a glimpse of them.'

Myrtle said approvingly, 'Starcross looks most genteel.'

'Well,' said Mother, 'perhaps we *might* go, for just a week or two . . .'

'Go for a month,' said Father, folding his copy of *The Times* in a decided manner. 'And I shall join you as soon as my business in London is complete.'

And so it was agreed. Trunks were packed, straw hats and shrimping nets fetched down* from the attic, and Mother ordered new bathing costumes for us all. And a week later we found ourselves bidding Father a fond farewell at the Port George aether-dock and going aboard the packet-ship *Euphrosyne*, outbound for Modesty and the Minor Planets.

* Or was it up?

Chapter Two

A Brief Description of the Asteroid Belt. By the
Good Offices of the A.B. & M.P. Rail Traction Co. Ltd
We Are conveyed to Starcross and Are Surprised at
What We Find There.

I wonder if you know the Asteroids at all. There are a
great many of them, and they tumble along in an orbit
which lies midway between those of Mars and Jupiter.
I have asked Mr Wyatt to provide sketches of a few of the
more interesting ones.

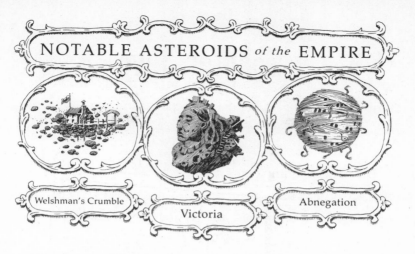

NOTABLE ASTEROIDS *of the* EMPIRE

Welshman's Crumble

Victoria

Abnegation

These worlds are home to countless millions of intelligent beings, mostly Earth people, Martians and Jovians who have travelled there in the employ of the big mining concerns. The asteroids are supposed to be the ruins of a planet which once swam there but was long ago destroyed, or else the building blocks of one which never formed – the scientific coves who study such things have never quite been able to decide. Several times on our voyage to Starcross I started to ask Mother about it, for the whole Solar System is her handiwork and I was sure that she would know the answer. But each time I began, I was rewarded with a vicious kick to the shins from Myrtle, and deemed it wiser to speak of something else instead. Myrtle does not like to hear Mother talking about her various previous lives, and would have been mortified if any of our fellow passengers had got wind of the many forms Mother had adopted over the millennia – a giant slime mould, a pre-Adamite reptile, a Martian princess and Heaven knows what else.

But one evening, about halfway through our voyage, while Mother and I were taking a turn upon the star deck and Myrtle was curled up in our state-room with her notebook, trying to think of things which rhymed with 'Havock', Mother raised the matter herself.

We were looking at the dim red lantern that was Mars, hanging in the dark just off the *Euphrosyne*'s port bow, and looking shimmery and ghostly through the ship's veil of alchemical particles. Suddenly Mother said, 'Did you know, Art, that our destination used to be a part of Mars?'

'Do you mean Starcross?' I asked.

'The very same. The rest of the asteroids are nothing but leftovers: bits and bobs which I half meant to build into another world, but never quite got round to. But Starcross is a mighty fragment of the Red Planet, which was blasted out to hang among the other asteroids by some immense collision or eruption about one hundred million years ago.'

'You do not know which?'

'I do not know *everything*, Art, dear. I was living in the seas of Georgium Sidus at the time it happened. How you would laugh if you could see me as I was then, all gills and fins! It was only several millennia later, when I returned to Larklight, that I noticed the new asteroid, and the crater on Mars which told me whence it came. Look, I believe you can see that crater still!'

And she showed me a sort of dimple on the ruddy cheek of Mars, a gentle depression perhaps a thousand miles across, and quite impossible to connect with the immense catastrophe of which she'd spoken.

I took her hand, and together we went for another turn about the star deck, nodding to our fellow passengers, Mother calling out cheerfully in Ionian to the startled sailors, who had never met an Earth lady who could master their complicated language before. And it felt very strange and wonderful to have a mother such as she.

The *Euphrosyne* docked at Modesty, one of the larger and more settled of the asteroids. In some parts of the belt thousands upon thousands of miles separate those drifting worldlets, but in others they clump quite close together, and

the twin asteroids, Modesty and Decorum, lie at the centre of just such a clump.

It would be neither economical nor prudent for aether-ships to fly to all those different little worlds, since some are very little indeed, and in the gulfs betwixt them all sorts of rock and grit and astral debris hangs, posing a danger to shipping. However, good old British know-how* has found a way around this difficulty. The Asteroid Belt and Minor Planets Rail Traction Company Ltd has constructed a splendid system of bridges and viaducts which link more than a hundred asteroids, with new termini being added to the system almost yearly. Some of these bridges span distances of well over a thousand miles, and make the beholder feel especially proud to be British.

* Huzzah!

It was upon this fine railway that we were to complete our journey to Starcross. We disembarked at the Modesty & Decorum Aether Harbour, bidding farewell to our fellow passengers, and set out across the busy docks to the ringing steel and crystal vaults of Modesty Station. Above the entrance a massive advertisement hoarding was being erected, bearing a picture of a top hat and the words, **TITFER'S TOP-NOTCH TOPPERS – NONE TALLER, NONE BLACKER**. I had not heard of such a make, and I asked Mother if the Titfer responsible was *our* Mr Titfer, at whose hotel we were to stay, but I could not make my question heard above the hubbub of the station.

'The train on platform 116b is the three o'clock to Chalcedony,' boomed a voice which sounded like that of God from fluted speakers on the roof. *'Calling at Vesta, New Rutland, Ivanhoe, Cribbage and Thring.'* The enticing smells of roasted chestnuts and fresh sprune drifted from vendors' booths, station staff blew whistles and fluttered multi-coloured flags, and a tricephalid muffin man stalked past with a tray of his mouth-watering wares balanced on each of his heads.

And through it all, with one eye on her *Bradshaw's Timetable* and the other on the ever-changing destinations which flickered upon the clattering mahogany departure boards, Mother led us unerringly to platform 237b, where waited a train of dark, windowless freight cars with a few passenger carriages attached at the end, their doors painted with a reassuringly sober coat-of-arms: **GRAND HOTEL STARCROSS**.

We went aboard and Mother paid our Ionian porters, who gave our luggage into the care of the train's attendant: a gleaming clockwork automaton, one of the latest models from Sir Waverley Rain's factory, and close cousin to the ones he had given us to help at Larklight. It seemed we were the only passengers that afternoon, for all the compartments were empty. We chose the one we liked the best, and arranged ourselves on its plush, well-padded seats, where we accepted the cups of tea which the auto-waiter served us, and prepared to enjoy the ride. It is almost ten thousand miles from Modesty to Starcross, but in the near frictionless aether the trains are able to reach enormous speeds, and I gathered that our journey would take but a few hours.

I settled myself next the window, looking forward to

spectacular views of such strange worlds as Vestibule, which is hollow, and inhabited by people who live upside down upon its inner surface, and Abnegation, which was woven out of brown string by Presbyterians.

But as the train started up and we began to pull out of the arched maw of the station, opening up thrilling views across the shunting yards towards the aether harbour, I saw something which startled me, and was to cast a little cloud over our trip. Moored at a launching tower there, among a gaggle of more ordinary ships, hung one that I should have known anywhere. That barnacled wooden hull and crooked bowsprit; those battered exhaust-trumpets and much-darned aether-wings. 'Why,' I blurted out, ''Tis the *Sophronia*!'

I regretted it at once, of course. Myrtle, who had been leafing happily through a journal called *The Young Lady's Orbital Miscellany*, sprang to my side at the mention of Jack Havock's ship, and stared out through the thick crystal of the window, quivering like a gun dog.

'Then he is *not* facing peril in some far-off corner of the sky,' she said, gazing out at the *Sophronia* until a passing train hid her from our view. 'He is here on Modesty, in the heart of British Space, and yet *still* he has not answered my letters.'

She slumped into her seat again, like a marionette with all

Moored at a launching tower there, among a gaggle of more ordinary ships, hung one that I should have known anywhere.

its strings cut. Honestly, I thought she was about to blub. I hope that *I* shall never form a Sentimental Attachment with anyone, for it seems to lead to nothing but tantrums and melancholia.

'Poor Myrtle,' said Mother, gently smoothing her hair. 'Perhaps we should ask the auto-porter if it is possible to turn the train back. We might find Jack aboard his ship, and –'

'No,' said Myrtle, with a deeply spiritual sigh. 'I would not think of it! It is clear that he does not wish to see me. I was his plaything for an idle hour, but now that he is out doing manly deeds in the aether again he has thought better of all those tender words which passed between us at Larklight.' A tear sneaked out from behind her spectacles and dropped into her tea,* and she lowered her head on to a handy hatbox, and remained there, like Isabella with her Pot of Basil,† for the next two thousand miles.

I must confess that I felt hurt by Jack's behaviour, too. I

---

* All First Class carriages on the Asteroid Belt and Minor Planets Railway are all fitted with gravity generators, though passengers who travel second class spend a great deal of the journey bobbing about on the ceiling with their luggage.

† This is a Clever Literary Reference to the poem by KEATS. I am not *entirely* ignorant, whatever Myrtle says.

had thought him a friend, and it seemed unamiable of him to act so aloof. If only he had written and told us the *Sophronia* was putting in at Modesty, I thought, we might have broken the journey there and looked him up! And I felt suddenly a strong desire to see again his crew, Mr Munkulus and Mr Grindle, brave blue Ssilissa, the Tentacle Twins and my good, true crab friend, Nipper!

However, time is a great healer, and after a minute or two I emerged from that fog of nostalgia, and sat with my nose pressed to the window and my hands cupped around my face to blot out the reflections of the carriage gas lamps and the mournful figure of my sister. Outside, whole worlds flicked past us in the wink of an eye: verdant asteroids like hanging baskets, covered in tulip fields or golden crops of wheat; manufacturing worldlets bristling with chimneys, where furnaces glowed through a pother of factory smoke. Sometimes our train plunged us through the interior of a tiny, hollowed-out world; sometimes it ran on for miles along singing silver trackways in the empty aether, and once, another train went by, roaring upside down along the underside of the same track, like our reflection. What could be more fascinating than to be whisked through the open aether aboard a speeding railway train?

Well, quite a few things, actually. Train travel in space is all very well while one is passing through a great asteroidal hub like the Modesty and Decorum clump, where worlds cluster thick and railway lines run alongside one's own, and entwine with each other like strands of spaghetti. But after a few hours we were out in the nether reaches, where the only things to see were mined-out rocks, dead, sere and drab, and even those were few and far between.

Somewhere nearby, back in 1804, Admiral Nelson had fought a famous battle against the aether-ships of some rebel Americans, and I looked out hopefully for the drifting wreckage of their flagship, the USSS *Liberty*, which had never been found. Naturally, I did not see anything nearly so romantic. Now and again I glimpsed a shoal of Aetheric Icthyomorphs, but they were small and far away, all the bigger forms having been hunted to extinction, or scared off by the trains. (The days when daring railway passengers used to roll down their carriage windows and take pot-shots at passing shoals of giant space jellyfish and aetheric manatee are long gone, worse luck!)

Mother, who has the knack of sleeping anywhere, was soon napping. Even Myrtle fell into a snooze, in which she sometimes murmured Jack Havock's name in a martyred

fashion. But I could not sleep, and I sat watching my own reflection in the trembling crystal of the window, and feeling my posterior become more and more benumbed.

At last the train began to slow, and the auto-guard came stumping along the corridor and slid open the door of our compartment to announce, 'Next stop, Starcross Halt.' We traversed a last, dark, echoey tunnel through the heart of a mined-out boulder called Scarcity, and I watched my own reflection in the window and waited wide-eyed for my first glimpse of Starcross.

'There!' cried Mother, just as eager as I, kneeling at the window as the train shot out from the shadows of the tunnel. Even Myrtle raised her head a little.

Ahead we could see the end of the line, a tiny world of reddish mountains with deserts of pale sand flashing in the starlight. I felt a great wave of excitement, and then, almost at once, a wave of disappointment even greater. I could see the roof of a small station, but precious little else. Starcross was just another old mining asteroid pitted with ugly craters. A few spindly aether-trees clung to the uninviting crags, while here and there some fragment of old pithead winding gear jutted up like a gibbet. Where was Sir Waverley's hotel? I wondered. For the only building I could see, apart from the station itself, was the ruin of some old mine-owner's mansion, which stood among the spoil-heaps, stark white and empty windowed, like a gigantic skull.

Chapter Three

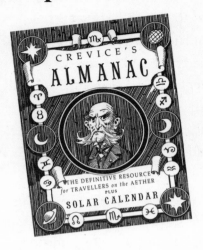

WE ARRIVE AT THE GRAND HOTEL AND ARE MADE
WELCOME BY ITS MYSTERIOUS PROPRIETOR.

'Oh, I declare!' cried Myrtle, as the train bore us
down a last long curve towards that dismal world,
with its lonely cluster of station buildings. 'We
have been practised upon! Mr Titfer's invitation was but a
foolish prank, and we have come all this way for nought!'

I was inclined to agree. Even Mother seemed downcast.
Then I looked again at the grim mansion, and saw that I had

been mistaken. Some trick of the light – some passing haze or optical illusion – had made it look a perfect ruin. Indeed, it still seemed to have a hazy, wavering, insubstantial look. But an instant later it stood out sharp and solid, and I could not understand how I had been deceived. It was no ruin at all, but rather a grand, elegant building, standing on a curved sweep of promenade which overlooked one of those dry, dead basins of white sand, its lofty Gothick turrets reaching up through the asteroid's thin atmosphere to touch the very tides of space.

The train descended a last long incline, and came to a halt beside a station platform with a painted canopy, hanging baskets full of song flowers, and its name,

STARCROSS HALT, picked out in white stones upon a bed of space thyme. I saw several liveried automata waiting on the platform to help us with our luggage, a three-legged water tower looking for all the world like one of those fighting machines the ancient Martians used to employ, and on a siding beyond it a small hand-car standing idle, with asteroid light glinting off its glass canopy. It was as pretty a station as you can imagine.

Myrtle, however, was still dissatisfied. 'Mr Titfer promised us sea bathing,' she said fussily, as we made our way to the door. 'And yet there is no sea.'

I knew why she was so vexed. One of the big trunks which the auto-porter was heaving down on to the platform contained her new bathing costume, a very fashionable garment ordered straight from London, and I knew she had been looking forward to a little graceful swimming in it.

'Perhaps the place is still under construction,' Mother said. 'I gather it is not unknown for these resort hotels to advertise themselves as their proprietors hope they will one day be, rather than as they really are.'

'Perhaps Mr Titfer plans to import some sea from another, more watery sphere, and set it down in that dry depression in front of the promenade!' I said, for I well knew that all manner of things are possible in this great age of engineering and invention in which we live.

We stood on the platform and looked towards the hotel. Behind us the train snorted and let out a single, shrill hoot before chuffing onward, past the station and on to a turntable where it would be spun about, ready to begin its journey back to Modesty. The station-master automaton who had waved it on its way turned and strode to where we stood, bowing low as he reached us.

'Welcome to Starcross,' he droned, and indicated a black metal carriage which waited nearby, with a pair of mechanical horses standing ready in the traces. 'The steam-brougham is available to convey you to the hotel, or . . .'

'I think we will walk, thank you,' replied Mother. 'We are all decidedly stiff after our journey, aren't we, children? I'm certain the exercise will do us good.'

'But do you not think,' asked Myrtle, as we left the station and started along a winding gravelled path towards the hotel, the porters following with our baggage, 'that the hotel has a rather silent, almost abandoned look?'

'Oh, that is easily explained,' said Mother, opening her purse and waving a thick buff pamphlet which she extracted from it. 'I have consulted Crevice, and I gather that here on Starcross it is the middle of the night.'*

We walked through the starlight of that sealess sea front, looking down over the promenade rail at where the bathing machines stood drawn up in a hopeful line at the edge of that bone-dry bay. About one hundred yards from the shore lay a knoll planted with shrubs and trees, and here and there on the slopes around the hotel stood spinneys of Martian

---

* Travellers among our extraterrestrial possessions have frequent cause to be grateful to Crevice's *Almanac*. After all, at any one time it might be three in the afternoon of the first of April on Mars, six in the morning on the third on Earth and twenty-five o'clock on the forty-fifth of Thribuary on Io. Professor Crevice's master-work provides useful tables for calculating what date and time it is, wherever you are in the Solar Realm.

birch, and other ornamental plantings. All else was drear, dead desolation. It was a melancholic vista, and I felt quite relieved when we turned our backs upon it and considered a more cheerful prospect: the entrance of the Grand Hotel,

where gas lamps were ablaze, casting a gentle amber glow down the red-carpeted steps. We climbed those steps, Mother pushed open the glass doors marked 'Reception' and we entered into a fairyland of gold and marble and gleaming Martian crystal.

Do you remember that poem which goes, 'In Xanadu did Kubla Khan a sacred pleasure dome decree'? Well, Mr Khan would have been as sick as a dog if he could have seen Starcross, because his old pleasure dome could not have held a candle to it for opulence and luxury. Fountains tinkled, chandeliers twinkled and startling works of modern art by Mr Rossetti and Mr Millais hung in gilded frames upon the walls. A herd of hoverhogs with the hotel's coat-of-arms painted on their spotless flanks snuffled about amid the finery, the faint poot-pooting sounds of their exhalations drowned out by the gentle voices of hanging baskets full of song flowers.

'Well!' said Mother. 'This is very grand!'

We approached the reception desk, a block of Martian mahogany polished like a mirror. An automaton behind it lurched to life as we drew near, and I heard clockwork whirr, and a needle drop on to one of the wax cylinders inside his head. But before he could speak, a human voice quite unlike the drone of an auto-servant, cried out, 'Mrs Mumby! And Miss Myrtle and Master Art as well!'

A door near the reception desk had been flung open, and a large, ruddy gentleman with black side-whiskers, tinted spectacles and a bottle-green coat came hurrying out to bow low before us and kiss my mother's hand.

'Mr Titfer, I presume?' said Mother.

'The very same, dear lady,' said the Titfer in question, straightening himself and beaming at us all, whiskers a-quiver. 'How very glad I am that you chose to accept my humble invitation. You've seen the promenade, I take it? As fine a stretch of sea frontage as a body could find anywhere in British Space.'

'Indeed, it is most picturesque,' said Mother. 'Tho' we could not help noticing the lack of –'

'Oh, here at Starcross you will lack for nothing!' boomed Mr Titfer. 'You need only ask! My hotel has a great number of staff, all eager to do your business. Not nasty, fallible human staff, mind, who would forever be falling in love with visiting valets and stealing the cufflinks of the Duke of ———. No, every last maid and bell-boy has been manufactured for me by Rain & Co. Why, even the manager is automatic! I am spending the summer here to ensure that everything is running smoothly, but once I return to London I expect the place to tick along quite nicely without any human guidance at all.' He checked his fob watch, and said hastily, 'But I must not detain you, for it is very late and I am sure you will wish to rest after your voyage. The auto-porters will take you to your rooms, and at breakfast you shall meet the other guests. The sea should be back by then, too.'

'Why, whatever do you mean?' asked Mother, smiling sweetly, as if she expected him to make a joke.

But Mr Titfer was in earnest. 'The sea, dear Mrs Mumby. I hope you do not think I had lured you here with the promise of a beach holiday only to make you look out at this dreary, desolate scene for your whole stay? No, no. My word is my bond. Starcross offers the finest sea bathing anywhere in the known worlds. It is simply that, ah, the *tide* is out at present.'

Still smiling, Mother turned to look out through the crystal windows at the promenade, and at the bone-dry, bone-white sandscape stretching away towards that hard horizon. A fitful breeze was blowing dust devils between the wheels of the bathing machines which waited mournfully in the starlight at the desert's edge. All else was as dry and still and silent as the land of Death.

'How long has the tide been out?' she asked.

'About one hundred million years.'

'And when does it come back in?'

'Oh, every twelve hours or so.'

'How *very* intriguing,' said Mother.

Chapter Four

IN WHICH I HAVE A CURIOUS ENCOUNTER, AND A LIGHT
BREAKFAST.

Our suite of rooms was at the very top of one of Starcross's airy turrets. One reached it by climbing a long spiral of stairs, a perfect cataract of blood-red carpet, barred with gilt stair-rods. You would hardly believe the view which we had from our sitting room! I flung wide the windows and stepped out on to the wrought-iron balcony outside, gazing up in wonder at a sky

full of tumbling asteroids. 'Look,' I cried. 'There is Vesta! And there is New Westmoreland, and Winnet, and the celebrated Ferrous Dumpling . . .'

But Mother and Myrtle only yawned, and declared that they wished to take a restorative nap before we all went down to breakfast.

There was a bed-room for each of us: the neatest, cleanest rooms you can imagine, each with a closet and a wash-stand and a brass bedstead. Myrtle and Mother retired to theirs, and I lay down in mine, but I could not sleep. I wanted to be up and *doing*, not wasting the first hours of my holiday in dull slumber! Oh, I put out the light and *tried* to sleep, but sleep would not come. I was aware of the distant humming of gravity generators deep in the hotel somewhere, and the gleam of asteroid light through the crack of my bedroom door. And I was aware, too, of a strange feeling that I needed to *open* that door and look out into our sitting room.

After a while I lit the lamp again, and gave into temptation. I eased the door open gently, for I could tell by the quality of the silence that Myrtle and Mother had both fallen asleep. The sitting room lay in darkness, except for the faint pale oblongs of the starlit French windows, and the lace curtains, which stirred like ghosts in a gentle breeze.

Cautious and expectant, I crossed the soft carpet and opened a closet. I had not noticed this closet earlier, yet now I somehow knew that it was there, and that I should find something intriguing inside it.

At first there seemed to be nothing inside but a dangle of wooden coat hangers, which I took care not to rattle, as I was afraid it would wake Mother and Myrtle. Then, on a shelf above me, I noticed a large hatbox. I lifted it down. It was made of stiff white card, and printed on the lid was this legend:

TITFER'S TOP-NOTCH TOPPERS

Taking the box into the glow of lamplight from my half-open bedroom door, I set it down on an occasional table, where I took off the lid. Inside, nestling in a lot of crisp crêpe paper, sat the tallest, blackest silk top hat I had ever seen. Even the lining was black, and without any label to say who had made it; but it did not need one, for I knew that Mr Titfer was the finest hatter in the Solar System, and a hat as splendid as this could only have been created by him.* I remember wondering what previous guest had left it behind in my closet, and why he had thought fit to bring such formal headgear to a beach resort.

---

* Which was odd, for you may remember that when I was at Modesty Station I was quite surprised to see an advertisement which connected his name with hats. But many odd things occurred at Starcross, as you shall shortly see.

And then, naturally, I felt an urge to put the hat on. But as I pushed aside the crinkling paper and made to lift it from its box a voice behind me whispered softly, 'Moob!'

I looked up, startled, the hat forgotten. 'Myrtle?' I breathed. But Myrtle was asleep; I could hear her maidenly snores through her bedroom door, and anyway, she is not the sort of girl who goes around saying 'Moob!' in the middle of the night.

'Moob?' came the voice again, sounding plaintive. Perhaps it was not a voice at all, I reasoned, but only the wind moaning around our turret. I went to the window, and found that I had left it ajar – that was why the curtains had been billowing in such a ghostly manner. I made to close it, then, on a sudden impulse, opened it wider instead and stepped out to stand upon the balcony once more. The air of Starcross was thin, and smelled like string.

'Moob!' whispered the voice, or the wind, or whatever it was. A shadow moved at the far end of the balcony and I almost yelped with fright. Then, telling myself not to be so funky, I edged towards the place. That part of the balcony was deeply shaded by the space ivy growing up the turret wall. Was it my imagining, or did two pale flames burn in the darkness there, no larger than the flames of safety matches, yet steady, and set side by side, for all the world like watchful eyes?

A cat, I thought, with some relief, and said, 'Here, puss, puss, puss . . .'

Suddenly I felt an odd lurching sensation and a wave of dizziness which made me snatch at the balcony rail for support. When it passed, the balcony was bathed in light. My own startled shadow was thrown against the wall, and another shadow, *a shadow cast by nothing that I could see*, slid like an oiled black eel between the railings of the balustrade.

I turned to search for it, and stopped, amazed. The inky sky with its scattering of asteroids was changed to a spotless dome of azure blue. Mid-morning sunlight filled it and shimmered on the waters of a bay which lay where, only seconds before, there had been nothing but a waterless sea of sand. The knoll was an island now, and the air was full of the invigorating scent of ozone. I could

hear the crisp sigh and snore of the little waves as they
curled in to break upon the shore, and see a troop of
burnished automata emerging from the hotel's side entrance
to pull down the awnings of the beach cafe, rake the sand
and untether the bathing machines.

I do not know how long I stood there, dumbstruck,
gawping at that sudden ocean. I did not move until I heard
the cheerful clamour of a gong, announcing
that it was time for breakfast.

In the breakfast room, just as Mr
Titfer had promised, we met some
of our fellow guests: a large,
flowery-looking lady, who beamed
most cheerfully at us as we entered, and
elbowed her small, meek husband so
that he looked up from his
scrambled egg and beamed too,
and an elderly gentleman with a
military air, who sat alone at a window-table, dividing his
toast into neat triangles and applying butter and marmalade
with brisk strokes of his knife.

Automated waiters saw us to our table and inquired in their flat voices whether we should like tea or coffee, brown toast or white?

'Why, tea, of course,' cried Myrtle, startled and mildly scandalised. 'We are English! And who on earth would want brown toast? White, with marmalade, if you please.'

The waiter executed a mechanical bow and went scudding silently off on well-oiled casters to fetch our breakfasts. As he left, my mother caught the eye of the military-looking gent, who seemed amused by Myrtle's outburst.

'We must tell Titfer to see if he can't make those clockwork men of his able to distinguish English guests from those from those of other nations, eh?' he chuckled. 'Pray permit me to introduce myself. I am Colonel Harry Quivering of Her Majesty's Martian Army (Ret'd).'

'Mrs Emily Mumby,' said my mother sweetly. 'And these are my children, Myrtle and Art.'

The colonel said that he was pleased to meet us, and that in his opinion it would liven the place up a bit to have some kids about. (You may imagine how this went down with Myrtle.) He went on to explain that he had been several weeks at Starcross. It was, he claimed, the best-appointed billet he had ever kipped in, and he had lived in his time everywhere from London to the wilds of Mercury. 'Titfer certainly knows his business,' he concluded.

'Indeed. I must say we are very impressed by the sea view,' said Mother, gazing out thoughtfully at the glittering blue expanse beyond the promenade. 'How does he do it, do you think?'

'I'm afraid I couldn't venture to say, ma'am,' said the colonel, spearing a kipper with the practised ease of one who has spent many years cactus-sticking in the badlands of Mars. 'Some sort of scientific miracle, I daresay. Science is advancing with such great leaps in the present age that it's impossible for an old soldier to keep up with it. One never knows what these brainy coves like Titfer will come up with next!'

'It is as if the hotel and the land about it, out as far as that small island in the bay, have been moved instantaneously through space to a warm and watery world,' mused Mother, looking out of the window at all the little dancing diamonds of light upon the sea. 'But short of a Shaper engine, I cannot think of a machine which could accomplish such a thing . . . And besides, what world has such oceans, apart from Earth, and we are not on Earth . . .'

'Oh, don't worry about how it comes to be here, ducks!' called the large, beaming lady. (She was addressing the colonel, but clearly hoping to be introduced to us. I felt Myrtle give a quiver of distaste at such forward behaviour.) 'Just 'op in an' enjoy it, I say! There's nothing like a nice dip for lifting the spirits, eh, Colonel?'

'Quite so, quite so,' the colonel chuckled, plainly approving of her good humour. He wolfed down a triangle of toast and introduced us. 'Mrs Mumby, children, this extraordinary lady is Mrs Rosie Spinnaker, that celebrated practitioner of the Terpsichore muse.'

'Ooh, 'ark at 'im!' cried Mrs Spinnaker, spraying toast crumbs over her companion. 'Don't you listen to his blandishments, my dearies. I'm just a simple songbird. "The Cockney Nightingale" they calls me, back 'ome in dear ol' London. Maybe you've 'eard that little ditty of mine . . .' and, beating time upon the table with a jam spoon, she launched into a chorus of 'My Flat Cat'.

Myrtle turned pale, and might have fainted had I not supported her. 'Can we never escape that abominable jingle?' she groaned.

'Eh?' asked the Cockney Nightingale, cupping a be-ringed hand to her ear. 'What's that? Speak up, dear! I'm quite deaf, you know!'

'Myrtle is something of a musician herself,' said Mother, to cover Myrtle's embarrassment. 'She is learning to play the pianoforte.'

'Ooh, so you tickle the ivories yourself, do you, ducks?' chortled Mrs Spinnaker. 'We'll have to have a recital, won't we, 'Erbert? My hubby, 'Erbert, is my usual accompanist, you see, but he's under the weather at the moment; sprained both wrists during my third encore at the Farpoo Apollo.' ('Erbert opened his mouth as if to add some explanation, but closed it again as his wife's stream of words went rushing on.) 'That's why we came here, see, for a rest cure. But if your Myrtle can play the old Joanna we'll be able to 'ave a lovely ol' sing-song, won't we? We'll do all the old

favourites – "My Flat Cat", "Were't Not for the Linnet", "Nobby Knocker's Noggin" ... Lord, what larks we'll 'ave!'

Myrtle glared at me as if it was all *my* idea, which I thought most unfair. But everyone else in the breakfast room seemed delighted by Mrs Spinnaker's proposal. Colonel Quivering raised his tea cup in a toast, and something which I had taken till then to be a large potted plant suddenly clapped its fronds together and said in a leafy sort of way, 'What an agreeable notion, Mrs S.!'

'Ah, Ferny!' called the colonel. 'Come and meet Mrs Mumby. Mrs Mumby, Art, Myrtle, this is Professor Ferny, the Educated Shrub.'

The professor, whom I saw had been standing with his roots in a large bowl of breakfast mulch, removed them, wiped them carefully upon a napkin and came rustling across the floor to our table. He bowed low and extended a broad leaf, which Mother, Myrtle and myself took turns to shake.

'Charmed, I'm sure,' he announced. 'I trust you will enjoy Starcross. Sea bathing is not to my taste, but perhaps you will do me the honour of visiting the gardens? Mr Titfer has asked me to help him with the planting there. Speaking of which, I fear I must leave you, ladies and gentlemen. I have some Screaming Lupin seedlings which will run quite wild if they are not potted up at once . . .'

'From Venus,' explained Colonel Quivering, as the sentient shrub departed. 'Grew from a seed brought back by Captain Cook. Turned out to be uncommonly intelligent. Director of Xenobotany at Kew Gardens now, I gather.'

Our toast and marmalade arrived, along with tea in a gleaming silver pot on clockwork legs, which poured itself. We ate, and drank, and Mother said, 'The hotel seems pleasantly quiet. Tell me, are we the only guests?'

'No, indeed, not quite,' said Colonel Quivering. 'There is a young French person, Miss Delphine Beauregard . . .'

'Such a sweet, beautiful young lady, poor thing!' cried

Mrs Spinnaker.

'She suffers from an Ailment or Malady,' confided the colonel.

'She is confined to a wicker bath chair,' said Mrs Spinnaker. 'And can go nowhere unless she is pushed about by her nurse . . .'

'The nurse is neither sweet, nor beautiful, I am afraid,' sighed Colonel Quivering.

'You shall see 'er for yourself quite soon, no doubt,' Mrs Spinnaker promised. 'She breakfasts early, and has 'er nurse push 'er along the promenade to take the morning air.'

'Perhaps you and Miss Beauregard may be friends,' said Mother to Myrtle. 'It would be an opportunity for you to practise your French conversation . . .'

'And don't forget the Honourable Ignatius Flint,' suggested Mr Spinnaker meekly.

'Oh, we had not *forgot* the Honourable Ignatius Flint!' cried Mrs Spinnaker. ''Ow could anyone forget the Honourable Ignatius Flint? We was merely saving 'im till last, as being the most exotic of our number and therefore the most interesting.' She leant closer to our table and said, 'The Honourable Ignatius Flint is a young gentleman who came 'ere but a week ago. A young gentleman of a dusky hue, but so 'andsome! I reckon he is travelling under an assumed name, and that 'is father must be one of them Indian rajahs.'

Myrtle perked up somewhat, as girls disappointed in love often will when they hear of an Indian prince in the offing. But she drooped again almost immediately as Mrs Spinnaker went on, 'Between you and me, dears, we think there is a little romance going on between the Hon. Ignatius and our Miss Beauregard. He, too, breakfasts early. He 'as been paying the most constant attention to her.'

'Aha!' said Colonel Quivering. 'There is Miss Beauregard now.'

Naturally we did not wish to stare, but the colonel and Mrs Spinnaker had painted such intriguing pictures-in-words for us of our absent fellow guests that we could none of us restrain ourselves from turning to peek out of the windows. There, approaching along the curve of the promenade, we saw a wicker bath chair propelled by perhaps the largest and ugliest lady I have ever seen. Mrs Spinnaker was large in an agreeable, floury-dumpling sort of way, but Miss Beauregard's nurse was quite enormous, and clad in a vast dress of black bombazine, which covered her right up to the chin, where the black ribbons of her

black poke bonnet were tied in a tight black bow. Out of the depths of this bonnet, like a goblin peering out of a coal scuttle, a little, sour, wizened face regarded the passing world with black button eyes.

But none of us looked long at this ogress, for we were far too busy gazing at her charge. Upon the embroidered cushions of the wicker chair reclined the loveliest young lady ever seen outside a painting of fairyland. She had pale skin and golden curls and forget-me-not eyes, and looked in all respects so like a porcelain shepherdess upon a mantel-shelf that it was hard to believe she was real, and alive. And yet a certain pallor in her cheeks, a certain restlessness about her manner, reminded us of what Colonel Quivering had said about her

suffering from a Malady or Ailment, and so our admiration for her beauty was sweetly mixed with pity.

'She is not all *that* beautiful,' said Myrtle, torn between delight at the prospect of trying out her French conversation on this Vision, and annoyance at finding herself no longer the prettiest girl at Starcross.

'Why, Myrtle,' I said, 'I do believe you're jealous!'

'Hush!' said Mother.

Colonel Quivering was drawing our attention to the far end of the seafront, where a second group of promenaders had come into sight. 'And there is our Indian prince and his servants!' he said proudly.

The Indian prince wore a suit of white linen, and was followed at a respectful distance by two servants in coats of black broadcloth, one an Ionian, the other some manner of small Jovian hobgoblin. A wide straw hat shadowed his face, so that all I saw of him as he strolled over to greet Miss Beauregard was his smile. But I saw the servants plain enough, and was so amazed I dropped my toast. The Ionian was my old friend Mr Munkulus, I was quite sure of it . . . And his goblin companion was none other than Mr Grindle!

I would have pointed out this strange coincidence, but

there was no need. The Honourable Ignatius Flint chose that moment to sweep off his hat and make a very low bow to Miss Beauregard, who offered him her perfect hand to kiss. And Myrtle, watching this, cried out in an indignant voice, 'Why, that is not an Indian prince at all! That is *Jack Havock*!'

Chapter Five

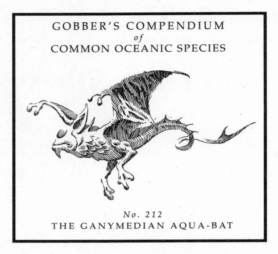

GOBBER'S COMPENDIUM
of
COMMON OCEANIC SPECIES

No. 212
THE GANYMEDIAN AQUA-BAT

IN WHICH WE DISPORT OURSELVES UPON THE PLAYFUL
BOSOM OF THE OCEAN, AND JACK'S EXPLANATIONS ARE
INTERRUPTED BY A DISTRESSING DISCOVERY.

N ow, I don't claim to be any sort of authority upon
matters of the heart, but it seems to me that if a
young lady has formed a Sentimental Attachment
to a young gentleman, and that young gentleman not only
fails to answer any of her letters, but then turns up at a
resort hotel under an assumed name, making himself

agreeable to beautiful young French women in bath chairs, then the young lady may be somewhat vexed. Myrtle turned bright red, and then stark white, and while I was waiting to see what other interesting colours she could go, Mother took her by the elbow and said, 'Excuse us, everyone; Myrtle is unwell. I think we should return to our suite of rooms.'

I started to protest, for I would far rather have run outside to greet my old friends Mr Munkulus and Mr Grindle, and Jack himself, once he had finished exchanging good-mornings with the fair Miss B. But Mother gave me a Commanding Look, and believe me, when you are on the receiving end of a Commanding Look from someone 4,499,999,989 years your senior, you tend to take notice.

Back in our suite, Myrtle closeted herself in her room with Mother, and a great deal of sobbing and consoling went on, while I kicked about in the sitting room, casting wistful looks at the sunshine outside and wishing I could be down on the beach, running in and out of the plashy billows, building sandcastles, etc., etc.

At last Mother and Myrtle emerged. Myrtle collapsed at once upon the sofa, looking pale but not particularly interesting. She must have been crying, because her nose

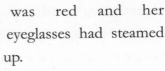

was red and her eyeglasses had steamed up.

Mother came to me, and, putting her arm about my shoulders, said softly, 'Art, do you think you could go and seek out Jack? Let him know that we are here, and see if there is some innocent explanation for his strange behaviour?'

'Oh, the explanation is quite clear,' said Myrtle, in a hollow sort of way. 'He prefers that French creature to me. It really does not matter. Let us go bathing.'

'Are you sure, Myrtle?' asked Mother.

'Oh, quite sure,' said Myrtle, with a sigh. 'Just because all the Hopes and Dreams of my Young Life lie in Ashes, it does not mean that you and Art should not be able to enjoy your holiday. Come, let us go down . . .'

And she picked up her patent bathing costume, which had been left draped over the sofa arm in its mothproof carrying bag, and led the way downstairs.

I still felt faintly troubled by the mysterious appearance of the ocean, and by my encounter earlier with that slinking shadow on the balcony. As Mother and I followed Myrtle out into the sunlight on the prom, I asked her, 'Mother, do you not think there is something queer about Mr Titfer and his hotel?'

'Of course there isn't,' snapped Myrtle, before Mother could reply. 'There isn't, is there, Mother? Art just sees mysteries and adventures everywhere. It is due to all those penny dreadfuls he reads, and the unsettling influence of our misfortunes in the springtime.'

Mother smiled, stopping on a landing to look fondly down at us. 'Well, my dears,' she said, 'there *is* something queer about Starcross, to be sure, and Mr Titfer certainly appears to be a most singular gentleman. But as far as one may tell it does not seem to be a dangerous sort of queerness. The Solar System is a very large place, after all, and there is room in it for all manner of oddities, I'm sure. So I propose that the best way of dealing with this one is to take an invigorating dip. However it comes to be here, the sea looks most inviting.'

I quite agreed with her, and yet part of me remained

wary. Perhaps Myrtle was right for once, and I had been unsettled by our adventure with the First Ones. At any rate, some sixth sense kept warning me that danger lurked near by.

But it's jolly hard to maintain a sense of lurking menace when the Sun is shining, and there are sand and sea to be enjoyed. There was no sign of Jack Havock and his friends, nor of Miss Beauregard, and as we walked down the ramp from the promenade I felt my spirits soar like a hot-air balloon. We each took one of the bathing machines which waited on the sand in front of the hotel, like a line of gaily-painted sentry boxes on wheels. As I stripped off inside mine, and hung the sailor suit I had been wearing on the hooks provided, a clockwork motor whirred into action and carried the machine gently down the strand and into the sea, so that when I emerged, resplendent in a wool serge bathing costume with red-and-white hoops, I had only to descend the three steps to find myself shoulder deep in the warm, gentle swell.

Soon Mother and Myrtle emerged from neighbouring machines to join me. Mother wore a simple bathing dress of blue worsted, while Myrtle modelled her new patent bathing costume, the Nereid, a quite remarkable garment which combined all the latest advances in dress-making and hydro-dynamics (see Mr Wyatt's illustration). Myrtle was so proud of it that she cut a neat little curtsey on the top step of her machine and called out across the water, 'What do you think, Art?'

Well, I thought that any Nereid who was silly enough to go sporting in the briny dressed up in all that clobber would sink straight to the bottom in a twinkling, and good riddance. But I have learned that it is sometimes best to varnish the truth slightly when Myrtle asks for my opinion (my shins are quite black and blue with the indentations of

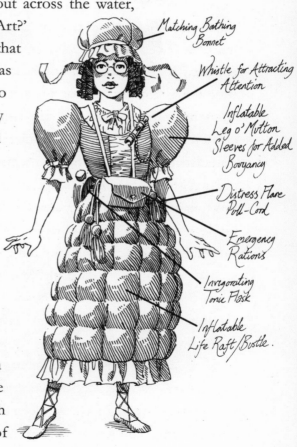

Matching Bathing Bonnet

Whistle for Attracting Attention

Inflatable Leg o' Mutton Sleeves for Added Bouyancy

Distress Flare Pull-Cord

Emergency Rations

Invigorating Tonic Flask

Inflatable Life Raft/Bustle.

her beastly boots). So I said, 'Very pretty', or words to that effect, and indeed there *was* something quite pretty about the way her over-skirts flowered out around her as she came smiling down the steps.

Oh, what fun we had that morning, there in the seas of Starcross! Even Myrtle soon forgot that her heart was broken. We both sploshed and frolicked and swam about, doing the doggy paddle just as Father had taught us in the main water tank at Larklight, and Mother circled us, gliding through the water as gracefully as any dolphin or Ganymedian aqua bat (she has been both in her time, of course).

When Myrtle and I grew weary we paused awhile upon a

tethered raft, where we sat in the shade of a parasol and ate ice creams, which were brought out to us by a mechanical mermaid with a waterproof ice box. We applauded Colonel Quivering as he sped past us in his regimental water-wings, a shark-like dorsal fin jutting jauntily from the back of his regulation army-issue swimming costume. We watched Herbert Spinnaker ascend the tall diving platform on the pier and perform a graceful swallow-dive. He fell in a slow, dreamlike way, turning over once, twice, thrice! before he splashed into the water. The gravity here, outside the influence of the hotel's generators, was gentle, and made us all feel light and buoyant. But it was still stronger than the one eighth or one tenth of British Standard that one would expect on a small asteroid like Starcross.

I pondered on this a bit, and then said, 'Myrtle, I believe

we are on the planet Mars.'

Myrtle gave me one of those Looks, over the tops of her spectacles, as if wondering whether it might not be kinder to have me confined in some form of Asylum.

'I have thought quite hard about it,' I explained. 'Starcross used to be part of Mars; Mother told me that. I think that Mr Titfer has some sort of machine in his hotel which transports the whole place back a few thousand centuries to a time when these hills and cliffs were still part of the Red Planet.'

'But there are no seas on Mars!' objected Myrtle. 'There is hardly any water at all on Mars! That is why they have had to build so many canals all over it!'

'That is true,' I agreed. 'But in pre-history, Mars had rolling oceans much like this.'

Myrtle considered this, and began to look alarmed. 'Mother!' she cried, and when our maternal relative surfaced alongside she complained, 'Art says we are on pre-historic Mars!'

'Does he?' asked Mother, wiping the water from her eyes and smiling sweetly at me. 'Jolly good, Art! I wondered when you would work it out!'

'But it's impossible!' Myrtle cried. 'How could Mr Titfer

do such a thing?'

'Oh, I doubt it was *his* doing,' Mother replied. 'It would require a science far more advanced than his mechanical tea pots and other toys. I should imagine that some strange natural phenomena affects Time here at Starcross. Do you not recall how ruinous the hotel appeared when we first saw it? I believe we must have been looking through some crevice in the face of Time, and seeing the hotel as it was twenty years ago, soon after the mines here were abandoned. I imagine that, every twelve hours or so, a larger crevice or cranny opens, and the hotel and its environs pass through it into pre-history.'

Myrtle looked most discomfited. 'Can it be safe? Surely there will be *Dinosauria*, and other creatures with insatiable appetites and ever so many teeth?'

Mother smiled her most reassuring smile. 'Evolution on Mars followed a somewhat different course to that on Earth,' she said patiently. 'The Martian oceans of this period were almost devoid of large predators. On shore, of course, it was a different matter; this was the age of the sabre-toothed sand clam and the terrible Crown of Thorns, a sort of land starfish which reached the most enormous size. But no doubt that is why Mr Titfer has erected that impressive-looking fence around his property.'

I think that when Mother took on human form she cheated a little, and gave herself the eyes of a hawk. I would never have noticed the fence if she had not pointed it out. It was a spindly affair of iron posts and taut wire cables, and it seemed to ring the hotel, running from the headland on the western side of the bay, up into the dusty hills behind and down to the sea again in the east.

'It looks a flimsy sort of fence, and barely capable of stopping an ordinary starfish, let alone a giant pre-historic Martian one,' said Myrtle, sounding fearful, and then, remembering her tragic position, 'Not that I should *mind* being eaten up, of course. Indeed, I should positively welcome it, as an end to my many sorrows.'

'Oh, chin up, dear,' said Mother. 'I should imagine that fence has a powerful electrical current running through it. It would hardly be in Mr Titfer's interests to expose his guests to danger.'

When we had finished our ices, and washed our hands in sea water, and Myrtle had dried hers upon a small hand towel which she withdrew from a waterproof compartment in her costume, she and Mother plunged once more into the waves, vowing to swim out to that small island, where the trees and flowering shrubs offered a pleasant shade. But I struck out for the shore, for trees and flowering shrubs don't interest me much, and besides, I had just seen Jack, Grindle and Mr Munkulus come out of the hotel and make their way over to the seaside cafe. I had not forgotten Mother's request, and I was determined to find out if Jack had an explanation for his actions.

When he saw me coming along the promenade, Jack looked first startled, then abashed. But Mr Munkulus and Mr Grindle did not hesitate to show how pleased they were to see me, leaping up and running to hug me and shake me warmly by the hand. And who was this emerging from the cafe with a tray of sandwiches and jugs of beer and lemonade and bowls of iced sprune clamped carefully in his powerful pincers? Why, it was none other than my dear friend Nipper, that amiable giant crab who has been Jack's friend since childhood!

'Art, my dear!' he cried, setting his tray down upon the table and scuttling over to lift me up in his claws and peer intently into my face with all four eyes. 'Why, how you've growed, and how glad we are to see you! Mrs Spinnaker told us there were Mumbys here, but Jack said that it could not be you; that it was a common enough name and that doubtless some other Mumbys had come to stay.'

'It is not *that* common a name,' I said, as Nipper let me down. I could not help thinking that Jack had *hoped* we were some different Mumbys, after the way he had been behaving with Miss Beauregard.

I turned to him and we shook hands, and he said awkwardly, 'I'm pleased to see you, Art. But please don't call me Jack. While I'm here I'm the Honourable Ignatius Flint.'

'But why?' I asked. 'Jack Havock is so much better a name . . .' And then the penny dropped. I glanced about to make sure no one had overheard me call him 'Jack.' 'You are here in disguise!' I said excitedly. 'Upon Her Majesty's service! I *knew* that there was something odd about Mr Titfer! No doubt he is a black-hearted villain, this hotel is but a front for his criminal activities, and you have come to bring him to justice!'

'Mr Titfer?' asked Jack, looking quite amazed. 'Why, no;

he's a good fellow, and makes the most wonderful hats. But there is something amiss here, you're right.' He sat down, and indicated that I should do likewise, and called out to a passing automaton for another glass, which he filled with lemonade for me. Then, leaning closer, he confided, 'Sir Richard Burton and Ulla thought there was something strange about this place, and came to take a look at it. That was several weeks ago. Since then, nothing has been heard or seen of them. So I have left the *Sophronia* at Modesty docks, with Ssilissa and the Tentacle Twins to watch her, and come to search for clues.'

'And is that why you were making yourself so friendly towards the French young lady in the invalid-chair?' I wondered. 'Myrtle is in a most terrible taking about it.'

'Ah, Myrtle . . .' Jack looked, for a moment, a great deal younger, and somewhat alarmed. He had fought space battles against Government gunships and gigantic spiders, but even he quailed at the thought of my sister in a bad mood.

'I think she would have liked a reply to her letters, too,' I told him.

'Yes, those ... I certainly meant to ...' Jack shook his head, setting aside for a moment the Myrtle problem. 'As for Delphine – I mean, Miss Beauregard – there does seem more to her and that nurse of hers than meets the eye.'

'Though what meets the eye is very agreeable,' said Mr Grindle, leering.

'Please, Grindle,' rumbled Mr Munkulus. 'Miss Beauregard's a lady, and it won't do to talk of her in that un-mannerly way.'

'Who was talking of Miss Beauregard?' protested Grindle. 'It was her nurse I meant, that Mrs Grinder. A fine figure of a woman.'

'I think they're up to something,' said Jack darkly. 'I don't know what, but they've come here for more than the sea air. She is forever having Mrs Grinder wheel her off on constitutionals among the rocks and scrub, and I have seen her measuring the air, or the temperature or some such, with all manner of curious instruments when she thinks no one is watching. That is why I befriended her; in the hope that I might find out why she has come here, and what she hopes to accomplish, and whether she had anything to do with the disappearance of Ulla and Sir Richard. If Myrtle chooses to take that amiss, then that is her look-out.'

'I'm sure Myrtle will understand once Art explains it,' said Nipper, that ever-hopeful crustacean. 'Myrtle is not one to cause a scene.'

But no sooner had the words emerged from his shell than we all heard my sister's voice, raised in a most piercing and unsettling shriek. We looked about – Jack sprung to his feet, and put a hand to his hip, where, in his piratical days, his revolving pistol had been wont to hang – and out upon that island in the sea we saw Myrtle and Mother. As we watched, they both plunged in and struck out for the beach.

We hurried down on to the sand, and were joined there by the Spinnakers, Prof. Ferny and Colonel Quivering, and even by Mr Titfer, who came running from some study or office in the upper regions of his hotel, in his shirt sleeves, with a clerical automaton hurrying behind him, making notes of everything he said.

'What the deuce is going on here?' he demanded.

Mother rose from the waves, looking like Aphrodite,* only better dressed, with Myrtle coughing and spluttering behind her.

'Myrtle?' cried Jack, running to her.

'I have nothing to say to you,' retorted Myrtle, folding her arms, turning her face away from him and elevating her chin to a steep angle.

'What was that dreadful scream?' asked Mrs Spinnaker, looking very flustered and tying nervous knots in her bonnet ribbons.

Myrtle forgot her anger at Jack and remembered what had caused her alarm. 'Oh, those trees!' she cried.

'What trees?' demanded Mr Titfer.

* Or whichever Greek Goddess it is who is supposed to have emerged from the sea, I can never remember which is which.

'On the island there,' said Mother, her brow creased by a worried frown. 'On that island, among the flowering shrubs, there are two trees growing . . .'

'Yes, I've noticed them several times,' said Colonel Quivering, squinting into the dazzle of the sunlit waves. 'They look rather like two people standing there.'

'Colonel,' said my mother, 'they *are* two people standing there. I am certain that those are Venusian Changeling Trees, and that until quite recently they were human beings.'

Chapter Six

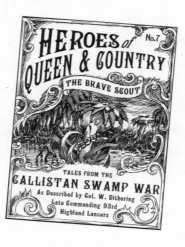

In Which One of Our Number Discerns the Hand of an Enemy at Work, and Is Struck Down by It!

There were gasps and cries of alarm from all about me, and I believe I gave a yelp, too. If you've been following my adventures you will recall the dreaded Venusian Changeling Trees, whose invisible spores wiped out our colonies on Venus by transforming the colonists into more Changeling Trees. Mother's words made me remember my own meeting with Jack Havock's family, who stood in a little spinney upon a headland there, with the sea wind sighing through their leaves, and when I looked at Jack I saw Horror etched on his face. The thought that Changeling spores might be drifting even now in the balmy airs of Starcross, and that Mother, Myrtle and the rest of us might soon be trees as well, was almost indescribably dreadful!

'Changeling Trees?' cried Professor Ferny, rustling his fronds in agitation. 'Impossible!'

'Are you sure, Ferny?' asked Mr Titfer. His eyes were wide behind those tinted spectacles he wore. 'You have imported many species of Venusian plant life. Is it possible that a Changeling spore was carried here along with them?'

'But that is not the worst of it,' said Mother. 'They're young trees, and wrapped about a branch of one of them, I discovered this.'

She held up for our inspection a small bronze tile, from which trailed two ends of a broken chain, as if it had once hung around someone's neck.

'Why,' cried Colonel Quivering, taking it and turning it over in his hands, 'that was Sir Richard's! An antique Martian piece! He told me that his wife gave it him, and that he wore it always, beneath his shirt!'

'Sir Richard?' exclaimed Myrtle. 'Sir Richard Burton was at Starcross?'

'Sir Richard stayed here a few weeks ago,' said Mr Titfer.

'A very good, handsome gentleman too,' said Mrs Spinnaker. 'He was here with his wife . . .'

'A d——d fine young woman,' said Colonel Quivering. 'Put me in mind of a lassie I knew when I was stationed on the Equatorial Canal back in '26 . . .' He looked wistful for a moment, then recalled himself and went on, 'I thought there was something odd about the way the Burtons left us so suddenly, in the middle of the night, without goodbyes.'

'Mrs Burton said goodbye to me,' insisted Mr Titfer. 'She told me that she and Sir Richard had been recalled to London. I remember it distinctly.'

'I heard shots that night!' cried Mrs Spinnaker, and, as her husband tried to calm her, 'No, no, 'Erbert, let me speak! I 'eard them most distinctly! Six pistol shots!'

'And yet you haven't mentioned them till now?' asked Mother.

'I mentioned them to 'Erbert,' said the Cockney Nightingale, glaring at her husband. 'And to Mr Titfer, and both of them said I must have been dreaming, and like a fool I supposed they must be right. But I *did* hear shots! And now Sir Richard has been turned into a tree, and so has his charming wife!'

'Nobody has been turned into a tree!' cried poor Professor Ferny, overcoming his natural diffidence and shouting loudly to make himself heard above the worried chatter of the other guests. 'It is quite impossible that a Changeling Tree should be growing here. I am confident that Mrs Mumby is mistaken.'

'Then let us go and look,' said Mr Titfer, starting towards the shoreline, where a rowing boat was drawn up.

'No, sir!' warned Colonel Quivering, catching him by the arm. 'If there is a Changeling Tree out there, you must not risk inhaling its spores.'

'Neither of the trees is in flower,' said Mother, 'so there should be no danger.'

'Nevertheless, dear Mrs Mumby, we cannot be too cautious. Tell me, Titfer, do we have any respirator masks about the place? Those elephant-nosed contraptions one wears when visiting a gas-moon?'

Mr Titfer shook his head. 'There is nothing like that on Starcross. No call for 'em.'

Professor Ferny stepped forward. 'Ladies and gentlemen, allow me to investigate. I am a vegetable already, and Changeling Trees can do me no harm. Wait for me on the terrace, and when I have got to the bottom of this puzzle I shall come and tell you my conclusions.'

And so saying, the noble shrub went rustling down to where the row boat lay, climbed in, and, wrapping a root about the handle of each oar, rowed himself out through the surf towards the island.

We watched him go, and did not look away from the dwindling shape of his boat until the *squeak, squeak, squeak* of turning wheels alerted us to the arrival of Miss Beauregard, who was approaching along the promenade. She had shielded herself from the Sun beneath a vast white parasol, and the wheels of her chair and the skirts of her nurse's black bombazine dress were brushed with reddish dust. I remembered what Jack had said about the two of them taking mysterious constitutionals among the unappealing bluffs inland. I could not help wondering, pretty and innocent though she appeared, whether Miss Beauregard was the author of whatever misfortune had overtaken Sir Richard Burton and his wife, and whether it was through her doing that those dreadful trees came to be sprouting upon the island.

But though I backed away from her, and Myrtle positively glared, the young woman in the bath chair seemed not to notice our reactions. She smiled delightfully upon us, and said, 'You must be the Mumbys; dear Mrs Spinnaker has been telling me all about you. Oh, but why does everybody look so wan? Ignatius, dear, do pray tell me! Whatever has occurred?'

We returned to our bathing machines, which had rolled themselves back up the beach in our absence. 'Try not to worry, children,' said Mother, as she climbed the steps to hers, and her smile was so gentle and reassuring that I was almost able to obey her.

As soon as we had dressed we hurried to the dining room

to rejoin the others. There, Mother and Myrtle greeted Grindle and Mr M., tho' Myrtle still refused to speak to Jack. 'You should talk to Miss Beauregard instead,' she told him tartly. 'I am sure *her* conversation is far more accomplished than mine.'

Miss Beauregard, meanwhile, who had been informed of the discovery upon the island, was busy telling the rest of us about other strokes of ill fortune which had occurred at Starcross. 'This asteroid is haunted!' she assured us, in her melodious French accent.

'Really, Mademoiselle? You astonish me!' said Mother, who was sat near to her. 'I simply adore ghost stories, and find that there is nearly always some truth at the bottom of them. Pray tell me what Starcross is supposed to be haunted *by*?'

Miss Beauregard shuddered, as if the room had taken on a sudden chill, and her nurse leant over and tucked her plaid blankets in around her. 'It's simply *haunted*,' she said. 'I made a study of it before I came. It seems there was once a mining camp here, owned by some rich English family named Sprigg. They built the railway and had Cornish miners brought in to extract copper and Newtonium, but it was always an unhappy place. The miners suffered from strange dreams, or found themselves of a sudden in other

parts of the asteroid, with not a notion of how they came to be there. Some vanished altogether, and nothing was found of them but their empty clothes.'

'How horrible!' exclaimed Mother. 'But it must have been a lonely spot. Do you think the miners may have imagined those occurrences?'

'I believe not,' said Miss Beauregard darkly. 'Something is wrong here. The way the sea comes and goes. It is not natural.'

'Sprigg, did you say?' asked Jack. He looked thoughtful, and I knew why. Sir Launcelot Sprigg was the name of the former Head of the Royal Xenological Institute, the man who had planned to have Jack and his friends dissected.

'That's right,' put in Mr Titfer, overhearing. 'I . . . ah . . .

bought this place from Sir Launcelot a few years back. It wasn't profitable as a mine. Couldn't persuade the miners to stay here, superstitious Cornish savages.'

'And yet you thought rich holidaymakers might be so persuaded,' mused Mother. 'How very interesting . . .'

Just then there came a murmur from those guests nearest to the door, and we saw Professor Ferny enter. The auto-waiters who had been trundling among us with glasses and decanters of lemonade and sillery put them down and fetched out a bowl of nutrient broth for the intellectual shrub, who stepped in gratefully and stood a moment in silence, as if savouring the flavour. Naturally, some of our number began to pester him for his opinion on Mother's Changeling Trees, but he held up a frond for quiet, and they fell silent.

'Ladies and gentlemen,' he said, 'I do not believe you are in any immediate danger.'

There was a sigh of relief at that, but only a brief one, for we could tell by his sombre tone that he had further news to impart, and that it was not good.

'Those trees which Mrs Mumby and her daughter saw are indeed Changelings,' he announced. 'Yet they are not *quite* like the Changeling Trees of Venus. I suspect they are some form of hybrid. I shall need to make further studies, and I shall require the use of my microscope and Mr Titfer's library.'

'Hybrids?' exclaimed Colonel Quivering. 'But how did they come here?'

Prof. Ferny rustled his fronds dolefully. 'When I say "hybrid", I do not mean a *natural* hybrid. I believe that some cunning person, well versed in botanical science, may have contrived a fast-acting Changeling spore, and inflicted it upon Sir Richard and his wife with malice aforethought.'

'You mean he is murdered!' gasped Myrtle.

'Oh, poor Sir Richard!' cried Mrs Spinnaker, and promptly fainted into the arms of her husband, who was unable to support her weight and had to call upon Colonel Quivering to help him.

'Then the same fate may yet befall us all!' wailed Myrtle.

'But what scoundrel

would commit such an outrage?' demanded the colonel, somewhat breathlessly, as he manoeuvred the insensate Cockney Nightingale into an armchair.

'Please, please!' called Prof. Ferny, above the hubbub of anxious voices. 'All may not be lost. While there's life, there's hope, and though Sir Richard and Mrs Burton are indisputably trees, they *are* still alive. If a mortal mind devised the spore which caused their transformation, then another mortal mind may yet undo its wicked work. Once I discern the nature of the spore which effected the change, I shall do my utmost to create another which may reverse it.'

'But, look here, everyone knows the Tree Sickness can't be cured!' shouted Mr Spinnaker.

Professor Ferny did not reply. Indeed, Professor Ferny seemed suddenly incapable of speech at all. His fronds made helpless flapping motions, stiffened briefly and then wilted. A brownish tinge spread over him, replacing his former healthful green. His brain-bole bowed on its thick stem, and he made muddy, unintelligible noises.

'The broth!' cried Mother suddenly. 'Fetch him out of it! It's poisoned!'

Mr Titfer and the colonel leapt forward at once and drew the wilting professor from his bowl. His roots were blackened and limp, and a greenish vapour rose from them, filling the dining room with a scent like that of damp socks.

'Oh Gawd! Is he done for?' asked Mrs Spinnaker, who had recovered from her faint but looked ready to fall into another at any instant.

'No, he's alive . . .' said the colonel doubtfully, as if he were about to add, *but for how long?*

'We must all pray for him!' said Myrtle earnestly.

'A nice tub of potting compost might be of more use,' suggested Mother.

'A sound notion!' agreed Colonel Quivering. 'I had a few of these shrub chappies serving as scouts with my regiment in the Callistan Swamp War of '39. Tough as old boots, they are. Good rich compost and regular feeding will revive him, God willing.'

'The plant nursery behind the greenhouse,' cried Mr Spinnaker. 'We will find all he needs there!'

And so they laid the poor shrub upon a table and bore him away, leaving the rest of us to wonder what evil was loose in this pleasant place, and which of us might fall victim to it next!

Chapter Seven

MODESTY AETHERGRAM OFFICE

In Which the Mystery Deepens Yet Further!

As you may imagine, we none of us ate well that night. Mr Titfer assured us that he would send an aethergram to the Chief Constable of Modesty and Decorum as soon as the hotel was restored to the Nineteenth Century. Indeed, when that happy event occurred (at about a half past six the next morning, according to his forecast) we should all be welcome to board the train and depart for safer asteroids if we wished.

But half past six seemed a long way off, and for the moment Starcross seemed suddenly to have become a lonely and dangerous place, very far removed from chief constables and railways and all the other comforts of our own era. *Who poisoned Professor Ferny?* we were all wondering, as we sniffed suspiciously at the soup the auto-waiters set before us. *Who had transformed Sir Richard and Ulla into trees?*

'I cannot believe that it was any one of us,' said Miss Beauregard at some point in the fish course. 'There is no one here who looks like a murderer to me.'

'Where is Mr Titfer?' asked Mother, contemplating the empty seat at the head of the long dining table. 'Does he not join his guests for dinner?'

'Not usually,' said Colonel Quivering. 'He is busy in his office. Or in the boiler room . . .' He frowned as he said this last part, as though the idea was one that he had stumbled upon, and it had surprised him to find it.

'The boiler room?' asked Mother.

'Yes, yes, it is below the hotel; there is a door to it in the corridor near the kitchens. I believe it houses the gravity generators . . . I have never been down there, of course.'

'Of course,' said Mother. 'I cannot imagine what a gentleman would find to do in a boiler room. That is why it surprises me to hear of Mr Titfer spending time down there. Surely he has automata to tend to his gravity generators and other such oily and bothersome bits of enginery?' She removed a few bones from her salmon and laid them neatly on a side plate. 'Does anyone know how Mr Titfer came by all the money to build this wonderful hotel?' she asked innocently. 'I have never heard the name of Titfer. All Titfer means to me is the Cockney slang, "Tit for Tat", meaning "Hat".'

'Aha!' cried Colonel Quivering, as if the word 'hat' had opened some floodgate in his mind. 'Well, of course, Mortimer Titfer is the maker of most excellent hats!'

'That's how he came by all his money, I dare say,' ventured Mr Spinnaker.

'The finest top hats in Known Space,' said Jack Havock, surprisingly, for he had been silent until now and anyway, I should not have thought him the sort of fellow who would care much about hats.

'I own one of his hats!' said Mr Spinnaker.

'So do I!' cried Colonel Quivering.

'Every gentleman in the Solar System should own one of Titfer's Toppers!' declared Mrs Spinnaker.

'Yes,' said Mother, in the same light yet thoughtful way. 'I recall seeing a large advertisement hoarding at Modesty, proclaiming their fine qualities. And yet, I am not sure that I recall ever hearing about Mr Titfer's hats before we came here. How odd.'

Jack looked at her curiously. 'Funny,' he said. 'I had a dream about hats last night ... Or *was* it a dream?' And he rubbed at his hair, with a most thoughtful expression.

Colonel Quivering said, 'No doubt there is a fascinating debate to be had about fashions in gentlemen's headgear, dear Mrs Mumby, but I would prefer to think about which of us attacked poor Ferny and turned the Burtons into trees. For despite what dear Miss Beauregard says, I believe it must have been one of us.'

'Unless it's them automatons!' whispered Mrs Spinnaker. 'Maybe one of them's gone wrong, just like the laundry-maid in that song of mine! Gone mad, maybe! Ready to slaughter us all!'

'Really, Mrs S., do please calm yourself,' Mother assured her. 'The automata are perfectly safe. There is no room in their mechanical heads for a thought, let alone a mad one.' But Mrs Spinnaker was far from reassured.

Still, it is a dark cloud indeed which has no silver lining, and at least her troubled mood meant we were spared her musical evening, and Myrtle's beastly old piano playing.

After dinner Mother and Myrtle and I took a stroll along the promenade for the sake of our digestions. It all looked very lovely in the evening light, with the crags like silhouettes cut from black card and pasted to a lilac sky, and the stars just starting to come out. But the shuttered beach cafe had taken on a sinister air, and the silent bathing machines and Punch & Judy shows which stood about reminded me now more of coffins than of sentry boxes. We stopped to peek at a fortune-telling booth, in which an automaton in the shape of a one-eyed gypsy woman sat staring into a ball of cloudy Martian crystal. Myrtle thought it a vulgar thing, and stomped off to strike wistful poses at the promenade rail, but Mother put a penny in  the machine's slot, and the gypsy clattered into life and droned, 'I foresee a long journey. You will meet a tall, dark stranger . . .'

That reminded me somehow of my encounter on the balcony the night before. The shadow-thing had not been tall, but it had certainly been dark and strange.

'Mother,' I said, 'what is small and inky black and goes "Moob"?'

'I don't know, Art,' she replied, thinking that I was trying to lighten the atmosphere with an amusing riddle. 'What *is* small and inky black and goes "Moob"?'

'It is no riddle, Mother. There was one nosing about on our balcony last night.'

I told her all about our strange nocturnal visitor, and she listened carefully. When I had finished she said, 'Well, Art, I do not know what to make of it, I'm sure, but there is nothing in this creature's behaviour to suggest it means us harm. Starcross has ventured out upon the ocean of Time, and I daresay as many strange fish swim there as in the oceans of Space. I am far more inclined to worry about the foul play which has befallen Professor Ferny and dear Sir Richard. I think it might be best if were to gather everyone together, and leave Starcross as soon as we can.'

I looked doubtfully towards the railway station, and the upward curve of the track which led from it, rising on its ornate iron pillars into the sky, where it suddenly ended, cut off from the rest of the railway by a hundred million years. It was like a reminder cast in steel of how very far we were from help.

We were just about to turn back to the hotel when we heard footfalls behind us and looked round to find Mr Munkulus, Nipper and Grindle hurrying to join us. I was exceeding glad to see them again, especially as they had not been able to join us for dinner. In keeping with their roles as the Honourable Ignatius Flint's servants they had to eat in the servant's quarters, and were very seldom seen in the parts of the hotel where the guests congregated.

'Well, Mrs Mumby,' said Mr Munkulus, when we had all greeted one another. 'This is a strange to-do.'

'Indeed it is, Mr M. What do you make of it?'

Mr M. looked bashful, clearly very proud that one of Mother's great age and wisdom should wish to hear his opinion. 'Mrs Mumby,' he said at last, 'there's oddness afoot. Jack's convinced himself that this Delphine person's at the bottom of it, but I'm not so sure.'

'There's something about that Mr Titfer that I don't like,' confessed Nipper. 'I know he makes very fine hats, but even so . . .'

'So you, too, admire this Titfer's Toppers?' asked Mother.

'Oh, yes,' they all chorused – though three beings less likely to don top hats it would be difficult to conceive of!

'I wish we was back in our own times,' muttered Grindle, 'I'd send word to Ssil and have her bring the *Sophronia* here and carry us all away. I've had enough of this spying lark; all sneaking about and pretending to be things you ain't. Give

me the open aether and a good clean fight any day.'

Mother patted his head. 'Don't be glum, Mr Grindle,' she said. 'By this time tomorrow we'll either be back at Modesty, or the villain whose hand we now but dimly perceive will have revealed himself –'

'Or *herself*,' said Myrtle.

'. . . and we shall have a chance to face him –'

'Or *her*.'

'. . . and whichever happens, I shall feel very glad to have you, and Mr Munkulus, and Nipper at my side. If we all stand together, I do not think that anything very terrible can happen, can it?'

We had been walking along as we spoke, and by this time we had reached the hotel entrance, and a parting of the ways – ours led inside and upstairs to our suite, while our friends must needs go round the side of the building to the servants' quarters, where they had their beds.

Mother said that the best thing we could do was try to get some sleep, so we set our alarm clocks and turned in. But after an hour or so I came awake, and found myself seized anew by the strange urge to open the closet in the sitting room. In all the excitements of the day before I had somehow forgotten that hat box on the top shelf, but now I saw it in my mind's eye, sharp and clear. I could imagine that fine black topper nestling inside it, and it seemed to be calling to me: *Put me on, Art! Put me on!*

As if in a waking dream I rose from my bed and lit the lamp. I went out into the sitting room, opened the closet and carried the box back into my own room. I set it down upon my bed and there undid the lid, and folded back the layers of tissue paper which protected the hat. But as I reached out for the hat itself, it seemed to *twitch*. The movement was very quick, and I might easily have missed it, but the round opening within the black brim seemed to narrow slightly.

I had the oddest notion that it had just licked its lips.

I took a step back, telling myself not to be so foolish. Yet I could not help myself. Suddenly I felt most terribly afraid.

I moved closer, and looked down inside the hat. And from its depths, two small white eyes looked back at me!

Suddenly, as if I had out-stared it and its nerve had snapped, the hat sprang from its box and hurled itself at my head! I ducked, and it twirled past me and struck the wall, flattening itself like one of those collapsible opera hats before springing back at me.

I wanted to cry out, but did not wish to startle my mother and sister, who would surely hear me. So I cried out very softly, 'Aaaah!', while reminding myself that Britons never, never, never shall be slaves, or the victims of man-eating hats, and wondering what Jack Havock would do in a position like mine.

A weapon was what I needed, I decided, as the creature darted across the room at me. I dived sideways to where a small bureau stood and snatched up a paper knife, its ornate hilt embossed with the Starcross coat of arms. As the thing readied itself for another attack I flung the knife at it, and transfixed it through the crown!

It gave a small, disappointed sigh and
dropped to the floor, where it twitched
for a moment and then lay still.
Dead, it looked not at all
like a hat. It
was a strange,
leathery thing, and
reminded me a little of those dogfish
eggs which are washed up from time to
time on English beaches, and known as
'Mermaid's Purses'. Except that a
'Mermaid's Purse' has a prong protruding from each corner,
while the thing on my rug had only two protrusions, and
each one ended in a tiny black hand . . .

Steadying myself, I quickly dressed and went to wake
Mother. But as I stood outside her bedroom door, poised to
tap upon it, I heard strange voices outside the suite. Several
men were coming up the stairs!

'We should wait a while longer,' said one.

'We have waited long enough already,' said another. 'She
did not come last night; she has not come tonight. She is
immune to our influence, and we must use more direct
means, otherwise she will leap aboard that supply train

tomorrow morning and we shall lose her.'

I stared at the door. I heard the soft click of a pass key in the lock and saw the handle start to turn.

Quick as a flash, I darted behind one of the curtains beside the balcony window.

From my hiding place I saw the door open. In came Mr Titfer, in evening dress, with a tall, black hat on his head. Then another person entered, and another, and I realised with a start that I knew *all* these fellows! There was Colonel Quivering, and Mr Spinnaker, and Grindle and Mr Munkulus, looking most curious in their evening clothes and toppers. And bringing up the rear, quite the wrong shape to wear tails or a waistcoat but with a top hat perched nattily atop his shell, was dear old Nipper!

Such was my relief that I stepped out from my concealment and said, 'Oh, I am so pleased to see you, I –'

Nipper struck me a blow with one pincer that sent me spinning backwards, knocking over the small occasional table as I fell. I think I was as much surprised as hurt. As I strove to rise, lifting a hand to staunch the blood that flowed freely from my nose, I saw that this was not the Nipper I knew. His eyes were the unseeing eyes of a sleepwalker!

Mother had heard the crash as I went down. Her

bedroom door opened. She stood there in her night-gown and cried, 'Good Heavens, gentlemen! What is the meaning of this?'

'Grab her!' said Mr Titfer, and it was clear that he held the others in his power. Like a well-dressed Rugby-football scrum, they charged at Mother. She realised much faster than I had that our friends were not quite in their right minds. She felled Colonel Quivering and Mr Grindle with

well-aimed blows, but the others proved too many for her. I stumbled forward to try and help her, but someone seized me, and I could only watch as Mr Munkulus pinioned Mother with his four strong arms while Mr Spinnaker pressed a pad of lint over her nose and mouth. For a moment she struggled violently, then the life seemed to go out of her; her eyes rolled upward, her lovely head drooped and she was bundled towards the door.

Good Lord! I remember thinking. *Chloroform!*

An instant later a pad of the same soft, scratchy stuff was crushed against my own face. A dreadful reek filled my nostrils. Through watering eyes I glimpsed a sliver of light widening as Myrtle's door opened, and heard her give a piercing shriek and slam it closed again. 'Myrtle!' I remember shouting, or *trying* to shout, lint-muffled and fainting. I struggled against unconsciousness with all my might – and it was not enough.

The last thing I saw was Mother being manhandled down the stairs. The last thing I heard was Grindle putting his shoulder to the door of Myrtle's room. Then I fell down and down into unutterable dark . . .

And there this portion of my tale must end, for I knew no more. So I shall hand over this account to another narrator, and we must all pray that she does not spend too much time going on about frocks – A.M.

Chapter Eight

IN WHICH THE NARRATIVE IS CONTINUED BY ANOTHER
HAND.

*M*y name is Myrtle Evangeline Mumby. My brother,
Arthur, has asked me to contribute my account of our
adventures at Starcross for publication in his latest volume
of memoirs. I was reluctant to do so at first, for it is so undignified to
have adventures, and even more so to write about them afterward so
that common people may read of them on omnibuses and the like.
However, it occurs to me that if I do not do as Art asks, he will simply

steal the relevant pages from my diary and publish them, as he did the last time, the little brute. So what follows is an account of all that befell me from the moment that Art and Mother were so rudely abducted. I present it here on the STRICT UNDERSTANDING that Mr Wyatt does NOT illustrate it with a picture of me in my night attire.

I was awoken on the night in question by a faint rapping or knocking sound. It took a while to rouse me, for I had been lost in the innocent wonderland of my girlish dreams. Indeed, I had been dreaming that Jack Havock, who until quite recently had been the unworthy recipient of my maidenly affections, was stood on my balcony in the starlight and was tapping at the windowpane.

At last the persistence of the noise roused me to wakefulness, and I leapt up, drew back the curtain and saw that Jack Havock *actually was* standing on my balcony and tapping at the windowpane!

Naturally, I do not approve of young men paying midnight visits to the balconies of young ladies. Especially if the young man in question has consistently failed to reply to the young lady's letters, and held conversations with attractive foreigners in public places. I made shooing

Myrtle in her night attire.

motions, and shut the curtains.

After a brief pause, the gentle, insistent tapping resumed. I went back to bed and pulled one of the pillows over my head, but I could still hear it. It was most vexing. Did Jack think that he could win back my affections by pursuing me in this unseemly manner? At last, driven almost to distraction, I stood up and opened the curtain again.

This time, he was pressing a crumpled scrap of paper to the glass. Upon it he had scrawled a single word:

DANGER

I opened the window and whispered angrily, 'Jack Havock, your handwriting is a perfect disgrace, and anyway, what do you mean, "danger"?'

Jack, with no regard at all for the niceties of polite behaviour, pushed his way into my chamber and said, 'I saw them starting up the stairs. Munk and Nipper and Grindle with 'em, and all in those d——d hats! They'll be here any minute!'

'Who will?' I hissed, flapping my hands at him to beg him to speak quieter, for fear my mother should hear him in my room. But before he could answer there was a commotion outside the door. I heard Art shout out something, and then a crash, as if a chair or table had fallen over.

Then footsteps, other voices, and Mother's voice crying, 'Good Heavens, gentlemen! What is the meaning of this?'

I ran to the door, and opened it to reveal a scene most indescribably alarming. The living room of our suite seemed full of persons in evening dress, two of whom were holding Mother, while another wrestled with Art. I uttered a loud yet ladylike cry, and in another moment Jack had slammed the door shut and locked it.

'But Mr Munkulus is out there!' I cried. 'And Mr Spinnaker! What are they doing?'

'They're not in their right minds,' Jack expostulated. 'Those d—— hats control 'em somehow!'

'Oh, Heavens! Then we must help Art and Mama!'

'We are too late!' he cried. 'Myrtle, you must come with me!'

I saw the sense in this suggestion, for someone had begun to batter against my bedroom door in the most intemperate way. So I followed Jack to the window and out on to the balcony. I did not entirely forget myself, I am glad to say, and as we passed the closet I reached in and snatched one of the mothproof calico bags in which I keep my dresses, so that I should have something decent to change into as soon as an opportunity presented itself.

Luckily a narrow fire escape descended from my balcony to the gravelled driveway behind the hotel, so there was no question of climbing down drainpipes or knotted ropes. Unshod as I was, my feet made no sound upon those iron stairs, though Jack, who was wearing a most disreputable-looking pair of old space boots, set up a dreadful clatter. Nevertheless, we reached the ground without further ado, and Jack hurried me across a starlit stretch of open promenade and stopped in the shadows of the beach cafe. The windows were shuttered. The canvas of a nearby Punch & Judy booth flapped softly in the wind, but all else was silent as the grave.

'What *is* going on?' I demanded.

'Wish I knew,' said Jack. 'It was your mother that put me on to it, talking about hats at dinnertime. Made me remember some dream I keep having, some strangeness about a hat . . . So straight after dinner I hunted about in my room, and there in my closet I found a hatbox: Titfer's Top-Notch Toppers.'

'What is so surprising about that?' I asked. 'Everyone knows that Titfer's hats are the finest in Known Space.'

'That's just it,' said Jack. 'They ain't! Think, Myrtle – can you honestly say you'd even heard of Titfer's Top-Notch

Toppers before you came to Starcross?'

'Well . . .'

'I guessed there was something strange about the hat in that box. So I didn't go to sleep tonight, but sat up and watched it. And about a half-hour back I started to get this strange sensation, like the hat was asking me to put it on.'

'Oh, come, Jack, a talking hat?'

'It didn't use words. It was just a feeling, an itch inside my head . . . I wish I'd brought Ssil or the Twins here – they might have been able to explain it. *I* can't. I only know that hat wanted me to put it on, and I wanted the same. But I restrained myself and stood a chair on top of that hatbox to stop it sneaking out, and ran downstairs. Because it had come to me, you see, that maybe Munkulus and Grindle had those things hid in their rooms too, and I wanted to warn 'em . . .

'But I was too late. Halfway downstairs I met the whole crowd coming up, and a look at their faces was enough to tell me the hats had 'em. Once you put one of those things on, you're gone; you're just a body, no better than an automaton, ready to jump to whatever order Titfer gives!'

'How horrible!'

'Horrible's right. I couldn't see any way of fighting them

all, not without someone getting harmed. And then I guessed where they were going, and I thought I'd best get there first, and rescue you and Art and your mum. Well, I was too late to stop them getting Art and Mrs Mumby, but at least I've got you . . .'

Then he smiled at me, that warm, dazzling smile, both shy and bold, which once made me feel so . . . well, I shall not say how it made me feel. For a moment I was almost inclined to forgive him, until I remembered how he had wronged me. Then I tilted my chin as haughtily as I was able, and turned away, and said very icily, 'What do you propose that we do now?'

'I don't know,' admitted Jack. 'I smelled chloroform up there, so at least they must have taken them alive. My guess is that they'll have carried them into the boiler room.'

'Perhaps if we wait until morning you might be able to creep down there unobserved and rescue them?' I reasoned.

Jack shook his head. 'Dangerous. Titfer did for Ulla and Sir Richard, by the sound of it. He's more than a match for us.'

I was relieved to hear him say it. I am far too weak and feminine to take part in daring rescue missions. 'We must fetch help!' I declared. 'I gather that a train is due to arrive in the morning. Perhaps if we conceal ourselves upon it we might return to Modesty and there alert the authorities. I realise that it would mean travelling without a valid ticket, but I am sure that in these calamitous circumstances . . .'

Jack grinned, as if unaccountably amused by what I had said. 'Sneak aboard a train, eh? You're thinking like a pirate, Myrtle!'

'I certainly hope I am not!' I retorted.

'Shhhh!' said Jack. 'What was that?'

I listened, but heard nothing except the canvas covers of the Punch & Judy show rustling. It seemed closer than it had been before.

Jack looked round. 'Myrtle,' he cried. 'Run!'

'A lady *never* runs.'

'Then walk d—— quickly! I reckon that tent is one of Titfer's sentinels, bent on our capture or destruction!'

And as he spoke, the flap at the top of the booth furled itself up; a horrid crocodile puppet fixed us with its glassy eyes, and two long, many-jointed metal arms reached out to snatch at us with clacking, scissory hands!

I am afraid I did run then, and may have screamed a little too. Despite my recent coldness towards Jack, I was glad that he was beside me as I hastened along the gravel paths

towards Starcross Halt. But we had not gone far when something moved ahead of us, and we saw another of those vulgar booths wheeling itself towards us, preparing to cut us off!

We turned towards the hotel, and there was a third, this one not a Punch & Judy show but the automated fortune-telling machine which Art and Mother had consulted earlier, its open front revealing that mannequin of a sinister gypsy woman with one all-seeing eye. As her booth creaked towards us on its spindly wheels, she rocked back and forth and a cackling voice issued from her, saying, '*I foretell danger!*'

'This way,' cried Jack, turning us in yet another direction, but there beyond a stand of ornamental cacti a fourth of those eldritch shapes loomed up. It was a mechanised speak-your-weight machine, rolling towards us on rattling casters. I tried to evade it, but I was encumbered by my dress in its calico bag and before I could turn aside it had lunged out with a silvery arm and dragged me on to its platform.

'*Eight stone and two ounces,*' it announced.

Jack punched it in the middle of its dial and pulled me free as it fell backwards.

'What an unspeakable lie!' I cried. 'I have never weighed above seven stone and five ounces!'

'Maybe it's the great sack you're lugging with you that confused it,' said Jack, hurrying me past the fallen machine and up a rocky, sandy hill behind the hotel. 'Why don't you let it go?'

'Certainly not!' I said. 'You may not have noticed, but I am undressed. I shall have to have some decent clothes to wear if we are to travel to Modesty and raise the alarm! If I burst into the office of the Governor in my nightdress, complaining of assault by seaside amusement engines, he may think me an eccentric!'

But how could we hope to catch the train now? Our mechanised pursuers seemed intent on driving us away from the hotel and its station! Each time we tried to veer in the right direction those wobbling booths began to gain on us.

Something whisked past me, and a rock exploded in a cloud of flying fragments.

'An air gun!' said Jack, and led me still further into the desert.

'Have you no weapon of your own?' I asked, feeling somewhat disappointed, for when I first knew him he had been positively bristling with swords and shooting instruments.

'Got my knife,' he grunted, 'but that won't be much good against automata . . .'

My words had acted as a challenge or spur to his manly nature, however, and after a few more steps he stopped and gathered up a few decent-sized stones, which he flung at the approaching booths. I saw the first strike a puppet of Mr Punch, which dropped out of sight like a coconut in a shy. The booth reeled sideways and toppled over, and an instant later a flash of flame leapt up into the Martian night as

some flammable substance within it
exploded.

'A hit!' I cried, clapping my
hands together. 'A palpable
hit!' But my elation was soon
extinguished, for the blazing
contraption simply used its
long arms to push itself
upright again and came on
as implacably as before,
quite unconcerned by the
flames which engulfed it.
Indeed, Jack's defiant stand
had made our plight seem worse, not better, for the canvas
which had shrouded the machine fell away in scorched rags
and flaming tatters, until we were pursued not by a jolly red-
and-white striped tent, but by a monstrous wheeled mass of
scorched metal, which sometimes brandished aloft a
blackened and half-melted puppet, crying out in a
squeaking, creaking voice, *Where's Mr Punch? Eh? Where's
Mr Punch?*

We came to the hilltop, and there ahead of us, just down
from the summit on the further side, lay that fence, the

seaward portions of which Mother had pointed out while we were bathing the previous day – oh, it seemed a thousand years before! I nearly tumbled into its thick strands of wire, but Jack held me back.

'Careful!' he cried. 'It is electrified!'

Almost as he spoke, the first of our pursuers crested the hill, only a few feet behind us! I shrieked (but in a refined way). Jack said something most unsuitable, and pushed me to the ground as the air gun concealed among those blackened struts and gears spat another bullet past us. The dress bag fell from my hand and, turning back to reach for it, I saw to my horror that its hanger had caught in the exposed metal framework of the machine, which was now almost upon us! I tugged at the bag to wrench it free, but succeeded only in pulling the machine towards me . . .

Yet in such apparent mishaps may Salvation lie, and sometimes even so small a thing as a coat hanger may be the instrument of Almighty GOD! For as it turned, the machine struck one wheel against a rock and lost its balance. I saw it teeter; I watched it fall past me towards the wires of that fence, through which the electrical fluid surged with a hum that was clearly audible. A vision of myself arriving at Modesty Station clad in nothing but my tattered nightclothes rose dreadfully before my eyes, and with an almost superhuman effort I unhooked the coat hanger and whisked my precious dress bag to safety as the booth, arms whirling like helpless windmills, struck against the fence.

'*That's the way to do it!*' it cried.

There was then such a crackling and sparking and hissing and shuddering as I have never heard before, and hope I never shall again! A blinding light made me shield my eyes and, when it was done and I could see again, the machine was a ruin indeed, a mere mass of half-molten scrap. The wires which had caught and fried it were blackened too, and several had parted, burned through by the force of the inferno.

'Huzzah!' I cried, sounding for all the world like Art in the momentary thrill of our victory. Then I recalled the two other machines. Sure enough they were just coming over the hilltop and advancing warily, as if they had noted the fate of their companion. From the gypsy woman's booth extended arms equipped with sharp, whirling blades, while from the mouth of the crocodile puppet in the second Punch & Judy show emerged the gleaming black barrel of a gun.

'Come on!' shouted Jack.

I could not imagine where he meant us to run next, with

the machines behind us and the fence ahead. Personally, I had been beginning to wonder if a prayer or other small act of Christian devotion might not be our best recourse. But Jack pointed, and I saw that where the bottom wires of the electrified fence had burned away there was a space through which we might pass, but which our lumbering pursuers never could!

Quickly, yet without sacrificing any of my feminine dignity, I crawled through, taking care not to brush the wires above me with any portion of my anatomy. Jack followed. Shots from the air gun sent spurts of sand leaping up all around us, but the machine was no marksman, and we were able to drop down into a gully out of its sight, and rest there, listening to the crunch and squeak of its wheels as it went to and fro along the fence, searching in vain for a way to reach us.

Rosy-fingered dawn was touching the fringes of the eastern sky with delicate shades of pink and red. Jack pulled out his watch and studied it. 'Five o'clock.'

'Jack,' I said, remembering something which Mother had mentioned, 'I believe that monstrous Martian wildlife may lurk without that fence. Sand clams, and . . . oh, I'm sure there was something else.'

Jack looked resolute and full of vim, which is exactly how one's gentleman companion *should* look when one is in a perilous predicament on an unearthly sphere.

'Never fear,' he said kindly. 'As soon as those machines give up we'll get back through the fence. I mean to make that train.'

There was a smudge of soot or ash upon his nose, which made him look like a naughty but loveable schoolboy. I longed to reach out and wipe it away, and began to wonder if I might not find it within myself to forgive him after all for his neglectfulness and his flirtation with Mademoiselle Beauregard.* But something about our close proximity

* Art had assured me that it was not really a flirtation, and that Jack was only making himself agreeable to that beautiful young person in the course of his duties as a secret agent of the British Crown. But there are duties and duties, and I still feel that Jack enjoyed that particular duty overmuch.

reminded me that I was still in my nightwear, so I said firmly, 'Turn your back, please, Mr Havock,' and he saw my intention and promptly did so. He does have *some* gentlemanly instincts, you see, (unlike certain people I might mention).

But, Oh! what a shock I was to receive when I unbuttoned my mothproof bag! And how I railed inwardly against my own folly and clumsiness! For in my haste to escape from our suite at the hotel I had taken from the closet not one of my day dresses, *but my bathing costume*!

'Jack,' I said, 'we must return *at once* to the hotel!'

'Shhh,' he told me, cocking his head to one side and listening intently. I listened with him. I could not hear anything, but I quickly realised that that was what intrigued him. The sound of the waiting machines had died away!

'Have they gone?' I asked.

'I don't know. It could be a trick.' Motioning for me to remain hidden, Jack stood up. I watched his face change as he scanned the hilltop beyond the fence.

'Are they gone?' I asked again.

'What? Oh, yes.'

'Excellent,' I declared. 'But, Jack, it is most important that I call in at the hotel on our way to the station. I have brought entirely the wrong outfit.'

'Can't do it,' he said. 'Look.'

I stood up. The machines were gone, as he had promised. But so too was the fence. Where its metal posts had stretched along the skyline there now lay nothing but the desert rocks and a few whispery clumps of Martian knotweed.

We walked together up the hill and looked over its crest, down to the darkness of the dawn sea. The fence, and all that had been contained within it, had vanished. The spot where Starcross had stood was empty. Along the curve of the bay, where the Starcross promenade had stretched so elegantly, and the flags of all nations had fluttered in the breeze, the waves now rolled in emptiness, making dainty lace doilies of foam upon the untouched sands of that ancient beach.

The hotel had returned without us to the Nineteenth Century, and I was marooned with Jack Havock on Pre-Historic Mars!

Chapter Nine

EXTINCT CREATURES
OF THE
PRE-ADAMITE RED PLANET

*Gentleman Drawn
to Scale*

No. 67
THE CROWN OF THORNS
(ASTRALIS MULTO POINTIUS)

IN WHICH VARIOUS HORRORS BESET MYRTLE IN THE DEPTHS
OF TIME, AND WHO CAN BLAME THEM?

Gentle reader, you may imagine my distress! Even if you are not gentle, but are merely a housemaid or labourer who has borrowed this volume from a lending library (in which case do *try* not to get BEER all over it), you may, I hope, grasp some faint inkling of the despair which threatened then to overwhelm me. My mother and brother had been kidnapped, Jack Havock and I were marooned on the planet Mars in the year 100,000,000 BC, we were without a chaperone and I had nothing to wear but my patent Nereid bathing dress!

Trying to make the best of our plight, I changed forthwith, for I reasoned that even bathing attire would be an improvement on the ripped, soot-speckled nightdress which was the only other garment I had brought with me into that remote era. And there was one small glimmer of good fortune, for in the bottom of the mothproof bag were my bathing slippers, so at least I would not have to walk any further barefoot across the sands of Mars.

'That's a pretty dress,' said Jack gallantly, when I had finished changing and he was allowed to look.

'You do not have to be kind,' I replied. 'I have learned not to expect kindness from you.'

He looked surprised, and then said, 'Ah, you mean all those letters you sent, and I never replied to. I'm sorry for it. I'm not much of a one for letters, see, and ... But anyway, it *is* a pretty dress.'

'It is a bathing costume,' I replied, refusing to be cheered.

'Are you sure? It has a bustle.'

'That is a safety feature. I believe it unfolds into a small life raft if you pull this tassel.'

'Good G-d!'

'Please do not blaspheme, Jack. This may be the year 100,000,000 BC but He Who Watches Over Us All is doubtless listening, and will be stung by the thoughtless way you take His name in vain. Who knows, at any moment a rampaging sand clam, or one of those other brutes which Mother spoke of, may charge us, and we shall have to call upon Him in earnest. And do you think He will be likely to notice our prayers if you go about saying His name just because you have seen an inflatable bustle?'

Jack shrugged.

'And don't shrug!' I added snappishly. (I fear adventures always leave me feeling somewhat irritable.)

We walked together down the hill, towards the shore, where that white line of breaking surf shone in the half-light like a supercilious grin. As we reached the hill's foot Jack noticed something in the sand nearby, and motioned for me to stop. I did so, and waited, with my heart beating swiftly beneath my bodice. Jack plucked a dead stalk from a nearby stand of Martian knotweed and poked the place which had caught his attention. Almost at once the ground heaved and something like a fanged trapdoor yawned open. Thin white teeth and strands of drool glistened in the

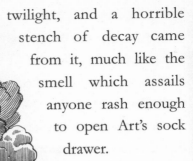

twilight, and a horrible stench of decay came from it, much like the smell which assails anyone rash enough to open Art's sock drawer.

'I suppose that must be a sand clam,' said Jack, as the thing slowly closed itself up and sank back into the sand. 'I don't think they'll be much trouble to us. Just look out for the little ridges where their shells break the surface, and stay clear of them.'

'Thank you, Jack,' I said, quite regretting my earlier harshness.

He smiled at me most kindly. 'I still say that's a pretty dress,' he said. 'What does the other tassel do?'

'I believe that releases a distress flare, in case one finds oneself adrift at sea,' I replied, and I looked down, blushing, for I suddenly found *myself* all adrift upon a sea of the most confusing emotions. And after a moment, I felt a light touch upon my hand, and guessed that Jack had sensed how I was feeling, and was standing close behind me. I could feel his breath against my neck, and I confess it made me tremble.

'Oh, Jack,' I said softly, 'why did you not reply to any of my letters?'

'What's that?' called Jack, and I raised my eyes and saw that he had walked on without me, and was already far down the beach towards the sea.

So whose was the breath I felt upon my neck?

I grew cold, despite the sturdy wool serge of my costume. Whose fingers were those, tracing aimless patterns on my palm? My trembling increased. With a great effort of will I made myself turn and look.

For yards around me the surface of the desert seemed to be undulating and crumbling and breaking open, and from beneath it was rising a fat, bag-like body, from which sprouted a myriad snaky, jointless limbs, one of which had come groping blindly through the air and found my hand. These limbs, of which there were far more than I could count, were studded all along their length with fearsome barbs, and as I stood there, staring in utter horror, the name that Mother had mentioned when she spoke about the predators of ancient Mars came back to me.

'Jack!' I screamed. 'The Crown of Thorns! A giant land starfish is upon us!'

And at my cry the monstrosity swung a broad, tubular trunk towards me, and a gale of wind seemed to grip me, fluttering the skirts of my bathing costume. I was dragged, still crying out plaintively, towards the ghastly opening. The horrid creature was endeavouring to suck me up, just as a hoverhog might suck up a drifting muffin crumb! A storm of sand flew all about me, and small pebbles and knotweed leaves went racing past and whirled up that trunk into the wet bag of the creature's body, which was palely translucent, and inside which I could dimly make out the forms of other luckless creatures like

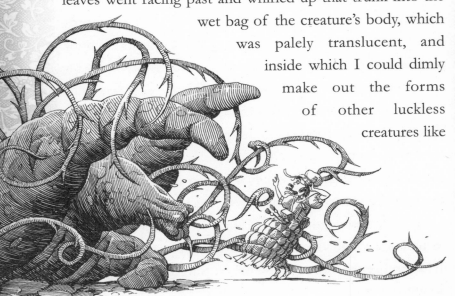

myself, churning and swirling in the acids of its stomach!

Suddenly Jack was by my side, helping me fight against the wind. As we were dragged closer to the feeding tube, he struck at it once, twice, thrice with his knife. Some glutinous liquid broke from it, and the trunk left off its sucking and withdrew, shrinking back into the creature's body like the eye-stalk of a snail.

Thorny limbs writhed over us, black against the pale sky as the Sun came up above the sea. One wrapped itself around Jack's arm. He severed it with his knife, then helped me up. A tentacle found my shoulder, but at its thorny touch one of my life-preserving leg-of-mutton sleeves burst and the hiss of expelled air made it flinch back, allowing me time to escape.

We ran towards the sea's edge, hoping that the Crown of Thorns would be too slow-moving to catch up with us. And for a few moments it seemed our hopes would be fulfilled, for the beast dragged itself cumbrously down the slope of the beach, and its tentacles and feeding tube wove about in a way which made me sure it was blind, and could not track us unless we made sounds that it could follow.

Then, as we hurried out on to the wet, shining sand where the small waves were breaking, disaster struck. Jack suddenly went down, almost dragging me with him. I thought that he had slipped, and made to help him up, but he gave a terrible cry, and I realised that he had fallen into the open maw of a sand clam! Weeping, I tried to pull him free, but the fanged lips of the trapdoor were closed tight on his left leg, just below the knee.

He tried to be brave, poor Jack, but the pain was terrible. He cried out again, and the Crown of Thorns heard him, and came slurping and flolloping towards us, and that awful suction tube swung down to snort me up.

'Oh, Jack!' I remember crying, as I was dragged backwards.

He held both my hands and pulled me towards him. The suction from the starfish's feeding tube increased, and I felt my feet rise up into the air. I was playing the part of the rope in a tug-of-war between Jack and the monster, and a most uncomfortable and undignified role it was!

'Myrtle!' cried Jack. Poor Jack, he looked quite grey with pain, and the left leg of his trousers was soaked through with gore! 'Myrtle,' he shouted. 'Just a bit closer, if you can . . .'

He was drawing me towards him, closer, closer, and I closed my eyes and raised my face to his, in expectation of one last kiss. I confess that I was somewhat disappointed when he let go of my hand and reached out to tug one of the tassels on my bathing costume.

'Jack!' I said indignantly – and an instant later he released my other hand, too, and I was whirling through mid-air in a most unseemly manner, sucked head-over-heels into the wet mouth of that hideous tube.

But Jack's plan, which I had been so slow to understand, had worked. Even as I flew, the inflatable raft concealed within my bustle expanded, so that by the time I reached the starfish I had become too large a morsel for it to swallow. I wedged in the feeding tube like a cork in a bottle, my head inside, my feet out in the open air, kicking frantically and all in vain, since they had nothing to kick against. For what seemed a distressingly long while I stayed there, shaken up and down by the thrashing of the tube and half smothered by the vile fumes from the monster's stomach. *Poor Jack,* I thought. *He tried so hard to save me, but he has failed, and once I am dead the beast will suck him up too, unless that wretched sand clam eats him first!*

And it seemed so dreadful to me that Jack should be eaten by a starfish *and* a clam that I had a quite uncharacteristic flash of inspiration. *The other tassel!* I thought suddenly, and groping about upon my bodice, I found it, and gave it a sharp tug.

In a spray of smoke and sparks my costume's distress flare was released from its concealment. The tube which held me captive filled with acrid, choking smoke as the flare went soaring through it into the very belly of the beast, there to explode in the internationally recognised colours of maritime distress.

The starfish shuddered convulsively, and collapsed. The tube in which I was stuck thudded into the wet sand. Tremors and quiverings still ran through the great corpse, but corpse it was! My action had destroyed it!

Some months ago, my brother Art contrived to cause a monstrous squid to explode in the upper airs of the planet

Jupiter, and he has been boring people rigid with the story of it ever since, oft remarking upon the sense of triumph it gave him, his resemblance to St George and other heroes, etc., etc. Yet I felt no thrill of victory as I contemplated the explosion and demise of the Crown of Thorns. Perhaps it is because I am female, and therefore above such primitive emotions, or perhaps because I was still stuck inside its slimy, stinking feeding tube.

At last I found the release valve on my life raft, and managed to deflate it. Beslimed and shuddering, I crawled out, and looked up in awe and wonder at the carcass of that great beast which Providence had lent me the strength to defeat. Bits of its stomach lay scattered all across the beach, and small pieces were still falling from the sky, landing with damp, sticky noises on the sand about me. At first I could not see Jack, and I thought that he had been eaten up entirely

by the sand clam. Then I realised that he lay just beyond the carcass, hidden from me by that hill of rent blubber and twitching tentacles. He had been trying to use his pocket knife to free himself from the clam, but his efforts had been in vain, and he had collapsed exhausted on the sand, his leg still clamped inside the creature's jaws, his blood spreading in a river down the sand to stain the waves pink.

The awfulness of our predicament almost overwhelmed me. 'Help! Help!' I shrieked, turning to shout across the empty beach, until my cries echoed plaintively among the bluffs and crags inland. But I knew that even if they echoed all the way to Earth it could do me no good, for in the remote era we were trapped in there would be no one there to hear me. How piteously alone I felt! And how I feared that I should soon be still more alone, for I did not see how Jack could long survive!

And then, miraculously (as I thought), my cries received an answer! Unexpectedly, impossibly, a voice called out, 'Miss Mumby?'

I looked about me and saw, emerging from the drifting smoke which still poured across the beach from the carcass of the dead starfish, a wicker bath chair.

Chapter Ten

MYRTLE'S ACCOUNT CONTINUES: STRANGE MEETINGS UPON
AN ANCIENT SHORE, MISS BEAUREGARD'S MOTIVES MADE
PLAIN AND MRS GRINDER REVEALED AS A WOMAN OF
MANY PARTS.

For a moment, as you may imagine, I stood quite
bewildered and astray, for the last people I had
expected to encounter upon this interminable
beach were the gentle Miss Beauregard and her lumpen
companion. Yet there they were, Miss Beauregard waving

graciously as Mrs Grinder propelled the invalid-carriage towards me o'er the shining sands. Its axles squeaked, and its wheels cut three deep grooves in the sand, which slowly filled with water and faded away once it had passed.

'Oh, Miss Beauregard!' I cried out as they drew near. 'Pray do not come any closer! There is a great deal of gore here; it is no sight for a lady and may cause you to swoon . . .' (I felt more than a little inclined to swoon myself whenever I looked down at the red wash of Jack's life-blood spilling down the strand into the surf. But I was determined to show no weakness in front of Miss Beauregard, who, for all her good breeding, was still a foreigner. I took deep breaths and told myself that I should show this daughter of France how brave a British girl might be, and somehow I was able to remain upright.)

'Ah!' cried Miss Beauregard, when she drew near enough to see Jack's predicament for herself. 'A sand clam! And it is eating the Honourable Ignatius Flint!' And with a graceful motion she sprang from her chair, pulled out a small silver revolver which had been concealed in her bosom, and fired six shots into the creature's maw. It spewed forth a quite horrible amount of stinking purple foam and its jaws went slack, allowing Jack to drag himself free.

'Why, Miss Beauregard!' I cried, staring at her through the thinning veil of pistol smoke. 'You can walk! I had no idea that sea air would effect so rapid an improvement in your condition!'

Miss Beauregard did not reply, but, stooping, tore a length of cotton calico from her underskirts, and used it to make a sort of bandage, which she tied tightly about Jack's leg. Glancing up at me as she worked, she snapped, 'Water! This wound should be washed in case the creature's fangs were envenomed.'

I hesitated a moment, thinking that it was really Mrs Grinder's place, as a servant, to fetch water. But Mrs Grinder stood stolidly behind the wicker chair, squinting out at us from the depths of her black bonnet, but making no attempt to help. I looked at Jack, who, though pale with pain and shock, was yet managing to smile gratefully at the fair Delphine as she tended his wounds. I am not sure why, but her attentiveness irritated me. Despite all that had come between us, I felt that it should be I who nursed Jack. So I undid the ties of my waterproof bathing bonnet and strode pointedly to the sea's edge, where I filled it with clean water and returned to help Delphine bathe Jack's poor, mauled limb.

Despite the blood, he had not been so badly savaged as I had feared, and soon declared that he could stand. But Delphine would not hear of it. 'You must take the chair,' she said. 'I do not need it.'

'*You* walk well enough, I see,' said Jack, grunting with the pain as we helped him to sit down in the chair. 'Handy with that pistol, too. I had a feeling there was more to you than met the eye.'

'As there is to you, *Ignatius Flint*,' said Delphine, emphasising that name in a way that showed she knew it to be false. 'I believe you to be none other than Jack Havock, an agent of the British Secret Service. What are you doing here?'

'We might ask you the same thing,' said Jack. 'And don't

tell me you were simply out for a walk when the hotel vanished. You ain't just some pretty invalid, are you? And you didn't come to Starcross for the sea bathing. Who are you really?'

Delphine laughed lightly, as if she and Jack were guests at some society function, and he had made a polite joke. 'It is supposed to be a secret,' she said, 'but since we are so *very* far from our own time, and you and Miss Mumby are so *entirely* at my mercy, I suppose I can tell you. I am an agent of the French Government.'

Naturally, dear reader, I was dismayed at this intelligence. The French are a most excitable race, forever having Revolutions and chopping one another's heads off. When not busy doing that they spend their time looking covetously skyward, quite green with envy because Britain has a splendid empire stretching all through the vaults of space, and they do not. To learn that we were keeping company with one of their spies was shocking news indeed!

More shocking still was Jack's reaction, for not only did he not appear horrified, he laughed, and continued to grin at Miss Beauregard in a most foolish and familiar manner. It occurred to me to wonder whether her considerable personal charms had got the better of his judgement, and I suddenly felt vexed that I was not dressed in a pretty gown of fashionable cut as Delphine was, but in a grimy bathing dress smeared with sand and starfish saliva, and a pair of bathing slippers which squelched comically with every step.

Suddenly I felt very weary of this adventure, and I am afraid my usual good humour quite deserted me. I lagged behind the others as Mrs Grinder pushed Jack on along the beach, towards a place where the cliffs rose steep and dour, haunted by small, see-through flying creatures with fat air-sacs and nasty dangling tentacles, which I believe are known as Martian Ghost-Jellies. Delphine strolled beside him, talking. I hung my head, and watched the long wheel marks unspooling from the chair's three tyres, and Mrs Grinder's deep footprints emerging from beneath her dragging skirts. I could not help noticing from the marks she made that Mrs Grinder seemed to have at least six feet, and I wondered if I should draw this odd fact to Jack's attention.

But Jack was busy listening to Delphine as she explained to him something of her history. I shall set down what she told him here, so that you may see what a nasty, vexing, deceitful, foreign young person she really was.

'My grandfather,' said Delphine, 'was Mr William Melville of Charlestown, Virginia. An American and an alchemist. Despite being a friend of freedom, and utterly opposed to Britain's empire, he underwent all the years of training that the Royal College of Alchemists insists upon. He lied about his own beliefs in order that he might pass the tests and checks and pitfalls which the College sets in order to keep the chemical wedding a secret known only to British gentlemen. For ten years he studied under the damp and dismal skies of England! But when he had learned every part of the process he fled home to Virginia, and there, with a few fellow patriots, he constructed the United States' first aether-ship: the *Liberty*.*

'My grandfather hoped that he might capture a British

---

* Back in 1776 a gang of American gents who were too stingy to pay their taxes decided to break free of old England, and declared the thirteen colonies independent, calling them 'The United States'. I believe they held a tea party to celebrate. King George promptly dispatched Lord Cornwallis with a squadron of aether-ships to teach them some manners, and that was the end of the matter. But from time to time in the years since there have been instances of odd, enthusiastic chaps trying to revive the designs of those old revolutionaries. Wild Will Melville was one of them. His aether-ship caused quite a panic when it first took flight in 1801, preying upon British shipping on the Earth–Mars run — A.M.

warship or two, and set up a free American settlement upon
one of the outer worlds, from where he might disseminate
the knowledge of the chemical wedding to all men. He
dreamed of founding a Rebel Alliance which would strike at
your empire from a hidden base . . .'

'It didn't come true, though, did it?' said Jack Havock.
'The British were better than your grandad. Better
alchemists, better aethernauts and better fighters. Their

Admiral Nelson beat him hands down.'

Delphine's eyes flashed fiercely, and she said, '*Liberty*'s wreck was never found.'

'Of course it wasn't,' Jack goaded her. 'She was blown to bits.'

Delphine laughed. 'That is what the British thought. That is what my grandfather *wanted* them to think. His ship was badly damaged, but somehow he managed to limp away into the reefs between the asteroids, where none dared follow him.'

Jack shook his head. 'That's just wishful thinking, Miss. You've no way of proving it.'

Delphine shot him a haughty look and went on with her tale. 'After my grandfather vanished,' she said, 'his wife and her young daughter, my mother, were forced to flee to France, and seek the protection of the Revolutionary Government there. My mother married a Frenchman, and settled down to live respectably near Paris. We had plenty to live on, for the Government of France awarded us a pension in honour of Grandpapa's great deeds. They would gladly love an aether-ship of their own, and they thought that Grandpapa's *Liberty* would suit them very well. They sent many secret agents out among the asteroids over the years, looking for the *Liberty*'s last resting place. But they found nothing at all.

'Then, a few months ago, they had word of Mr Titfer's new venture, and of the way that his hotel seemed able to fling itself into the past. They told me of it, and suddenly I understood. My grandfather's ship lies on Starcross, but hidden where no prying British eye would ever see it! He must have taken advantage of this asteroid's curious time-holes to sail the *Liberty* back into the depths of pre-history, and there some calamity befell him, or else I am sure he would have reappeared to light *Liberty*'s flame among the Heavens . . .

'Well, I spoke of my theory to my friends in the Government, and they furnished me with Mrs Grinder, and with my fare to the asteroid belt. As soon as I arrived at Starcross I began searching for a way into the past. That invalid chair which serves as my disguise also contains a number of concealed instruments with which I was able to cut a way through Mr Titfer's electrical fence, and Mrs Grinder has a powerful sense of smell, which I hope will lead us to the place where the *Liberty* lies moored. We were searching for it when we saw your distress flare, and heard Miss Mumby's pathetic cries. Naturally we hastened to investigate.'

'Very good of you,' said Jack. 'But hold hard; what about the goings-on at Starcross? Was it you who kidnapped Mrs Mumby and young Art? And poisoned Ferny? And turned Sir Richard and Ulla into trees?'

Delphine frowned. 'Certainly not. Something strange is happening in that hotel, but it is not my doing.'

Throughout this latter part of the conversation I had

been repeatedly distracted by Mrs Grinder, who had taken to sniffing loudly every few seconds. Suddenly she stopped, and pointed to a dark cleft in the cliffs which rose behind the beach. 'There!' she said, in a gruff and oddly accented voice. 'The smell is strong there!'

'We have found it!' cried Delphine. 'The hiding place of the *Liberty*!' And she started to run over the dunes of dry, piled sand while Mrs Grinder shoved Jack's chair along behind her, and I struggled in my squelching shoes to keep pace with them all.

I caught them up at the mouth of the canyon, where the warm sunshine gave way to dim, chill shadow. All I could see in there were a few of those drifting ghost-jellies, but Delphine and Mrs Grinder stood staring into the gloom, and even Jack had pushed himself upright so that he might stand staring with them. I stumbled up to the abandoned invalid chair and leant upon its handle to catch my breath, wondering what held them so transfixed. And then I looked past them, and I saw it too.

On the canyon's floor sat an aether-ship, even older and filthier than Jack's *Sophronia*, and from her flagpole hung a faded, ripped and shot-torn banner, striped red and white, with a blue square in one corner containing a ring of stars.

*On the canyon's floor sat an aether-ship, even older and
filthier than Jack's* Sophronia.

'The *Liberty*!' cried Delphine excitably. 'We shall fly her out of here and find our way back to the Nineteenth Century, and there she shall become the flagship of a new armada that will blast Britain's navies from the heavens!'

As she spoke these wicked words, I noticed a silvery gleam among the tumbled blankets of the empty chair. In her haste, Delphine had cast aside her revolver! Spurred on by patriotism and a desire to show Jack that I was every bit as plucky and resourceful as this young French person, I snatched it up and aimed it at her, hoping that she would not notice how much my hands were trembling.

'Hands up, Miss Beauregard!' I cried. 'You shall do no such thing! You will return with Jack and I to the year 1852, and there we shall hand you over to the proper authorities!'

I had hoped that Delphine would recognise the justice of my proposal, and would simply raise her hands and say something such as, 'I'll come quietly.' Instead, she shrugged, and shook her head as if to say, 'What is this Mumby girl doing now?' Then she glanced at Mrs Grinder, and raised one perfect eyebrow in what I gather was a secret signal, for Mrs Grinder suddenly surprised me very greatly by exploding.

I suppose she did not actually explode. She did not fly

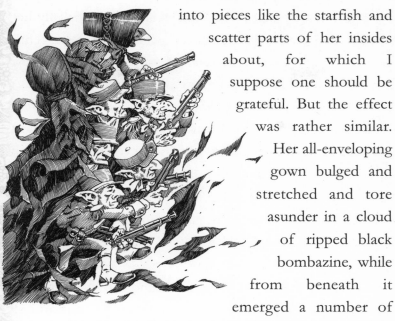

into pieces like the starfish and scatter parts of her insides about, for which I suppose one should be grateful. But the effect was rather similar. Her all-enveloping gown bulged and stretched and tore asunder in a cloud of ripped black bombazine, while from beneath it emerged a number of very small goblin-like beings, who must have been standing all piled up upon each other's shoulders like a band of circus acrobats. And every one of them clutched a tiny carbine, and every one was clad in the navy-blue caps and coats and scarlet trousers of the French Army!

Naturally I shrieked, and dropped Delphine's pistol. The horrid goblins leered and chuckled, surrounding Jack and I with their carbines raised, and prodding us with the muzzles. Delphine just stood laughing at my discomfort.

'Oh, Miss Mumby,' she said, 'your face is a perfect picture! Did you really think that the French Intelligence Service would send me here without the means to defend myself, or take Starcross by force if it seemed needful? Do please take care to keep your hands raised, and to make no sudden movements. You are a prisoner of the Legion D'Outre Espace.'

Chapter Eleven

BLACKWOOD'S MAGAZINE
No.79 in Our Exciting
'Savage Rites of Sundry Tribes'
Cut-Out-and-Keep Series

The Grand Ipsissimus of Threlfall
Prepares the GREAT PURLING Ceremony.

IN WHICH MYRTLE EXPLORES A LONG-LOST WRECK AND IS
NOT MUCH ENCOURAGED BY WHAT SHE FINDS.

Here I must ask Mr Wyatt to provide you with a sketch or etching of some sort (overleaf), for I can barely describe in words the ugly faces and squat, lumpish persons of our captors, nor the strands of multi-coloured wool which protruded, for some reason, from every flap and pocket of their knapsacks!

I had thought from the first that Mrs Grinder seemed an

odd sort of person, and I believed her odder still when I saw how many footprints she left upon the sea-sand, but I should never have guessed that she was made up of *quite* so many dwarfish legionnaires. Impertinent little beasts they were too; I suppose they were weary of being so long contained inside that black bombazine dress, and felt inclined to make the most of their new freedom to dance about making fun of people's bathing costumes and prodding the inflatable parts thereof with their bayonets in the hope of popping them. Fortunately, the Nereid proved more than a match for French steel!*

---

* If only Myrtle would pay attention to the *Boy's Own Journal, Blackwood's Magazine,* etc., she would have known that these creatures were Threls, who come from a worldlet called Threlfall on the far side of the asteroid belt. This Threlfall is a cheerless, chilly spot, and the whole history and religion of the Threls has been concerned with their quest to knit a nice woolly coverlet for it. This great

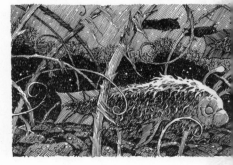

work, which they call the World Cosy, will, if ever it is completed, be the largest piece of knitting anywhere in Known Space. Progress upon it has been troublesome and slow, however, for until the arrival of British trading ships in 1829 the only yarn the poor Threls had to work with was some skimpy stuff which they spun from the fleece of the hairy space monkfish, shoals of which cruise past their asteroid each spring and sometimes leave clumps of their scraggy wool snagged upon the branches of its briar forests. Indeed, after nearly sixty centuries of steady knitting, the World Cosy still covers less than an eighth of Threlfall's surface!

Naturally, the Threls were awed and delighted by the varieties of woollen stuff our aethernauts brought with them, and our Government purchased the mining rights to the entire asteroid in exchange for a few shiploads of old socks and half-unravelled jerseys. These rights were then leased to a French concern, the Grande Compagnie pour l'Extraction des Minerales Extra-Mondiale. It seems to me that this was a MISTAKE. The Grande Compagnie must have been a mere front for the French Secret Service all along, and those Frenchies had undoubtedly been tempting the peaceable Threls with promises of yards and yards of wool, and had turned them, not into miners, but into soldiers! — A.M.

At last the duplicitous Delphine called them to heel, and drew our attention back to that ancient ship, which lay there in the canyon looking as silent and derelict as some ruined castle, with ghost-jellies drifting in and out of its various holes and hatches, and Martian ivy growing in dense clumps about its hull and upperworks.

'The USSS *Liberty*!' said Delphine, gazing in such a rapt way at it that she looked quite transfigured, like a saint in a picture. No doubt it had sentimental value for her, having once belonged to her grandfather. I remembered how touchy Jack Havock had been on the subject of his own tatty old aether-ship, so I refrained from making any comment about the *Liberty*'s condition, and followed meekly as Delphine and her goblin soldiers hurried through the knee-deep sand towards her hatch.

Even if it had been locked, we should have had no trouble gaining access, for dozens of gaping, splinter-fringed holes pierced the old ship's planking, where broadsides had smashed into her during the Battle of the Asteroids. And yet Delphine's soldiers hesitated before we went aboard.

'Looks haunted,' said one.

'Sure to be,' agreed another.

'Ghosties and goblins and Tebbits,' muttered a third.

Delphine looked vexed, as any young woman might who found her servants so reluctant to perform a simple chore. She set her hands upon her hips and scowled at them and said, 'There are no such things as ghosts, and you are goblins yourselves, so I don't see how *they* can frighten you. And whatever is a Tebbit?'

'Ooh,' muttered her soldiers all together. 'Ooh, a terrible thing, Miss . . .'

'A haunter of caves.'

'A night-hopper!'

'Big as an armchair!'

'Smells like damp corduroy!'

'Bite your head off soon as look at you!'

'And it eats wool! Nibbles and nobbles it! Unpicks and unstitches!'

Delphine gave a cry of irritation. 'Ach! So *that* is all that troubles you, is it? Well, if a Tebbit does lurk within this ship (which strikes me as

most unlikely) I shall more than recompense you for any wool it nibbles. Indeed, I shall offer an extra fifty yards to the first man to follow me aboard!'

At which the goblins gave her a rousing cheer, and began fighting among themselves to be the first through the hatch behind her.

In their haste they forgot Jack, and it was left to me to help him climb in after them. I suppose you will say that we should have taken the opportunity to escape, but neither of us thought of doing so. I think we both felt drawn to that ship, old and filthy and shattered as she was; in all the worlds of the Sun she was the only artefact yet built by human hands; she was as out-of-place in that era as ourselves, and we felt that we belonged aboard her.

'But I do hope Wild Will Melville and his crew are not waiting to pounce upon us,' I said, as we climbed inside.

'I reckon they're long dead,' said Jack.

'Oh dear,' I exclaimed. 'Then I hope we shall not find skeletons! I am always exceedingly alarmed by skeletons!'

'Dead bones can't harm us, Myrtle,' Jack said boldly, and went limping ahead of me into a great cabin filled with the voices of Delphine's legionnaires.

The light poking through the shot-holes in the hull filled the place with the most confusing shadows. Delphine's goblins charged about, overturning baskets and opening lockers, searching, I suppose, for treasure. One found an old spaceman's jersey, and held it aloft with a hoot of triumph, crying, 'By the flashing needles of Grodqol the Mighty!'* Another, upon opening a trunk to find nothing but a few frayed strands of greasy wool and a papery mass of moth pupae, stamped his foot and let out dreadful curses, crying, 'Tis like the Nibbling in there!'† Delphine ignored their ill-discipline, and glided serenely past them, gazing about her at the interior of her grandpa's ship, and Jack and I went after her, up a stairway which opened on to the main gun deck.

It was deserted. An upturned bucket rolled across the planking, squat space cannon sat watch at every gunport and ramrods stood like winter bulrushes in racks beside them . . . but there were none of the dead men I had feared.

* A Threllish folk hero.

† Threllish prophets speak darkly of a time to come called the Moth Storm, or Great Nibbling, when they fear a cloud of gigantic interstellar clothes moths will descend upon Threlfall and undo in a few instants the work of all those generations — A.M.

'It was quite a feat of aether-faring, bringing her all that way in such a wretched state,' said Jack, in a hushed and reverent tone. 'She must have had a good captain and a sturdy crew.'

'But where are they?' I wondered. 'What has become of them?'

We moved on through tight passageways, looking sometimes into the cabins which opened off them. In several we saw men's clothes laid out upon the bunks and hammocks, as if ready for them to put on when they rose from their sleep – but the men themselves were nowhere to be seen.

We looked into the galley, where a cauldron of stew had dried and solidified. 'Well, they did not starve,' said Jack, jabbing his pistol at a heap of lemons in a bowl, shrivelled to hard, brown shells like outsized walnuts. 'And wherever they've gone, I'd say they left in a hurry.'

Something moved, startling me and making Delphine whirl round with pistol raised, but it was only a shadow slipping across a bulkhead. I was pleased that I was not the only one to be afraid of my own shadow!

'Moooob,' sighed the rising wind, muttering through chinks in the planking, stirring the ropes of a mouldy old hammock.

We crept on, whispering like visitors in a cathedral, until at last we found our way into the captain's cabin at the stern. The wall of windows, which must once have looked out over the *Liberty*'s wake, was gone, and the ragged gash where they had been was patched with timber and sheets of taut tarpaulin. A heap of clothes lay on the bunk. An upturned tea chest made a table. There was a candlestick set upright on it, but the candle had burned out long ago, leaving nothing but ribbons and puddles of wax. On a pewter plate beside it sat a half-eaten hunk of bread and a glass with an inch or so of red dust in its bottom, which might once have been wine. A thick book lay open on the floor beside an upturned chair. A fallen inkwell had let out a splash of ink across the whitewashed deck.

'Oh, what happened here?' I whispered, and I'm ashamed to say my voice sounded exceeding shrill and fearful.

Delphine circled the room, opening doors that led off into other cabins, but finding nothing there.

'Will Melville was eating his supper, and writing up his logbook,' Jack reasoned, studying the dusty tableau before us. 'And something happened that made him leap up. He

knocked the chair over. The logbook fell, knocking over the ink pot . . . He ran from the cabin . . .'

'And he never came back,' I said. I picked up the book. Page after page of neat entries, in an old-fashioned, swirling hand. Then something written more urgently, underlined with an inky splatter . . . But what it said I could not see, for all over that page had been stamped what looked like tiny, sooty handprints.

'*Sacre bleu!*' said Delphine suddenly, (which I believe is something rather blasphemous in French). She was staring at the heap of garments which lay thrown across the bunk.

'It's just like the clothes in the other cabins. Look!'

I had sensed that there was something strange about those mounds of clothes we'd glimpsed all through the ship. Now I saw what it was. If Wild Will Melville had just thrown down his clothes before changing into his night attire, why would he have taken the trouble to stuff his shirt inside his tunic, or tie a stock around his shirt collar? Why would his stockings still be trailing from the tops of his boots? Why would his glove be wrapped like that around the hilt of his sword, which lay in the shadows beneath the bunk?

'He vanished from inside his garments!' I cried. 'They all of them did! They disappeared, and there is nothing left of them but the clothes which they stood up in!'

'That is not possible,' said Jack. 'What could cause such a thing?'

I looked at the book, at that frantic pattern of tiny hand-prints. I rubbed at one with the tip of my finger and it smudged. I rubbed harder, using the side of my hand and the cuff of my bathing costume, and soon wore a gap through which I might just make out the words scrawled upon the page: the final entry in the *Liberty*'s log, which those strange little prints had all but obliterated.

They are aboard the ship!
They are at the door!
THE MOOBS! THE MOOBS ARE COMING!

Heavens, is it not almost unbearably exciting? Yet I do find Myrtle can become quite trying after a few pages, so I shall return you to my own narrative for a time, and we shall worry about her later — A.M.

Chapter Twelve

INTERESTING FLORA & FAUNA

Callistan
Snapdragon

Nº 9

In Which Mother and I, All Unaware of the Perils
Which Face Poor Myrtle in Pre-History, Pay a Visit to
the Boiler Room, There to Meet with the Author of
Our Misfortunes!

I awoke rather pleasantly, with my head in Mother's lap,
while she sang to me one of her ancient Martian
lullabies, which sound like a tuneful breeze sighing
across an unusually musical sand dune. For what seemed a
long time I lay in that delicious, drowsy state, not quite

dreaming and yet not properly awake. And then I started to realise that the strange sensation I could feel at my wrists and ankles was the bite of cords which bound me hand and foot, and that the odd, ebbing scent I could smell was that of medicinal chloroform, and all my memories of our abduction came flooding back to me.

I struggled upright with some difficulty, and Mother said, 'Please, don't be alarmed, Art.'

She was bound as I was, and sitting on a hard floor of reddish stone, with her back against a wall of the same unpromising material.

'Where are we?' I said, my mouth dry and full of the taste of chloroform.

'I have not long been awake myself,' said Mother, 'but I suspect we are in the boiler room beneath the hotel.'

'And Myrtle?'

'I do not know.'

'Was she not chloroformed along with us?'

'I do hope not; she would doubtless have thought it most unladylike. I have not seen her since I regained consciousness, so perhaps she escaped safely.'

'But why have they brought us here?'

'I imagine they are going to ask for my help with their

boiler,' said Mother. 'It looks somewhat familiar, don't you think?'

I had been looking at her face till then, and could see nothing besides but more red rock, where two walls came together behind her to make a corner. At her words I twisted myself about so that I could see what manner of place we had been dragged to.

It was large and shadowy, more cavern than basement, and I recalled that Starcross had once been the site of many mines, and guessed that the hotel had stood above one of them. In one place a flight of metal stairs went up steeply to a door, which I supposed must lead into the hotel itself. In another, a lesser cavern opened out, sealed off from the one in which we sat by thick glass doors. It held tables and workbenches cluttered with a great many brass microscopes and other instruments, and many retorts and stoppered flasks in which mosses and seedlings appeared to be growing. And in the centre of the cavern stood a veritable mountain of machinery. My eyes crept over it, struggling to understand what it might do. I saw wheels and flanges, pipes and ducts and cables, mysterious upside-down pyramids and strange hanging spheres ... And slowly, as I took it all in, I started to realise that it *was* familiar.

'Heavens above!' I exclaimed. 'It is our old gravity generator from Larklight!'*

'Yes indeed,' said Mother. 'Naughty Sir Waverley! He assured me he had destroyed it, but it seems he simply removed it secretly to Starcross and rebuilt it. Or *tried* to rebuild it. He has made rather a mess of it. Clearly Mr Titfer has found a way to make it convey us through time.'

'Then your people knew the secret of travel in the fourth dimension?' I asked. 'Larklight was a time machine?'

* Of course, what we called the gravity generator at Larklight was not just a gravity generator. It was a Shaper machine, capable of transferring Larklight clear across the Universe to bring Mother to the early Solar System, and of re-shaping with fans and rays of gravitational force the drifting clouds of gas and matter she found when she got there.

'Well, not exactly,' said Mother. 'I don't believe Shapers ever tried to travel in time, particularly. It's rather a complicated business, and can be quite dangerous. But gravity and space and time are all connected, you know. I suppose the poor old engine still wants to move, and since I disabled the parts that make it move through space, it moves through time instead. That must be the cause of these strange temporal effects: the sudden appearance of pre-historic bits of seaside, the hauntings, etc.'

'But those occurred long before the machine was set here!'

'Yes, Art, but the machine was still the cause. When it was switched on the surge of energy shattered time, like a spike driven through a mirror. Now there are all manner of rents and passageways drifting about this part of space, leading into all sorts of eras. No doubt most are very tiny, and perhaps stay open only for a second or so, but others, such as the one which transports this hotel into the Martian past, are both stable and sizeable . . .'

Footsteps echoed among the aisles and cloisters of the ancient device, and our captors appeared.

'Those villains!' I cried angrily.

'Well, at least they are properly dressed,' said Mother.

'But Grindle and Nipper and Mr Munkulus! I thought they were our friends!'

'Don't feel too betrayed, Art,' Mother said. 'They cannot help themselves. I believe there is something very strange about those hats.'

'Yes!' I gasped, remembering. 'There was one in my closet! It tried to leap on me!'

Mother looked concerned. 'Oh, Art! You must have been terribly frightened!'

'Not a bit,' I said bravely. 'I had forgotten it, what with being chloroformed and kidnapped and all.'

They were almost upon us, and Mrs Spinnaker was with them now, also wearing one of the black top hats, and looking every bit as blank and glazed as the others. It was clear that what my mother said was true; they were not in control of their own thoughts or actions.

The only hat present which looked like the work of a decent, Earthly hatter sat on the head of Mortimer Titfer. He walked ahead of the rest, with a sort of triumphant smirk upon his fat red face, and as the others stopped he stepped forward, removed his topper, and sketched a satirical bow.

'Mrs Mumby!' he said, in a voice full of false friendliness, his black 'tache and whiskers bristling with self-satisfaction. 'And Master Art!'

'Mr Titfer!' said Mother, sounding as old and cold as space itself. 'Where is my daughter, sir?'

'Myrtle slipped away somehow, along with that villain who calls himself Ignatius Flint,' said Titfer. 'But they shall be tracked down by my machines.' He tossed his hat aside and hooked his thumbs in the pockets of his waistcoat. 'Of course,' he went on conversationally, 'Titfer is not my real name. I have had to sail under false colours to set up this place, and to distribute my hypnotic hats to those I wished to influence. Why, even my whiskers are but a cunning disguise. Observe!'

So saying, he tore off his black whiskers to reveal a smaller, more gingery set beneath. Mother and I looked blankly at him, for he clearly felt he had performed an amazing transformation, yet we neither of us had the faintest idea who he was.

'What?' he cried. 'Don't you know me? Well, perhaps not. I haven't had my picture in the *Times* or any other journal these past few years, thanks to your friend Havock. My name is Sprigg. Sir Launcelot Sprigg, former head of the Royal Xenological Institute!'

'That villain who wanted to dissect Jack, and Ssil, and the Tentacle Twins!' I exclaimed.*

'The very same,' said Sir Launcelot. 'And a deal of trouble it would have saved everyone if I had been allowed to go ahead and do it. But never mind. Soon I shall be the most powerful man in the Empire, and *then* we shall see some fun, eh? Then those fools in Government will tremble, and regret dismissing me from my position, and letting that mongrel sky-pirate Havock make a laughing stock of me!'

'And was it in your time at the Royal Xenological Institute that you came across these mysterious living hats?' asked Mother sweetly.

'Oh, the RXS knows nothing of *them*,' chuckled Sir Launcelot. 'A small colony was found here on Starcross a few years ago, when my family were shutting down the mines. I was able to hush up their discovery. Thought they'd come in useful, and so they have. They disguise themselves

* I wondered at the time how Jack and Nipper had failed to recognise their old oppressor, but they told me later that they had very few dealings in person with Sir Launcelot during their time at the RXS, and so much had happened since that neither of them had a clear memory of him, and so his black whiskers and tinted spectacles were quite a sufficient disguise.

as headgear so that they can sit on the heads of higher animals and feed upon the electrical impulses generated by their brainwaves. It appears to do the host no lasting harm, but while the hypno-hat is feeding they are in a state of trance, and terribly suggestible. Watch this.'

He turned to poor Mr Spinnaker, who stood nearby looking quite numb and mindless beneath his hypno-hat. 'Herbert!' he barked. 'You have soup all down your front!'

Mr Spinnaker's waistcoat was as white as fresh snow, but he looked down and gave a little cry of vexation, then began trying to wipe off the imagined spillage with his pocket-handkerchief.

'See that?' chuckled Sir Launcelot. 'Never fails to amuse. During the day, while the hat's off, he doesn't remember a thing. But come the night, when he's asleep, that hat starts calling to him, and then he's my creature. Him and all the others. They think they're asleep in their beds, when all the time they're doing my bidding.'

Mother did not look amused. She said, 'The other thing I should like to know is, how did you come by the old gravity engines from Larklight? When I dismantled them, and handed over the parts to Sir Waverley Rain, he assured me that they would all be melted down in one of his steel mills. Does he, too, wear one of these strange hats of yours?'

'Sir Waverley Rain?' Sir Launcelot fairly chortled. 'Why, Rain's such a squirt I didn't need a hypno-hat to bend him to my will! As soon as I got wind of the fact that he was carrying those strange old machines of yours to England aboard one of his ships I hurried to find him. "Melting down other-worldly miracles of engineering, Rain?" I said. "There's some who'd think that dashed short-sighted. Unpatriotic, even." "But Mrs Mumby's a friend of mine," he whines, "and I gave her my word." "Who knows *what* Mrs Mumby is?" I told him. "Some kind of unearthly monstrosity, I don't doubt, with a house that can fly about faster than any of our aether-ships, and who can say what her word's worth, or her friendship? She could turn nasty and eat us all up, and then you'd look a proper flat for not handing over the secrets of her machines to those who know what to do with 'em, when you had the chance.'"

'Oh!' declared Mother, quite shocked. 'I have never eaten anyone! At least, not since I was a Callistan snap-dragon, and that was absolutely *ages* ago . . .'

'Long and the short of it was,' went on our host, not listening, 'that Sir Waverley Rain was persuaded to fly his ship out here instead, where I took delivery of all your mysterious contraptions. Rain did his best to put them back in working order, and I set about using them to further my own ends. The hotel makes a useful disguise, and the guests the hotel attract have been my labour force. Why, even Sir Richard Burton was toiling away for me for a while, though he thought he was here to spy upon me! But he worked out what was going on at last – him or that Martian wench of his – and I had to dispose of them.'

'So it was you who turned Sir Richard and his wife into –'

'Changeling Trees!' laughed Sir Launcelot. 'Professor Ferny created the hybrid spores for me, working away under hat-hypnosis in a laboratory I had constructed down here for the purpose.'

'So the spores he discovered yesterday were his own invention? And, of course, you had to dispose of him too,

in case he succeeded in reversing their effects ...' Mother looked fiercely at Sir Launcelot, as she understood the depth of his villainy. 'And what of me and Art, and Myrtle? I presume that you had some purpose in luring us here. What part do we play in your plans?'

Sir Launcelot sniggered. He was one of those villains who was forever gloating, and most amused by his own feeble jokes and schemes. He even rubbed his hands together like some wicked uncle in a melodrama, as he said, 'The children have no use, except perhaps to persuade you to help me.'

'But what persuasion do I need?' replied my mother. 'Surely you need only set one of your hats upon me and I shall be entirely at your bidding.'

'Ha!' exclaimed Sir Launcelot bitterly. 'There was one concealed in a hatbox in your suite. For two nights it has been calling out to you to put it on . . .'

'I never heard it,' said Mother.

('I did!' I said, but no one noticed.)*

'No doubt it was unable to influence your weird, unearthly brain, madam.'

'I protest, sir!' retorted Mother. 'There is nothing the least bit weird about my brain!'

'Nonsense!' barked Sir L., losing his sense of humour in a flash. Turning, he stood looking up at the spire of machinery which silly old Sir Waverley had given him. His foot tapped impatiently. He said, '*This* carried Larklight from the Trans-Lunar Aether all the way to London in the blink of an eye, I gather. But when I switch it on, it just hums.'

---

* I have often wondered why Myrtle was not affected by the siren-song of the hat in our sitting-room closet. I heard it, as you have seen, and as for Mother her age-old brain is so mighty that it could not be easily influenced by such a brute. But Myrtle has barely any brain at all, and I should have thought a hypnotic hat would have found her easy prey. The only explanation I can find is that she is so concerned with appearances that, even when fast asleep, she finds the notion of donning gentleman's headgear completely unthinkable.

'That is not quite all it does, is it?' said Mother. 'I think it is having all manner of effects. Why else does this asteroid keep falling back through time to pre-historic Mars?'

Sir Launcelot shrugged. 'Starcross has always been prey to time-slips. It's a freak of nature. That's why the miners ran away, superstitious blighters. Nothing to do with the machine.'

'And it's not just pre-historic Mars, is it?' said Mother. 'That's the most powerful slip; the one that happens most regularly. But there have been others. Art and Myrtle and myself experienced a minor one as we arrived. And then there are these horrid hats . . . I can assure you that they are like nothing I have seen in all my years, and I have been around for a quite surprisingly long time. No such peculiar creature could have evolved without me noticing. I suspect that they have come from the future, and have dropped into our own era through some rift which you have opened with your meddling. The fabric of time is just like any other fabric, you know; it can be crumpled and torn and rendered quite unwearable if you do not treat it with due care.'

'Be silent, woman!' bellowed Sir Launcelot, and bent forward, so that his plump, ruddy face was close to Mother's pale and lovely one. Patches of dried spirit-gum showed on his cheeks, with strands of his false whiskers still clinging to them. 'Make it move, Mrs Mumby,' he commanded. 'Make this machine of yours move, and give me the knowledge to control it . . .'

'I can sense an "or" coming,' said Mother. 'Tell me, are *all* the Fellows of the Royal Xenological Institute insane megalomaniacs, or is it just you and Dr Ptarmigan?'

Sir Launcelot Sprigg struck her with the flat of his hand. 'Or your precious brat will be putting down roots at Starcross,' he growled, 'just like Dick Burton and his Martian girl!'

He turned away and barked another command. At once Grindle and Mr Munkulus came forward and dragged me to my feet, while the others went into a far corner and returned bearing an enormous urn of potting compost. I tried not to let Sir Launcelot see how scared I was as I realised what he planned to do to me.

'Ferny's new Changeling spores,' he said. 'Faster acting than the natural variety, and they lose power once their work is done. Imagine what a weapon that will make when I put it into production! And when we combine it with the space ironclads I plan to build, powered by engines like this one here, I shall be unstoppable! Then the Government will see what fools they were to dismiss me! I shall be appointed

Prime Minister, and Generalissimo over all the forces of our Empire! There will be no more pussyfooting about once I am in charge! I shall bring every nation of the Earth and every world of the Sun under Britain's heel! I shall set our flag flying everywhere from the tin moon of Mercury to the mountains of those nameless planetoids beyond Georgium Sidus!'

Mr Spinnaker wheeled a small set of library steps over, while his companions lofted me up to stand in the urn. Mr Grindle produced a box of respirator masks, and everyone clamped one over his face, and buckled its thick leather strap around the back of his head. Mrs Spinnaker did the same for my mother. Then Sir Launcelot drew a perfume spray from inside his jacket and climbed the steps so that he was holding it out on a level with my face.

'Sadly we have only produced a few batches so far,' he said, his voice muffled and rubbery behind the respirator. 'But the spores are quite effective, as Dick Burton and his Martian bride could tell you if they weren't so busy swaying gently in the breeze. So what will you say, Mrs Mumby?'

His hand reached for the dangling rubber bulb of the spray.

'Shall you give me dominion over Space of your own free will, without any tricks or foolish attempts to outwit me?' he asked dramatically. 'Or shall you watch this boy of yours become a Changeling Tree?'

Chapter Thirteen

FUNDAMOLE'S BESPOKE
HATBOXES

10/6
in this
style

As Recommended by
TITFER'S TOP-NOTCH TOPPERS

IN WHICH MOTHER DECIDES.

Mother tipped her head on one side to think over Sir Launcelot's ultimatum. It was a girlish gesture that she often made, but it looked awful and grotesque, masked as she was in that ugly respirator.

It's really an awful bore being held hostage by mad geniuses and threatened with this or that in order to make one's mother do their evil bidding. It sometimes seems as if never a week goes by without some reprobate or other pointing a revolving pistol or a Changeling-spore disseminator at me and insisting that Mother share with him some ancient secret or other. It makes a chap feel a little hard-done-by, and inclined to ask, 'Am I a boy, or a mere bargaining counter?' And then there's always the worry that one day, when asked to choose between the safety of her Art and the future of the Solar System, she might plump for the Solar System for a change . . .

But this time, she chose neither, for that few seconds of thinking time had been enough for her to see a way out of our predicament. She tore off her mask and declared, 'Gentlemen, you forget yourselves! You are in the presence of a lady! Be so good as to *remove your hats*!'

Her voice was so loud and sudden and commanding that I would have obeyed her myself had I had a hat to remove, and had not my hands been tied. My fellow guests all jumped to do as she asked, and as Sir Launcelot looked round at her in momentary surprise she sprang at him. Somehow she had managed to undo the cords with which he'd bound her! One hand lashed out to strike him on the chin – she has a very creditable uppercut, my mother – while the other snatched the dreadful spores from him.

Sir Launcelot crashed to the
floor and lay there, dazed and
groaning. Mother placed a foot
upon his shirt front to stop him
getting up, and reached out to
tear the hat from off the head of
Mrs Spinnaker.

The gentlemen all
stood looking about
them, and down
at the strange
hats in their
hands, and
blinking, and
wondering how in the
worlds they came to be there instead of safe in their beds.
The hats, for their part, seemed to sense that they'd been
rumbled; they wrenched themselves from their former
wearers' hands and flapped off to cluster in a high corner of
the cavern like so many bats.

'Great Scott!' cried Colonel Quivering, who was the first
to recover. 'Whatever's afoot, Mrs Mumby? What place is
this? What are those beasts? And who is that gentleman

upon whose chest you are standing?'

'This is the author of our misfortunes,' said Mother. 'At least, he *thinks* he is.'

'It's Mr Titfer!' cried Mrs Spinnaker.

'But what has become of his whiskers?' asked her husband.

'He's not a Titfer at all! He's *Sir Launcelot Sprigg*!' gasped Nipper, looking most confused, and not a little ashamed, at letting his old enemy deceive him so successfully.

'The very same,' Mother said. 'Now, if you would help me to secure him, I have to ask him something rather important.'

Sir Launcelot struggled indignantly as the others set about him, but before long they had him pinioned between them. 'This is an outrage!' he shouted angrily.

'No, it isn't,' said Mother patiently. 'The only thing that is outrageous is the way that you are planning to spread your hats across the Solar System.'

'Nonsense! I have no such plan!'

'Oh, how can you deny it?' cried Mother. 'I saw for myself that vast great advertisement at Modesty Station –'

'I know of no such advertisement! It is not *my* doing!'

'And ever since I arrived here,' Mother continued, 'I have been distracted by thoughts of Titfer's Toppers and their shiny blackness, and resolving to buy one for Edward and for everyone I know.'

'Well, they *are* simply *splendid* hats,' said Colonel Quivering.

'I'm sure we all think so,' agreed Mr Grindle.

'Exactly,' said Mother. 'And yet I guarantee none of us had even *heard* of a Titfer's Topper before they came here. There is only one explanation. You have had Professor Ferny devise an advertisement spore which will persuade people to buy your horrible hypnotic hats. No doubt you should like to see half the gentlemen in British Space wearing one, and wandering about in trances as a consequence, obeying your every command.'

'No!' cried Sir Launcelot quite plaintively. 'The thought had never crossed my mind! There are only a dozen of the hats in existence. They were handy for persuading these fools to do my bidding, but I could hardly set out to hypnotise the whole Empire!'

Mother frowned and looked thoughtful. 'No . . . no, of course. And yet *someone* is hoping to persuade people to invest in Mr Titfer's hats.'

'What are you suggesting, madam?' asked Colonel Quivering.

'I am not sure,' replied Mother. 'But it seems to me that there is something going on here far more serious than Sir Launcelot's attempts to make himself powerful. Indeed, his whole approach seems rather curious. Why bring the Larklight engine here, and set it up upon an asteroid known for its time-slips and other curious phenomena?'

'Well, that is quite simple,' declared Sir Launcelot. 'I . . . I . . . I . . .'

'And why go to all the trouble of starting up a hotel?'

'Ah, I have a reason for that, a very good and cunning one . . . But I have forgotten what it is . . .'

'Surely,' Mother went on, 'you would wish to keep visitors *away* from the scene of your crimes, not to encourage them? It makes no sense.'

'Yes, it does . . .' protested Sir Launcelot, but he seemed unable to put his finger on quite *how*.

Mother turned to the rest of us. 'My dears, this foolish man is nothing but a pawn in some far greater scheme, devised by . . . Well, by whom? In whose interest would it be to meddle with time, and open a hotel here, and lure all sorts of guests to it so that they might travel home wearing one

of these strange hats?'

We all looked at one another, wondering, and then raised our eyes towards the cavern roof, where the defeated hats had stopped bothering to even try and look like hats, but had melted into sinuous smoky shapes like the one I had glimpsed upon the balcony that first night at Starcross; tadpoles of black smoke with white stars for eyes.

'Sir Launcelot,' said Mother thoughtfully, never taking her eyes from the creatures, 'do *you* own a top hat?'

'What? You think I'd let myself be hypnotised like these weak-minded dupes?' Sir Launcelot laughed, flecking poor Mother's face with spittle. 'I *do* own a top hat, madam. There it sits, upon that table. Examine it if you wish. You shall find that it was made for me like all my other hats by

Lock & Co.'

'An excellent establishment,' said Mother, 'utterly above suspicion. And yet, if it is not your *hat* which controls you, then what?'

She paused a moment, pondering, then, lightning quick, reached out and snatched the black satin cravat from around Sir Launcelot's throat. There was a tearing sound as the pin which had held it in place ripped his shirt linen, and then another noise – a fierce, animal hiss. The cravat writhed like a serpent in Mother's hand. She tried to hold it, but it slid through her grasp and, changing shape, flapped off to join the other creatures which hung rustling in their high corner.

'Great G-d!' Sir Launcelot wailed, clasping both hands to his throat where the creature had nestled. 'What is it?'

'It is one of those hat-creatures in another form,' said Mother. 'It may only have been wrapped about your neck, but clearly it was still close enough to your brain-stem to influence your thoughts and deeds. I wonder how long it has been controlling you.'

'It was not controlling me!' insisted Sir Launcelot. 'I control the hats! I used them to make these other fools do my bidding!'

'Yes, yes,' said Mother. 'The hat-creatures have made you believe that you are a criminal mastermind, but you are really just a buffoon. Poor Professor Ferny has been down here creating spores, all right, but not just for you; we know now why he found time to create only a few of your nasty Changeling spores. His real work has been on an advertisement spore which infects unwary minds with the desire to wear a Titfer's Top-Notch Topper!'

'But Mrs Mumby,' protested Colonel Quivering, 'what does all this mean?'

Mother rounded on him, pale and beautiful and looking far more worried than I had ever seen her.

'Elementary, my dear colonel,' she said. 'When every sensible explanation has been disproved, then whatever remains, however silly, must be the truth. And the truth is that the British Empire stands on the brink of an invasion by highly intelligent hats from the future!'

Chapter Fourteen

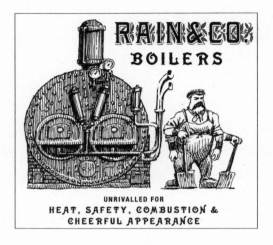

THE BATTLE OF THE BOILER ROOM.

They were not really hats, of course. When you looked up at them, clustered in their lofty corner, it was easy to see that. Ink-black and pale-eyed, they shifted shape like blobs of oil, extending small black hands to clutch the cavern roof, slithering like lizards through the passages between the stalactites. 'Moob, moooob, moooob,' we heard them whisper. It was really jolly unsettling to look up at them, and to think that, given half a chance, they'd form themselves back into hat-shapes and leap upon our heads.

'Keep an eye on them!' ordered Colonel Quivering. 'I'm going to fetch my shotgun!'

'Now, Colonel, dear,' said Mother, 'violence may not be the only answer!'

'Well, I hope you can tell us another, then,' said Sir Launcelot Sprigg rather rudely, from the corner where Mr Munkulus and Mr Spinnaker were restraining him.

Mother did not heed him, but turned to me. 'Art,' she said, 'now that we see those creatures in their true form, would you say they are the same as the one which you encountered on our first night here?'

'They are,' I vowed.

'And yet that one showed no wish to hurt you? It did not try to leap upon your head?'

'No,' I said, frowning as I tried to recall exactly what had happened.

'Perhaps it *did* leap upon his head!' Mrs Spinnaker pointed out. 'It might have mesmerised him into *thinking* that it hadn't.'

'I am sure it didn't,' I promised her. 'Indeed, it *saved* me from being mesmerised, for there was a hat in the closet in our sitting room, and I would have put it on had not that creature on the balcony said "Moob" when it did.'

'*Moob*,' mused Mother. 'Whatever can that mean?'

'Perhaps it is their name,' I ventured. 'Perhaps they are Moobs.'

The Moobs (if that is what they were) were gathering together like blobs of black mercury, combining to form a larger pool. Mother stood beneath them, frowning upward.

'One of these creatures has been controlling Sir Launcelot for a long time,' she said. 'It caused him to bring my old engine here. But for what purpose? What do they hope to achieve? I think they mean to use the machine to open a pathway to their own time ... A stable pathway, through which an invading army of Moobs will swarm!'

The black Moob-pool on the cavern roof quivered, as if it heard and understood.

'But you cannot make the machine do what you want, can you, poor Moobs?' she went on. 'And so you caused me to be brought here, thinking that you could make me do what you could not. But I won't help you, you know. I like all my worlds the way they are. I do not think the various races of the Sun would be half so interesting if they all wore top hats and did what they were told.'

From the darkness of the Moob-pool, a dozen pairs of eyes gleamed down at her. A ripple ran across it, and, all of a sudden, it came unstuck from the cavern roof and fell. Mother flung up her arms to protect her head, but the Moobs came down on her like a douche of oil, and she fell to the floor engulfed in slithering blackness.

'Mother!' I shouted, leaping forward.

Colonel Quivering held me back. 'Steady, Art! Your mother is more than a match for those devils. Remember what Sir Launcelot said? They have no effect on her. Too strong-willed, I reckon, to give herself up to their mesmeric powers . . .'

But he was wrong. One single Moob had not been enough to enslave Mother, but she was at the mercy of a dozen now, and soon her struggles ceased. She rose upright, clad in Moobs. Moobs on her hands like long black gloves, a Moob about her throat like a black choker, a gown of Moobs covering up her nightdress, a Moob upon her head stretching itself into a hat. Twelve pairs of Moobish eyes glinted like seed pearls amid the blackness. For a moment, as she stared at me, I saw a ghost of her old self behind her eyes. Then it was gone; she looked as lifeless as her own waxwork.

She rose upright, clad in Moobs.

'Moob!' she murmured.

'Mother!' I howled, running to her, but she swatted me aside, and knocked aside the colonel too when he ran to my aid. She strode to the old engine, and her black-gloved hands seized the controls.

'Stop her, someone!' cried Mr Munkulus. But my Moob-clad mother had eyes quite literally on the back of her head; when Mr Spinnaker and the colonel ran to wrest her from the controls, she kicked them to the floor without even looking round from her work. Exultant little black hands reached out of the caul of blackness that enwrapped her, tickling and pinching Mr Grindle until he shrieked for mercy.

The cavern was filling with a weird music as the ancient engine began to work. I saw the strange spheres and pyramids and various nameless shapes which make up its workings begin to turn and shimmy and do the other unlikely things they do when it is working. Waves of dizziness spilled through the cavern, and Sir Launcelot clutched his hands over his ears and fell grovelling on the floor with his bottom in the air. I wish I had taken the opportunity to give it the kick which it so heartily deserved, but I was distracted at that moment by a most disagreeable sight.

In the air above the machine, without so much as a puff

of smoke or any fuss or bother, a Moob appeared. It hung quivering there, as if surprised, and then, quick as a flash, dived down and settled on the head of Colonel Quivering, who was closest to the point where it had sprung into being. In its place appeared another, and another, and suddenly a black geyser of the creatures seemed to be pouring into the chamber, whirling about like black leaves in a tempest.

I saw one leap upon Mrs Spinnaker's back and swarm up on to her head, transforming itself into a topper as it went. Mr Spinnaker lunged at it, but his wife caught him by both hands and held him tight while Colonel Quivering came up behind him and set a hungry hat upon his head. The two of them turned upon Sir Launcelot, who took aim at the colonel with a revolver, crying, 'Keep away, you devil, d'you hear?'

'Oh, you mustn't shoot the colonel!' shouted Mr Munkulus, dashing the revolver from Sir Launcelot's hand, and a moment later a Moob had each of them; they struggled for a moment, and then turned, blank-eyed, on those of us who had not yet been possessed.

Mr Grindle snatched up the fallen revolver, using it to put a bullet neatly through the middle of Colonel Quivering's hypnotic hat.

'Good gracious!' said the old soldier, as the dying Moob dropped limply from his head. 'The cheeky blighters! They had me again! I trust I did nothing regrettable while I was under their influence?'

The pistol rang out again, again, and for a time it looked as though we might yet win, for old Grindle was a splendid shot and hats toppled from the heads of our hypnotised friends like targets in a shooting gallery. But the Moobs were too many and, one by one, each of our friends was caught again, and that sleep-walking look came back into their faces as they fell once more under the influence of those dreadful living hats, and at last poor Grindle was behatted, too.

Through the midst of the fray came my own mother, white-faced and clad in Moobs, looking like a wicked witch in a fairy tale. She reached for me, and I saw Moob eyes glittering on the palms of her hands, but I whisked past her and dived into the shadows under the machine.

It felt almost homely there. If I ignored the fading sounds of the battle in the cavern I could imagine myself back at Larklight in the old days. Yet I knew it would be only moments before a Moob found me.

A half-glimpsed black shape on the floor made me cry out in horror, but it was only Sir Launcelot Sprigg's hat, which had been knocked off the table in the fighting, and rolled under the machine. A perfectly normal, respectable hat, made in dear old London . . .

A sudden hope came to me. I put the hat on, and squeezed my way back out into the cavern.

'There is the Mumby boy,' said Mrs Spinnaker, not in her own jolly voice but in a sort of ghostly sigh; a voice from the unimaginable future of the Moobs.

'Are all accounted for?' asked my mother, and it was horrible, horrible to hear her speaking Moobish thoughts in that flat, Moobish voice.

'Not all,' said Colonel Quivering flatly. 'The girl, Myrtle, and the Frenchwoman and her companion, and the Honourable Mr Flint are still at large.'

'They will be found and controlled.'

'We must begin the next stage of the plan,' announced Mr Munkulus.

'Starcross has returned to 1851. The train will be ready. The first batch must be delivered to Modesty at once.'

In the midst of this terrible council I stood with Sir Launcelot's too-big hat upon my head, hoping that the others wouldn't spot that it was not a Moob, praying that they would not see how I shook and quaked, and doing my utmost to maintain a look of dull indifference. And when they began to move, when they started marching up the metal stairs to go and find Myrtle and Jack and Miss Beauregard and subject them to the same strange transformation, there was nothing I could do but go with them.

Mother did not even glance at me; she was intent upon

the machine and already unscrewing the bolts which held its inspection panels in place. I passed her by and climbed the stairs with all the others.

Oh, how I wanted to look back at her when I reached the top! But I knew a Moob would not look back, and if I had, and she had happened to glance up, she would have seen the tears which were running freely down my cheeks!

So I stepped through that door and left her there, not knowing if I would ever see her again. The others spread out through the hotel, calling in their ghostly Moobish voices, 'Myrtle! Myrtle! Miss Beauregard! Mr Flint!' Even the hoverhogs now wore top hats and had left off their truffling after crumbs to glide about grunting, 'Moob, moob!' and peeking into corners for some sign of the fugitives. I hoped for a moment that Jack might spring out and save us all. But the hope was in vain; the Moobs got no answer to their calls, nor did Jack appear. And so I went out through the front door and down to the promenade, and ran.

For, you see, I did not think I had any hope of saving Myrtle from those Moobs. I could but pray that she was hiding somewhere they would not find her, and that, if they should, they would not make her do anything unladylike which might cause her embarrassment when she found out about it later.

As for myself, the only thing that I could do was to find my way to Modesty, and trust that I might alert the authorities there to the coming storm.

Chapter Fifteen

SLAUGHTER & CO.
IRONWORKS

'THE OLYMPIAN'
PATENTED HAND-CAR
INCORPORATING A TREVITHICK
GRAVITY GENERATOR

In Which I Make Good My Escape and Gain an
Unexpected Ally, Only to Find Myself Pursued across
the Gulfs of Space!

I ran through the night, feeling very fearful that Starcross might return to ancient Mars at any moment and leave me with no means of escape. But it did not; the sky remained the sky of 1851, jet black and polka-dotted with asteroids, and I reached the railway station without incident. The train from Modesty had come in, and had already been unloaded and refuelled and turned about, ready to make its long return trip. The railway automata who had done all the work were nowhere to be seen, having presumably beetled off to refuel themselves. I crossed the rails in front of the idling locomotive, and saw ahead of me, on a siding, the hand-car which I had noticed on the night we arrived.

I wonder if you have ever seen a hand-car? They are used by railwaymen who have to go out to check the line, or search for lost trains. They generally resemble a flat railway wagon, with a sort of see-saw arrangement in the middle that has a handle on each end in place of seats. Two men may stand on either side of this contraption and, by pumping it up and down, propel the vehicle along the rails at a fair speed. Naturally, being adapted for use in the open aether, the hand-car I was preparing to steal had a glass cabin with its own air supply and a small gravity generator, but in all other respects it was the image of an earthly one.

I doubled back to pull the lever which changed the points, so that the hand-car would be able to leave its siding. I had just succeeded in shifting it when sounds from behind made me look round, and then seek concealment in a handy pool of shadow beneath the water-tower.

On the road from the hotel lights were showing, and in another moment a mechanised wagon came clattering and steaming into the station. My poor Moob-hatted friends piled out, intent on some fresh errand for their masters. I cursed my ill luck, for if they had arrived five minutes later I should have been safe on my way, but as it was I had no choice but to crouch there and watch as they began unloading stacks of round white objects from the wagon and carrying them in teetering piles to the waiting train.

I could not understand at first what those white things were. Giant pills? Wheels of cheese? No! A chill of pure terror run through me. They were hatboxes! And every single one, no doubt, held a Moob, waiting to spring upon the head of some unsuspecting person when the train reached Modesty and Decorum, and bend them to the Moobish will!

If I had not been so alarmed, it

might have been quite comical to spy upon my friends as they stumbled to and fro with those heaps of boxes. Hypnosis seemed to have made them clumsy, and they were forever dropping boxes, which drew indignant cries of 'Moob!' from those inside.

Nipper, even clumsier than the rest, at last tripped over his own feet and measured his length upon the station platform, and the hat rolled off his head and dropped with a cry of annoyance on to the rails beneath the train.* At once the dull light of mesmerism vanished from his eyes; they rose up on their stalks and peered about in great fear and confusion. Then, as understanding dawned, he sprang up and started to run, shouting out, 'Help! Help! The Moobs! The Moobs are upon us!'

It was horrible to see the cold way in which the poor crab's friends and fellow guests pursued him, and, producing a Moob from one of the boxes, forced it down upon his shell and made him meek and obedient once again. More horrible still, from my point of view, was the fact that this pursuit brought them close to where I was hiding. I

---

* The Moobs seemed to have some difficulty controlling poor Nipper's limbs, either because he has so many, or because the thickness of his shell made it harder for the Moob to gain control of his thoughts.

tried not to breathe or even move as the Moob-slaves turned to resume their task. But I must have made some small noise – or else Moobs can detect the thoughts of their prey – for the Moob that sat upon the head of Mrs Spinnaker, who was the last to go, suddenly swivelled around like one of the gun turrets on those new iron-clad aether-dreadnoughts, and I knew that it had sensed me.

Mrs Spinnaker turned and walked towards the water-tower, closer and closer to the shadows where I was crouched. I felt about upon the ground for some weapon I might use to defend myself, but found none. Then I saw the dangling chain which operated the tower. As Mrs Spinnaker saw me, and turned to call out to the others, I leapt up and pulled it. The tower's hose swung out like the trunk of a helpful iron elephant, and a white cataract of chilly water engulfed Mrs Spinnaker and myself, quite blinding us both for a moment and knocking us to the ground. As I had hoped, it startled Mrs Spinnaker's Moobish hat, which fell from her head, losing its hat-shape, coughing and spluttering and choking and waving its tiny hands about.

'Oh lawks!' exclaimed Mrs Spinnaker. '*Now* where am I?'

'Run, Mrs Spinnaker!' I shouted, for already the Moobs' other slaves were hastening to where we sat. 'That hand-car is our only hope!'

A lady as large as Mrs S. does not rise easily, especially when her clothes are sodden with water, and Colonel Quivering and Nipper were almost upon us by the time I had her upright. But she felled Nipper with a firm punch upon the carapace, a technique she had no doubt picked up in the East End pubs where she had started her career, and, taking my hand, let me lead her across the confusion of starlit rails and sleepers to the waiting car.

It was unlocked, thank Heaven! We leapt aboard – I seized a handle and Mrs Spinnaker seized the other – and together we began to heave for dear life. With painful sloth at first, but swiftly gathering speed, the hand-car started to move. It wiggled its way over the points I had set for it, and started up the long slope of the bridge, which was not as hard a climb as I had feared, for Starcross's gravity soon released its grip upon us, and we were in space, where there is neither up nor down and precious little friction, so that an object once set in motion may carry almost for ever. We continued working the car's handle regardless, until it was singing along the rails at a speed of several hundred miles per hour.

Then, breathless, we paused in our labours and, avoiding the handles, which continued to pump up and down on their own, looked out through the back of the car's glass canopy. Starcross was a speck astern, dwindling into the asteroid-freckled sky.

'My poor 'Erbert!' sighed Mrs Spinnaker, wringing out the wet hems of her skirts. 'He never did 'ave much brain, and now what 'e 'ad's been stolen.'

'Don't worry, Mrs Spinnaker,' I said bravely — for it is the duty of a British boy to keep up the spirits of those about him at times like that — 'we shall return, and save him. We'll get to Modesty and Decorum, and let the authorities there know what's what.'

'We'll have to hurry, then,' said Mrs S. 'Look!'

She pointed out through the glass. Far behind us, where the bright rails narrowed towards distant Starcross like a diagram of perspective in a drawing class, I saw a white cauliflower-shape bloom against the dark.

'Steam!' I cried.

'The train!' said Mrs Spinnaker. 'They're coming after us!'

'We're done for!' I said despondently. 'Now I shall never save Mother, nor find out what has become of poor Myrtle . . .'

Then it was time for Mrs Spinnaker to raise *my* spirits, which she did by directing me to take my place again at the handle. 'How fast can we make this contraption go?' she wondered. 'Pretty fast, I reckon. Faster than that train? Well, maybe. And let's 'ave a song to cheer us on our way; those Moobs won't be singing, and perhaps that's how we'll best 'em, eh, Art?'

And so we sang. We sang 'My Flat Cat' and 'Nobby Knocker's Noggin'. We sang 'Tom O'Bedlam' and 'Ganymede Fair'. We sang and pumped, and pumped and sang, and our wet clothes steamed, filling the cabin with a smell of damp serge, while the asteroids and spatial reefs turned to the merest blur beyond our windows.

What a race that was! The hand-car had no speedometer, so I cannot be sure, but I am willing to wager that it was moving faster than any hand-car has in the whole history of the Solar Realms, or ever shall!

And yet, for all our songs and striving, the Moobs' train moved faster. Mrs Spinnaker had her back to it, but when I looked past her through the hand-car's canopy I could see it drawing ever nearer. At first it was a mere cloud of steam,

then steam and lights. For a while, on a long bend, it must have slowed, for it fell back and I felt sure that we were winning. But then it began to gain on us steadily, until I could see the brass handle gleaming on the front of its boiler and the grid-like catcher it carried to shove luckless aetheric wildlife from its path.

'Mrs Spinnaker?' I ventured.

'What's that, dearie?' The good woman's face was quite glowing with the effort of her exertions. 'Sing up!' she advised.

I joined her in another merry chorus of 'Dearest Margaret, You Are Danish and Your Dog's Not Very Well' (that old music-hall favourite) but it was no use; the train looming behind her posed too much of a distraction. And as she commenced the next verse, the locomotive surged up

in a pother of steam and cinders and gave our hand-car a nudge with the tip of its aetheric cow-catcher, such that we were thrown about inside our glass canopy, and even Mrs Spinnaker grew too distracted to sing any more.

'But this ain't so bad!' she said brightly, as the train barged us along. 'They are just pushing us ahead of them. I don't see how they can reach us, an' make us put on those 'orrid tiles again. They'd burn themselves on that great steamy boiler if they tried it!'

I did not reply. For one thing, I did not believe the Moobs would be much troubled if our friends burned themselves in order to recapture us. For another, I had just noticed something strange outside the glass.

It was hard to see at first, what with all the steam and sparks gushing about, and the reflections of me and Mrs Spinnaker and the frantically see-sawing mechanism of the car filling every pane. But after a few seconds the gas lamp in the hand-car roof failed, which cut out the reflections somewhat, and by the ruddy glow of the locomotive's fires and the lightning-blue glare of the sparks which leapt up betimes from its hurrying wheels I saw the new phenomena quite clearly. An Aetheric Icthyomorph was keeping pace with our hand-car, very close. And out in the dark behind it swam another and another – a whole school of them, tails flicking frantically to and fro as they drove themselves through the aether at the same speed as the Moobs' locomotive. They were common red whizzers (*Pseudomullus vulgaris*) such as I had oft seen swim in and out among the chimney stacks at Larklight – but I had never seen them whiz quite so fast as this. And when I looked closer I soon saw the reason why they were so interested in us and our hand-car . . . For each of those fishes wore a sinister grin, and upon the head of every one there sat a *black top hat*!

'Oh, Mrs Spinnaker!' I cried – but there was no time for me to explain this fresh peril to her, for at that instant the leading Icthyomorph suddenly dived in and struck its bony pate against our canopy. I saw, as it dinged against the glass, that the Moob upon its head had braced itself for the shock by extending its little arms and clasping its small black hands together beneath the fish's chin, so that the impact should not hurl it off. The glass was thick, and the fish swam away dazed, having done no damage, yet there were a great many others, and their heads came battering against the canopy like the blows of tiny hammers. It was not long before one pane cracked, and then another, and our ears filled with the ominous hiss of air escaping from the canopy.

A human being may breath pure aether for a while, as all those fishes and other creatures do, but not for long. An hour or two at most, I believe. Yet countless miles still separated us from our destination! If all our air escaped, we should expire long before we reached it!

And now the train that bore us on was slowing, and along the sides of the locomotives, clad in tarpaulin suits and fireproof gloves which they must have found in the guard's van, Colonel Quivering and Mr Grindle came scrambling, each with his hat in place and a spare Moob hanging at his waist, ready to fit upon the heads of myself and Mrs Spinnaker!

But they never reached us. For the mechanism of the hand-car, which had been pumping and see-sawing away so furiously all this time, chose that instant to break. A spring gave way somewhere beneath the floor with a dreadful crack, an axle parted, and the hand-car pitched forward and flew clean off the track, tumbling over and over through the empty aether, leaving a trail of nuts and bolts and wheels and shards of glass, while Mrs Spinnaker and I were hurled helplessly about inside like two dried peas in a rattle.

And far behind us, along that shining silver thread which was the Asteroid Belt and Minor Planets Railway, that train with its cargo of ungodly hats went thundering on its way towards Modesty, Decorum and the wider Empire!

Chapter Sixteen

IN WHICH OUR NARRATIVE RETURNS TO ANCIENT MARS,
AND WE LEARN OF THE SURPRISING THINGS WHICH HAD
BEFALLEN MYRTLE IN THE MEANWHILE.

Horrid and eerie as that empty ship had seemed
before, it seemed ten times eerier and more
horrid once I had read those dreadful words in
Captain Melville's log. *The Moobs! The Moobs are coming!*

'Whatever is a Moob?' I asked, trembling a little, so that
the dry old pages of the logbook in my hands rustled like

dead leaves, adding even more to the general atmosphere of Gothick dread.

'I do not know,' said Jack. 'I never heard of such a thing . . .'

'I have,' said Delphine, reaching up in a hesitant and confused manner to touch her hair. 'I had a dream, I think, about a Moob, on our first night at Starcross . . . Or was it a hat? Oh, the picture of it will not stay in my head!'

Jack, meanwhile, had been stirring the sad heap of Captain Melville's clothes with the toe of his boot, so that a small quantity of cobweb-coloured powder tipped out upon the deck.

'Whatever they were,' he said, 'it seems they've consumed your poor grandfather and his men, and eaten them up inside their clothes, bones and all. And there's a chance they might be lingering still in these parts. So if you've some plan for flying this ship out of here, without an alchemist to start her engines up nor any place to go, you'd best begin. For I don't wish to be lingering here when these Moobs return.'

Delphine nodded. She was a woman of action, as I suppose one must be if one is to make a living as a mistress of intrigue. She went at once and shouted to her goblins to leave off their wool-gathering and set a guard upon the ship. She snatched the logbook from my hands and riffled inquisitively through its yellowed leaves. Then she went to the bookcase above Captain Melville's bunk and took down first one, and then another book. '*Spatial Geography for the Aethernaut*,' I heard her mutter, glancing at the titles. '*The Poems of Dryden . . . On Jove and Its Many Moones* . . . It is not here!'

'Pray what are you searching for, Miss Beauregard?' I asked politely.

'Alchemy!' returned the young lady. 'My grandfather had vowed to publish the secrets of his art that all might learn it. I had imagined that I might find his notes here, and use them to teach myself how to pilot this vessel. But I see no notebooks here, only poems and atlases . . . Oh, did all his knowledge die with him?'

'A pretty slender hope, even if it were there,' Jack opined. 'Gentlemen study for years and years to learn the arts of

Alchemy; I doubt you could pick it up from a book in the short time we have.'

'Indeed,' said Delphine, looking cross, as Delphine always did when someone ventured to contradict her. 'But my grandfather held that that was quite unnecessary. The Royal College erects all manner of barriers about the secret of the chemical wedding, and makes its students sit through years of dreary examinations, and learn reams of Latin words and alchemical signs and symbols, but the truth is that the chemical wedding may be performed by anyone who has a talent for it. It is no harder, and no easier, than singing.'

'Good Heavens!' I protested. 'What a horrid, democratic notion! Why, if that were true, then *anyone* would be able to do Alchemy – foreigners of all sorts might set up as alchemists!'

'Indeed, Miss Mumby,' replied Delphine, turning to me with a triumphant look, as if I had proved her point for her. 'Did you yourself not travel through the heavens by means of Alchemy performed by the creature Ssilissa, who was not even a human being, but some unknown breed of lizard?' And then her expression changed. Her eyes remained fixed upon me, but they took on a cunning, calculating look, which made me grow quite uneasy.

'And did not your own mother, Miss Mumby, steer a whole house across the Heavens, despite the fact that she has no accreditation from the Royal College of Alchemists, or any other learned body? Oh yes, my masters in Paris were most interested by that news. We are not entirely sure what Mrs Mumby *is*, but she clearly has a talent for Alchemy. And is it not possible that you, as her daughter, have inherited that talent?'

'Most certainly not!' I cried. 'Young ladies do not perform Alchemy!'*

But Delphine was not to be put off. She opened a door in the panelled wall and thrust me down a tight spiral of stairs behind it. She had no doubt studied plans and models of the *Liberty*, and so knew that this stygian stairway led into the ship's wedding chamber, but I had no notion of what lay

---

* Myrtle is wrong, as usual. The alchemist of the aether-ship HMS *Minerva* was found out be a lady in disguise, and there was a person named Miss Dunkery, who, in the last age, passed all the Royal College's exams with flying colours and became ship's alchemist upon a trading vessel; but since she wore men's clothing and smoked cigars she does not perhaps count as a true lady — A.M.

below me, and cried out most piteously to Jack to save me.

'Unhand her!' I heard him say gallantly.

'Stow it, Havock,' replied Delphine, displaying that shocking want of feminine delicacy which was so typical of her. 'I still have my revolver here, and if you try anything heroical I'll smash your other leg.'

Still, Jack followed us down, and I was glad of him, for at the stairs' foot I found myself in a most curious room, filled with pipes and tubes. Long lines of bottles gleamed dully in racks around the walls. In the midst of it was an alchemical oven or *alembic*, looking for all the world like a large pot-bellied stove.

Keeping her pistol trained on us, Delphine prowled about lighting the candles which stood in brackets upon the walls. Their gathering light raised dim reflections through the cauls of dust on all those bottles, and showed us the colours of the substances within: red Mercury, green Antimony, silver-white Newtonium and dozens more whose names I did not know.

Then, lighting a taper from the last of the candles, Delphine stooped down and kindled a fire beneath the alembic (it was an old-fashioned sort, of course, not one of the modern gas models). She bellowed for her goblins, and

told them to get stoking. Soon a veritable chain of them were passing fuel up from some store beneath the deck and feeding it into the under-parts of the alembic, which began to glow deepest cherry red and give off a dry heat which might have made me perspire, were I not so well brought-up.

'Now,' said Delphine (perspiring freely, of course, and pushing a curl of dampened hair out of her eyes), 'to work,

Miss Mumby. Which elements must we combine to bring this old ship to life?'

'I do not know!' I cried, almost in tears, for I could not imagine how she expected me to do this incomprehensible thing.

'Then *think*, if you please,' she said, 'before the Moobs come and turn us all to heaps of clothes, and you to a mere empty bathing suit!'

I stumbled to the rack of bottles and took down one, and then another, trying to read the crabbed writing and mysterious alchemical signs upon their labels. I could not; the words made no sense to me, and my tears made them hard to see. I snatched up a blackened rag which hung upon a peg beside the alembic and dried my eyes, then used it to tie back my hair, which had come quite undone with all that running about.

'Quickly, Miss Mumby!' my tormentor insisted, and when I looked at her, meaning to tell her that she was quite mistaken and that I had no talent, none at all, for Alchemy, she raised her gun and, pressing it against poor Jack's temple, repeated, 'Make my ship fly! You are your mother's daughter, aren't you? You *must* have the skill!'

I looked down again in desperation at the two bottles in

my hands. I did not know if it was the heat of the alembic, or some other thing, but suddenly it seemed to me that the chemicals within were brighter than before: one a vivid, acid green, the other a pleasing russet. It occurred to me that if I mixed a very little of the first with a generous portion of

the second, then the green would be rendered less offensive, and the russet more pleasant still.

Knowing not what else to do, I took down a pewter scoop which hung upon the wall and began shovelling quantities of each substance into a heavy iron pot which rested beside the oven, its surface scorched and rainbowed by the intense heats it had endured. After the russet and the green I found some red Mercury, like crumbly cake. Its very smell told me that it was poisonous, and so I put on some heavy fireproof gloves and broke it up between my fingers, dropping the fragments into my mixture of powders until some womanly instinct told me that the proportions were just right.

For it had struck me as I worked that this Alchemy was very like cooking, and might therefore be a ladylike thing to do after all — not so much a science as a *domestic* science. I began to grow quite elated as I sought along the racks of phials and bottles for the colours and textures which I felt my mixture lacked, and added them, and stirred them in.

And when at last all seemed ready, I used a handy shovel to push my pot inside the alembic, and shut the door upon it.

And . . . nothing happened.

It was most embarrassing. I had become quite carried away with my cookery, and had almost convinced myself that Delphine was right and that I had a natural talent for things alchemical. She and Jack were both looking at me most expectantly, and even her goblins ceased shovelling to stare at me, until she scolded them and ordered them back to work. Yet nothing happened, and slowly Delphine's wide, waiting eyes narrowed, and her mouth widened into a most disagreeable sneer, and she drew back the hammer of her silver pistol and set it once more against Jack's head, enquiring, 'Well?'

I turned to the mass of pipes and dials and levers which grew like ivy on the wall behind the oven. Oh, how I have always *loathed* pipes and dials and levers! They are so very Modern, and Lack Soul. I should much rather have lived in olden times, in Merrie England, when a girl had to concern herself with nothing more complicated than a little light dulcimer-playing and the occasional lovelorn swain. Dials, levers, pipes – these things mean nought to me! But in my helplessness I chose a dial, quite at random, and gave it a sharp rap with my knuckles, which set the needle within it a-trembling. And, thus encouraged, I settled upon a lever, and pulled it. And at that, every pipe in the place set up a strange lowing, a howling song, quite unearthly, which rose and fell and twisted itself into the strange harmonies I had heard before aboard *Sophronia*, when Ssilissa was preparing to loft us into space.

'She has done it!' cried Jack. 'The engine sings!'

'I hope it does rather more than that,' Delphine said. 'To the helm, Mr Havock. Sergeant Tartuffe, keep watch on him; Boke, Gaggarat, Sneave, go along and assist Mr Havock in the working of the ship. The rest of you, keep shovelling! Shovel for all you're worth! Get this ship spaceborne and back to our own time, where there are fat

British ships to prey upon, and you'll have wool beyond the dreams of avarice!'

The goblins hastened to do as she commanded, and Jack had no choice but to let them hustle him up that spiral companionway and away to whatever part of the old ship the helm was housed in. Yet he shot me a look as he went which seemed full of pride and affection, as if I had surprised him with my cleverness.

He could not, of course, have been half so surprised as me!

Delphine remained in the wedding chamber. 'Now take us aloft!' she said.

I was about to say that I couldn't, when I realised that I could. If I closed my eyes I could see the ship beneath me, a golden pod shining in my mind's eye. I could sense the alchemical power which strained to escape and drive her upward, free from the shackles of Mars's gravity. And I knew that if I just adjusted the controls of the alembic by a whisker, she would obey me.

'But where will we go?' I asked. 'There cannot be much fuel aboard, and there is nowhere in this desolate era where we may find more!'

'Then let us leave this desolate era,' vowed Delphine. She

had out her pocket watch, and was consulting it. 'We shall find the rift in time which brought my grandfather here, and use it to return to 1851.'

I could sense the pressure building inside the ship. It made me feel quite unwell – a sensation which I had often felt aboard *Sophronia*, but had put down to simple space sickness. Unable to restrain myself, I reached out and touched the controls, and at once the old ship rose, trembling, creaking . . .

'Careful!' cried Delphine. 'Do you wish to run us upon a mountainside?'

I suppose that that is exactly what I should have done. Being a patriot and loving Britain, as I do, much more dearly than my own life, I should have steered the USSS *Liberty* to her destruction, rather than return her to Known Space to begin her campaign of piracy and revolution against the established order. But I was carried away by the strangest emotions. I felt as if the power of the Alchemical Realm, which lies beyond the world we know, were surging through me in a golden tide. Not only that, but I could feel the pull of other tides: the great slow tug of the planet's gravity, the warm yearning call of the mighty Sun, and amid it all, just a few miles away, and as ugly as a grease spot upon a

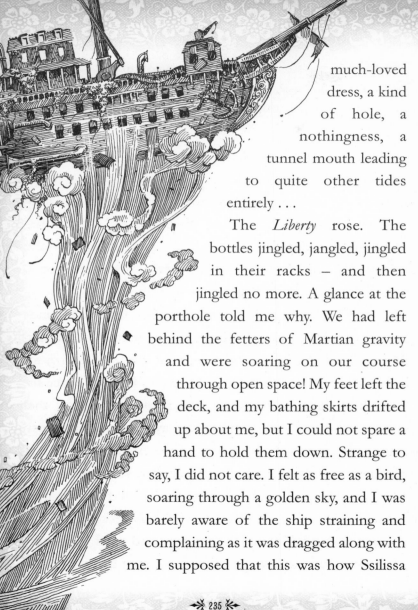

much-loved dress, a kind of hole, a nothingness, a tunnel mouth leading to quite other tides entirely . . .

The *Liberty* rose. The bottles jingled, jangled, jingled in their racks – and then jingled no more. A glance at the porthole told me why. We had left behind the fetters of Martian gravity and were soaring on our course through open space! My feet left the deck, and my bathing skirts drifted up about me, but I could not spare a hand to hold them down. Strange to say, I did not care. I felt as free as a bird, soaring through a golden sky, and I was barely aware of the ship straining and complaining as it was dragged along with me. I supposed that this was how Ssilissa felt each day as she helped the *Sophronia* across the aether's seas, and I am sorry to say that I felt envious of her, and most regretful that I had not known such splendour until now.

Ahead of us I sensed again that hole, its ragged edges trailing threads of lost time. I cried out for Jack to steer us a mite to the left, if he pleased, and Delphine translated my request into more nautical terms and barked them up the speaking trumpet to Jack without troubling to add the 'please'.

He did as she asked. The *Liberty* seemed to hesitate for an instant on the boundary of that gash in time. In that instant I fancied that she had become a million, million ships, all laid one atop the other, some smelling of fresh paint and new-cut timber and full of the voices of American buccaneers, some mere rotted hulks, whose rusted nails were turning to powder and letting her mouldy timbers fall away into the blackness of the night. A wave of dizziness o'erwhelmed me! I thought at first that it was because my simple, feminine mind was too weak to comprehend the grandeur and the mystery of Time. Then I realised that I had felt that sensation before, at Starcross, each time the hotel had plunged back or forth through history; it is the sensation aroused in a mortal body when it travels through the Fourth Dimension.

Then it passed. We were through the rift, we had crossed a gulf of many centuries, and all, all was changed! Instead of the simple tides which had swirled about the planet Mars I faced the churning rapids of the asteroid belt. Wherever I turned there was a gravity field or a reef of dreadful rocks, which seemed to me like hard, dark points in a great confusion of light. 'Oh!' and 'Eek!' I cried, and I felt the ship swerve this way and that as Jack, far above me, responded to the alarums of a goblin look-out and swung us narrowly past each obstacle.

'I do not know which one is Starcross!' I said, bewildered by all the different gravity fields, which seemed to want to pull the *Liberty* in every direction at once, but none strongly enough to actually capture her. 'Miss Beauregard, you must find your grandpapa's atlases and star charts and work out a course . . .'

'There's no need for us to call at Starcross,' said Delphine, prowling the shuddering deck like a panther.

'But Art, and Mother!'

'A fig for Art and Mother,' said Delphine. 'Find us a path to Modesty and Decorum, so we can fill our holds with

stolen fuel and vittles and burn a ship or two to let the British know they don't have Heaven to themselves any longer!'

'But I cannot tell which one is Modesty, either. Nor Decorum.'

'Then follow the railway line,' said Delphine.

I sought through the gaudy washes of light and gravity which filled my mind with most upsetting, garish effects, like one of those disagreeable modern paintings by Mr Turner. At last, amid it all, I sensed the gaunt, gleaming straightness of a railway line, and felt the *Liberty* settle into a course quite near it. I relaxed a little then, and pushed myself back from the alembic, feeling quite faint from my exertions, yet filled with a sort of happy tiredness. Beyond the porthole sable space rushed by, flecked with asteroids. I was disappointed to see that the ship was not enfolded in the golden veils that I had seen sometimes trailing around *Sophronia*. Ssilissa had more experience than I, and must have been able to accelerate Jack's ship to vastly greater speeds. But we were moving fast enough, I thought, quite pleased by what I had achieved. Judging by the way the railway tracks kept sliding by outside, we should reach Modesty and Decorum within a few more hours.

And *then* what? I wondered, and my complacency began to fade. How could I prevent Delphine from blasting and burning Her Majesty's settlements there, and her goblins from looting every wool shop in the place, and unravelling all the inhabitants' cardigans?*

Delphine, meanwhile, had glided over to the porthole, and was peering out of it with her telescope, perhaps hoping to confirm that I really had brought her to our own time, and not ten years ago or the middle of next week. 'There's a train ahead,' I heard her say. And then, 'Why, what's this?'

Glad of anything which distracted her from her

---

* Cardigan (n): a curious knitted garment with buttons up the front, named after Lord Cardigan, who had one made to keep him warm when he went on aether fishing expeditions off Vesta — A.M.

rebellious mission, I took the opportunity to slide a cold-shelf into the alembic. This cooled the reactions within somewhat, and I felt the *Liberty* slow accordingly. The pipes about us gave out strange moans and creaks as the alembic's heat faded. (One seemed to murmur 'Moob!', but I assured myself that it was only my overwrought imagining.)

Delphine did not notice. She was intent upon whatever distant object had caught her attention. 'D——d extraordinary!' she muttered. 'Miss Mumby, there is a train upon the track ahead. Two men in top hats are scrambling about upon its boiler, and it is pushing ahead of it a hand-car in which I can clearly see your brother Art and Mrs Spinnaker.'

'Art?' I said. 'Oh, whatever mischief is Arthur about now? Do let me see!'

'Oh!' cried Delphine, ignoring my request. 'They have jumped the rails! They're done for! A wheel is off – glass breaking – what a smash! They are off the track, and falling free in space! The train will stop and help, surely? But no! It races on! It vanishes, and leaves them to die!'

'Then *we* must rescue them!' I cried.

Delphine glanced round at me, and I thought for a moment that she was about to forbid the notion, and insist that I drove on towards Modesty. But even in Delphine's unwomanly breast there still beat some semblance of a heart, and within that heart there yet survived some trace of feminine compassion! She could not fly on and leave poor Mrs Spinnaker to breathe her last in the vastness of the empty aether. (I say nothing of Art, of course; she did not know him well, and so it is quite possible she might have stopped to rescue him even if he had been quite alone.)

Delphine snatched up the speaking tube mounted on the chamber wall and shouted up it, 'Alter course! Lay us alongside that hand-car!'

I knew, somehow, that only the ghost of power would be required for such delicate manoeuvrings, and so, despite Delphine's protests, I left the alembic to attend to itself. I heard Delphine shout out something as I scurried upstairs, but it seemed hardly likely that she would put a bullet through me now that I proved myself so useful. The knotted cloth which held my hair came undone and fell, yet I did not look back, but hurried up to the top deck, where I found Jack turning the wheel, while Delphine's goblins clustered at an open hatch.

There I joined them, and watched as they slung skeins of their precious wool out into the night and used them to reel

in first Mrs Spinnaker, who seemed to have swooned, and then Art, who, not noticing me, but spying the carbines which the goblins wore on slings over their shoulders, cried out, 'Those fish! Shoot those fish! Whatever you do, don't let those fish come aboard!'

The goblins all gaped at him. There were indeed a number of red whizzers flitting about outside, but whoever heard of a fish boarding an aether-ship, unless it had been hooked and reeled in by a hungry aethernaut? I was about to push my way to the front of the little crowd and make myself known to him when Delphine came up the companionway behind us and called out in a loud and strangely altered voice, 'Do as he says! Shoot down those fish!'

I covered my ears as the goblins raised their carbines and started firing. Really, I thought, looking at Delphine, she was a very peculiar person. Why was she speaking in that ridiculous, hollow-sounding voice, and what had made her decide to humour Art in his strange whim of massacring red whizzers?

And whatever had possessed her to put on that enormous top hat?

Chapter Seventeen

IN WHICH WE LEARN THE HISTORY OF A MOOB.

I was jolly surprised to find myself being rescued when I had been prepared for certain death in the chilly immensities of space (although I suppose I should be used to it by now, for it seems to happen to me quite regularly). But I had not noticed that ship until it came swooping in to save me and Mrs S., so it came as rather a shock when its hatch suddenly heaved open in the darkness and a parcel of goblins in red trews and blue jackets started hullooing and throwing out woolly ropes for me to clap hold of.

It was a strange old tub, too: like a warship from Admiral Nelson's day, all dusty and beaten up and overgrown with ivy, and from its jack-staff flew the banner of the old American rebellion. I wondered if it were a ghost ship as they hauled me in, but I would sooner face ghosts than Moobs any day, so I set aside such fancies and started hollering at the goblins to shoot those Moobified fish before they came whizzing in to make mad hatters of us all.

While they set about the shoal with their carbines I flopped on the deck beside poor, insensible Mrs Spinnaker, gasping for breath and feeling for all the world like a landed fish myself. It was only then that I noticed (surprised) that Myrtle was present, in her swimming things. And not just Myrtle, but Jack Havock, too, manning the wheel and looking most heroic. And before I could greet either of them I saw that the person who had given the order to fire upon those fish was Delphine Beauregard, and that she was wearing upon her head a Moob!

Mustering what strength I had left, I sprang to my feet, snatched a ramrod from a nearby rack and swung it at the malevolent hat. I thought I had a chance to knock it down and trample on it before it could betray us to its chums.

But Delphine, to my surprise, called out, 'Please! Do not strike me! Listen!'

I was so startled to hear such politeness from a Moob that I missed it, and as I was trying to recover myself (for there was no gravity aboard that old ship, and the effort of swinging the ramrod had set me tumbling head over heels in the middle of the cabin) a thought struck me.

Had not Delphine called out and told those soldierly types to shoot down the Moob-infested shoal of whizzers? Could it be that the hat upon her head was on our side, not theirs?

The gunfire had ceased now, and the goblins were securing the hatch and turning to stare at Delphine, as if they were puzzled by her choice of headwear. I guessed that they had not met a Moob before, and nor had Jack and Myrtle.

'Keep away from her!' I warned (for I still couldn't quite trust that hat of hers). 'She is not herself! That thing on her head is a sort of vampire-hat. It has taken control of all her thoughts and actions.'

'Well, it is high time *somebody* did,' sniffed Myrtle.

The goblins nervously raised their guns, but once again Delphine called out, 'Don't shoot! I am a friend!'

Jack jumped down from the steering platform. 'That's for us to say,' he said. 'Who are you? *What* are you? Where do you come from?'

'Moob, Moob, Moob,' said Delphine – or rather the Moob, speaking through her mouth. 'That is to say, my *name* is Moob, I *am* a Moob, and I come from a *place* called Moob. Moob is the only sound that we can make, you see. Indeed, it was the only sound I knew existed, until I met Wild Bill Melville and his men.'

'And *ate* them,' said Jack angrily.

'No, no!' said the Moob. 'It was

not like that! Let me explain . . . !'

'All right,' said Jack. 'But make it good, or I shall be throwing you overboard before we go on our way.'

Delphine drifted towards us, so that the light of the cabin lamps shone on her face. Her eyes were dull, her gaze indifferent; she was not Delphine at all. But still she spoke, and this is what she said.

'The place we come from exists far, far in the future, at the very end of time. It is a mournful place; a realm of nothingness, where nothing lives but Moobs. For we are the Last Ones. When all else is darkness, and the last stars are guttering like candle stubs, and the great cold is spreading out across the Heavens, we are what remains. We have none of the vim and vigour of life forms in your era. We do not love, or dream, or hope, or have adventures. We are the Last Ones, and all such passions have been washed out of us. All we ever do is eat, and what we eat are thoughts.

'There are beings who live inside the stars, you see. Inside all the suns of space those golden beings swirl and sing, and their thoughts go scattering out across space like a pale sleet. It is the habit of us Moobs to stretch ourselves very thin, like nets or sieves, and catch these thoughts as they go soaring through the aether. But they are meagre fare, for all the sun-beings think the same thing; they are very sorry that their sun is going out, and so their thoughts are mournful, and rather stringy.

'Then, one day (I do not mean "day" precisely, for there are no days and nights in Moob, but that is the best word I can find in Miss Beauregard's mind) I found a sort of tear or rent in the fabric of Moob. I slipped through it, quite by accident, and found myself upon the world that you call Mars, in a period of history far removed from your own. Several other Moobs came through with me, intrigued by the scent of fresh thoughts which emanated from the place. But no sooner were we there than the rent or tear snapped shut again, leaving us marooned!

'We were not worried or afraid, for Mars had much to offer us. There were the sand clams, whose slow, vicious thoughts seemed new and spicy to us. There were the starfish, whose predatory dreams tasted hot as cayenne pepper. And if too much of that rich diet disagreed with us, we simply spread ourselves out and drank up the yellow, buttery thoughts of sun-people that were blown in on the solar wind.

'And then, one day, this ship appeared. It had fallen, I believe, through another of those fickle rifts. We did not know what it was. We settled on it and tried to eat its thoughts, not realising that it was not alive. The other Moobs lost interest, and drifted off, but I had scented something strange beneath the whiffs of gunpowder and Alchemy which clung to these old timbers. And my curiosity was rewarded, for at last a hatch opened, and out stepped the crew, looking about in wonderment at this strange place that they had fallen in.

'That night, I slid into Will Melville's cabin and tasted his dreams: dreams of battle, peppery and sharp; dreams of his family, like pudding and warm custard; sometimes a nightmare, sour as curdled milk. I'd never known such variety, such wonders! I hurried to find my fellow Moobs, who were spread out like pools of tar upon the beach, drinking up passing sun-thoughts. I told them of the ship and its cargo of tasty thought-food, and soon we spent all our time there. We grew tired of dreams, and found a way of eating waking thoughts. We'd noticed the objects these newcomers wore upon their heads. "Hats", they called them. So we turned ourselves into hats . . .

'When a man wakes in the morning and reaches for his hat and grasps a Moob instead, he often puts the Moob upon his head without realising. And once we were on, we found that we could control the man's thoughts, and make him believe he was going about his usual business, when all the time he was just thinking thoughts for us. And it seemed a fair trade, for they were in a sad pickle, those men, marooned so far from their own time, without a hope of rescue. It seemed that we were doing them a favour by taking their thoughts away.

'Sat on Will Melville's head, I came to know and cherish him. He was a brave, good man, an enthusiast and an adventurer . . . None of those words would have any meaning to most Moobs, and I am grateful to Will Melville

for teaching them to me.

'But alas, the rest of the *Liberty*'s crew were not such paragons. They were rough, angry, thoughtless rogues, who'd signed aboard for deviltry and plunder, with never a care for Will's republic. And just as, by drinking Will's thoughts I grew thoughtful, so by drinking theirs my fellow Moobs grew churlish, rough and sullen. And, worse, I began to realise that we were harming our hosts. To take a sip of their dreams from time to time had caused them no ill effect, but to drink up all their thoughts, day in, day out, was horribly harmful. The men turned pale and dusty-coloured; they grew thin and their thoughts took on the taste of porridge made with dirty water. One by one, they started to crumble into dust.

'I tried to persuade my fellow Moobs to give up their feasting. I quit Will's head. I hadn't yet learned how to talk through someone else and so explain to him, as I am doing now to you, but Will could see what was happening. He was strong enough still to act, and tore the Moobs from the heads of his surviving men.

'But the Moobs had grown wily, as Moobs will who feast too well upon the thoughts of pirates. They crept back, and seized the ship, and when I tried to stop them they had their slaves stuff me in a locker and batten it down. Miserable and alone, I lay trapped in that locker like a forgotten sock. I heard them climb the stairs to Will's cabin, and the final struggle as they pinioned him and crammed a Moob upon his head. Then nothing more.

'At last I escaped my captivity and went in search of the other Moobs. I thought to find them on the shore, supping upon the thoughts of starfish or the small dreams of barnacles. But I had underestimated them. They had a taste for human thoughts now, and they had gone whirling off like dust-devils across the sands of Mars to search for more. They found none there, of course, for intelligent life had not yet appeared upon that sphere. But they found something better; another of those rifts in time. It carried them forward to the year seventeen hundred and something, when the part of Mars where Will Melville had landed had been blasted far into space, and had a new name:

Starcross.

'I followed them there, and found them haunting its deep mines like ghosts, leaping down upon the heads of unsuspecting miners to drink their thoughts. The miners grew fearful, and the mine was abandoned, but not before its owner came to examine it, no doubt to see whether he might make any other sort of profit from that lonely rock. My fellow Moobs, who had grown particularly cunning and crafty, allowed themselves to be discovered and carried away by him. I was left alone.

'For many years I crept about the crags and glens of Starcross, subsisting on the thoughts of passing Icthyomorphs. Then, at last, Sir Launcelot Sprigg returned, with a crew of workmen, and began renovating the old mine manager's house, extending it, turning it into a hotel. And to my surprise I found that he had brought my fellow Moobs with him; that he was using them to control the actions of other men, and that, although he did not know it, one was wrapped about his own neck in the guise of a cravat, controlling him!

'What their scheme is, I do not know, for they no longer trusted me and would not share their plans with me. All I know is that Sir Launcelot has been installing some manner of ancient machinery in one of the caverns beneath the hotel, and that when a gentleman from Earth came to investigate, along with a young Martian lady whose dreams taste like nougat, he and those wicked Moobs transformed them into trees!

'I stayed at the hotel, sick with anxiety as I waited to see what would happen. And what happened was young Art arrived with his family. I could not bear to see them transformed into trees, too, so I crept on to their balcony and tried to warn them of the danger, but of course I was still in Moobish form, and all that I could say was "Moob".

'Soon afterward, the other Moobs discovered me and drove me away. Like some revenant spirit, I found my way back to Wild Will Melville's ship, on pre-historic Mars. And there I found you, Miss Myrtle, and Master Jack, and Miss Delphine, and, well, you know the rest.'

Now, as you may imagine, I had been shuffling about like a cat on hot bricks while the Moob told us the last part of this tale, for although *he* might not know why the other Moobs had made Sir Launcelot install that old machine in the basement of Starcross, *I* did.

'They are opening a pathway to the future realm of the Moobs!' I explained, my words all stumbling over each other in their haste to get out of my mouth and climb into the ears of my listeners. 'They have the old Larklight gravity engine, but they have made Mother turn it into a time machine, and Moob after horrid Moob is popping out of it! They are loading them into hatboxes. There were hundreds of them aboard that train!'

'On their way to Modesty?' said Jack, catching on at once. 'Then we must hurry there, and stop them before they can spread out across the entire Empire!'

'No!' I said. 'First we must turn back to Starcross! Mother is a prisoner of the Moobs, and at their bidding she is bringing ever so many more of them into our era.'

Jack thought on this a moment. 'Art,' he said firmly, 'Modesty first, then back to Starcross. For the Moobs there can do no harm until the train returns to them, but those who have already left pose a danger to us all!' He turned to my sister. 'Myrtle, will you start up the chemical wedding again?'

I could not have been more surprised if he had asked, 'Myrtle, can you turn yourself into a fish and swim out of the window?' I had thought that my sister was looking somewhat pleased with herself, and a bit pale, and generally even more like a demented owl than usual, but it had not occurred to me that it was *she* who had been mixing the elements in the *Liberty*'s great alembic, nor that it had been *she* who had driven this old ship through so many leagues of Space and Time to rescue me and Mrs Spinnaker!

'Myrtle?' I cried. 'Have you become an alchemist?'

She looked down her nose at me, haughty-like. 'It is a talent that some of us possess, Arthur,' said she. 'I find that I have inherited a feel for the chemical wedding from Mama. It is somewhat like cookery. Now, if you will excuse me I shall go downstairs and bring the fiery elements to a nice rolling boil, so that we may hasten on and stop that train.'

'Erm,' said Delphine, or rather, her Moobish hat.

'What does it mean, "erm"?' asked Myrtle, addressing the rest of us rather than the Moob – I suppose she thought it wasn't ladylike to converse with headgear.

The Moob said, 'It was not you who set the alembic going, but Wild Will Melville.'

'Oh, what nonsense!' cried Myrtle. 'You saw me, Delphine — I mean, you saw me, Jack. And Wild Will Melville has been dead for ages.'

'He has,' said the Moob-Delphine. 'But some of his memories still linger on in me, and the memory of his alchemical studies are among them. When Delphine asked you to perform the wedding for her I saw that you could not, so I wrapped myself about you and took control of your actions, for a while.'

'Wrapped yourself about me?' cried Myrtle, quite appalled. 'About which part of me did you wrap yourself, pray?'

'About your hair,' the Moob confessed. 'I was the black cloth you used to tie it back.'

Myrtle turned paler still, and put a hand to her hair as if she feared to find a dozen more Moobs lurking there. 'But I felt nothing!'

'I hypnotised you into *thinking* you felt nothing.'

'And all those things I saw while we were flying along — the Tides of Space, and so forth?'

'Those were the things *I* saw. I shared them with you.'

'Oh,' said Myrtle. 'Oh. Well, perhaps it is for the best. I am not certain that Alchemy is a suitable occupation for a young lady.' But she looked quite downcast about it, as I suppose anyone would who believed they had acquired some superhuman talent, only to find it was not real.

'Perhaps if you would permit me to perch upon some part of you, we may resume the process?' asked the Moob politely.

'Quite definitely not!' gasped Myrtle. 'It would be most irregular!'

'Myrtle,' I said, 'we have to reach Modesty somehow. Heaven knows how much damage will be done if that train gets in before us, and starts to disseminate its freight of vampire hats.'

'Whatever the reason, Art,' Myrtle retorted, 'a young lady does not grant permission for the quaint denizens of Futurity to go gambolling about her mind and person. Why cannot one of Delphine's goblins be this creature's puppet and perform the alchemical chores, if it is so very important?'

'Threls,' I said.

'Don't be coarse, Art.'

'I'm not! That's what they're called!' I said, for of course, being a boy, I had recognised our blue-coated companions at once from the chart of *Odd Races of the Empire** which I kept pinned to my bedroom wall at Larklight (though why they should have joined the French Army I could not then guess, and looked forward very much to learning).

'Miss Myrtle is quite correct,' said the Moob. 'I can perform the chemical wedding just as well in any other body. I shall remain upon Delphine and press on towards Modesty. You know the place, which I do not, so I shall leave it to you to decide how we frustrate my fellow Moobs when we arrive there.'

'Now hold on!' called out one of the Threls, a thickset fellow with sergeant's stripes upon his sleeves. 'What about us? We obey orders from Miss Beauregard, not some talking hat! And we signed up to fight the British, who don't sound half so scary as these Moobs you've been going on about!'

'That's right!' the others growled mutinously. 'You tell 'em, Sarge!', etc., etc. Some of the Threls shook their carbines, some drew their bayonets, and things might have turned quite ugly, I believe. But thanks to Messrs Gargany,

* Published by Messrs Gargany, Nisbit and Stringg of Clerkenwell Road.

Nisbit and Stringg and their informative wallchart I knew what a Threl values above all else.

'Wool!' I cried, which soon got their attention. 'If you help us stop these wicked Moobs, why, Queen Victoria herself will reward you with all the wool you need! Shiploads of wool! Whole fleets full of wool! A flock of fine Merino sheep to call your own, who'll provide you with wool in endless supply!'

'You sure?' asked a Threl, looking sceptical.

'You have my word as a Briton and a Gentleman,' I said.

The Threls all looked at one another, and then, as one man (or one Threl, I suppose), they threw their kepis in the air and cried out, 'Three cheers for Queen Victoria and Confusion to the Moobs!'*

After that, things seemed to go swimmingly. Delphine's hat marched her down to the wedding chamber, and soon the ship was singing through the aether again.

---

* This is why the better sort of countries do not employ mercenaries: they change sides in an instant if you offer them more gold. Or, indeed, wool.

Jack kept to the wheel (his injured leg made it awkward for him to move about the cabin) and I relayed his orders to the Threls, who busied themselves nailing more oiled tarpaulin over the old shot-holes in the *Liberty*'s sides, cleaning their carbines, sharpening their cutlasses and generally preparing for whatever lay ahead. Mrs Spinnaker, who had been revived with a few sips of brandy, became a great favourite with them, for once she had had the situation explained to her she became as peppery as any of us in her desire to smite the Moobs, and urged the Threls on in their labours by leading us in such rousing old aether-shanties as 'Yo Ho Ho and a Bottle of Qrg' and 'My Grandfather's Sqallaxian Bogusoid Was Too Tall for the Shelf', etc.

Only Myrtle failed to rise to the spirit of the expedition. She spent her time instead peering at passing space through the leaded windows of the captain's cabin, and occasionally letting out a heartfelt sigh.

'You and Jack have not settled your disagreement, then?' I said when I looked in on her to let her know that Modesty was in sight.

'It is not a disagreement, exactly,' said Myrtle dolefully. 'It is simply that he is a piratical adventurer and I am a young lady and we have nothing whatever in common. I was foolish ever to think that we had.'

'Still,' I said brightly, 'at least you aren't an alchemist.'

She threw a candlestick at my head. She is a most peculiar creature.

Chapter Eighteen

We Arrive at Modesty but Find Ourselves Both Out-Paced and Out-Witted by the Dreaded Moobs.

Try as we might, we could not catch up with that train. I have spoken before, I think, about the many floating rocks and reefs which make sailing an aether-ship among the asteroids so trying. Well, not only did we have to creep around those, but we had to be wary of the *Liberty* herself, for long neglect had left her fragile, and whenever we came close to full speed her old timbers would

begin to groan,
and her metal bindings
squealed like scalded cats, and all sorts
of bits and pieces dropped off and were left bobbing in her
wake. So we were never able to reach top speed and soar
along Sir Isaac Newton's Golden Roads, and as a result, we
could not catch the train.

But we kept on following that shining rail, and at last we
reached a hub where a dozen other rails joined it, coming in
at all angles from other stations in the asteroid belt, and
soon after that we came down to Modesty docks through a
blanket of drifting fog.

'Fog in space?' I hear you cry. Why, yes. You see Modesty
was too small a world to hold on to its own atmosphere
until we colonised it and set up patent gravity generators in
its centre. Even now, there is a certain amount of seepage,
and so the oxygen must be replenished every seven months
or so by a delivery of comet ice. And when this fresh, cold

oxygen is first unleashed into the Modestine atmosphere, it causes a billowy, swirly, blind-folding fog as dense as any London pea-souper.

Out of that fog we watched the gantries and mooring-pergolas of the aether-dock appear, and the bright pin-point of a swinging lantern guided the *Liberty* towards a berth. I found a telescope and peered warily at the dockhands as they caught the ropes the Threls threw them and made us fast to the pergola's bollards. And the dockhands peered back, looking amazed, as well they might, for the *Liberty* must have been a most curious spectacle. But none of them wore hats, or any other

garment which might be a Moob in disguise – at least, none which I could see. And Delphine, propelled by the Moob upon her head, came to my side and said, 'There are no Moobs there.'

'Then where?' asked Myrtle. 'If there were as many on that train as Art says, what has become of them? What are they planning?'

'We'll find out soon enough, I'll warrant,' Jack declared, arming himself with some old American's cutlass and kicking open the *Liberty*'s hatch. 'First thing to do is get to the *Sophronia* and warn Ssil of the danger. Then the Tentacle Twins can help us find those Moobs.'

Before we set off, the Threls disguised themselves once more as Mrs Grinder, for it would hardly do to have a whole band of armed hobgoblins in the uniforms of the Legion D'Outre Espace charging about a British port. Like circus tumblers they jumped and scrambled and somersaulted up on to one another's shoulders until they had formed a teetering pyramid, whereupon the topmost Threl took from his pack a spare black bombazine dress and, fitting it over his own head, shook the skirts down to cover all his comrades. There was a certain amount of struggling to get arms through sleeve-holes and the like, but it was all accomplished jolly quickly, and once the fellow on the top had put on his black poke bonnet again nobody would have believed that the large, respectable-looking lady who followed us out into the fogs of Modesty was really ten cut-throat Threls.

We explained ourselves as best we could to the puzzled dockhands – luckily I'd thought to send a Threl aloft to haul down that stars-and-bars banner before we docked, or I think they would have taken us for Yankee rebels and roused out the marines. Even so, they eyed us most suspiciously, until they recognised Mrs Spinnaker, at which they quite forgot the rest of us and began asking for autographs and demanding that she give them a chorus or two of 'My Flat Cat'. Honestly, it was a stroke of luck that we had reached Modesty in the middle of their night, for otherwise I do not doubt but that the whole harbour should soon have been filled with sightseers and admirers of the Cockney Nightingale.

As it was, there seemed almost nobody about. As soon as she could fit a word in edgewise Mrs Spinnaker asked the adoring dockhands whether they had seen 'some "mates" of ours, what were due in aboard a train from Starcross a few minutes back'?

The honest fellows looked quite blank, until Jack explained that these 'mates' would have been travelling with a large number of hatboxes.

'Hatboxes?' cried the foreman, hearing that. 'Why, some folks are loading hatboxes aboard an old aether-ship called *Sophronia,* over at Number 9 Pergola . . .'

You may imagine what dismay that caused us! It had been one thing to imagine an abstract threat to the Empire as a whole, quite another to realise that the Moobs might be menacing our own dear friends aboard the *Sophronia*! Breaking free of the dockworkers as politely as we could, we hastened through the labyrinths of the docks behind Jack Havock, who knew his way between those wooden warehouses and stacks of tarry rope and sap-smelling timber as well as the back of his own hand. It was not long before the familiar, comforting outline of the *Sophronia* emerged from the fog ahead, looking as colourless and insubstantial as if she had been sketched in watercolours. And, sure enough, a hatch was standing open under *Sophronia*'s stern, a wagon was waiting at the foot of her loading ramp – and going up and down that ramp, dimly discernable in the light that spilled from the old ship's cargo hold, were our beMoobed friends from Starcross, carrying their piles of hatboxes aboard!

''Ere! There's my 'Erbert!' exclaimed Mrs Spinnaker, but Jack hushed her, bundling her into an empty shed. We all went after her, and peered out through the smeary windows at the work going on in the shadow of the *Sophronia*'s exhaust-trumpets.

'They are here already!' whispered Myrtle. 'They have enMoobed poor Ssilissa and the others!'

She was right. We could not see Ssilissa, but we could hear the low warbling song of the *Sophronia*'s alembic, which told us she was busy in the wedding chamber, no doubt at the bidding of a Moob. And on the boarding ramp, helping the others with their hatboxes, we could discern Yarg and Squidley, each with a shining topper clinging to the middle of his stalk (which is where those anemone-folk of Ganymede keep their brains).

'I see everyone but

Munkulus,' said Jack, watching grimly as his captive crew went about the Moobs' work. 'Where is Munkulus?'

'He was not at Starcross Halt when they were loading the train,' I remembered. 'I believe they have kept him behind at the hotel for some reason . . .'

'But what are they doing?' asked Mrs Spinnaker, as her husband and the others went to and fro, carting those heaps of boxes into the *Sophronia*'s hold.

'Taking that first batch of hats to England, I'll be bound!' Jack said grimly. 'I'd lay a bet those Moobs're bound for London, to set themselves upon the head of the Prime Minister and the Chief Alchemist and the First Lord of the Admiralty and a hundred other high-up men in Government. Then their friends can set about snacking on the brains of us lowly types out here in the black, and no ships will ever be dispatched to stop 'em, for the reins of Empire will already be in their little hands!'

'But why choose the *Sophronia*?' I demanded. 'Of all the aether-ships they could have loaded those hatboxes aboard, why her? It's awfully rotten luck, isn't it?'

'She is the only ship they know,' said Delphine, turning her blank face to us. 'Remember, they have ate the thoughts of Munkulus and Grindle and the crab, Nipper. That is how they knew where your *Sophronia* was moored, and that is why they chose her to take them to England. For I am sure you are right, Jack; those Moobs are bound for London town.'

'Not if I have anything to do with it!' declared Jack, reaching for his sword, but Delphine held him back.

'Not here!' she said. 'There are many, many Moobs in those white boxes. If you attempt to rush the ship, they will catch us all.'

'Then where?' demanded Jack, looking fiercely into Delphine's eyes, and then recalling that it was not she to whom he spoke, and glaring at her hat instead. 'Those are my crew! My friends! I have to save them!'

'We must fetch help!' exclaimed Myrtle.

But we were too late. The last of the hatboxes had been loaded aboard, and the song of the *Sophronia*'s engines was gathering strength. I saw Yarg and Squidley heave the cargo hatch closed, and the cart horses in the traces of the wagon tossed their heads restlessly as the old ship started to tremble and rise skyward.

Jack stared, and scowled, and said something which made Myrtle go, '*Jack! Language! Please!*'

The *Sophronia* lifted into the sky, and the curtains of the fog swayed and stirred in the wind from her flapping wings, while her engines trilled like some other-worldly choir.

''Erbert!' wailed Mrs Spinnaker. 'They've gone off with my 'Erbert again!'

Jack, looking grim yet resolute, said, 'Mrs Spinnaker, you must go directly to the authorities, and tell them what has been happening. Take care to trust no gentleman wearing a top hat.'

'If he is a *real* gentleman,' my sister said, 'he will remove his hat in Mrs Spinnaker's presence, and then she will know it is not a Moob. But, Jack, would it not be better if we all went together to the authorities?'

Jack shook his head. 'No time. We're going back to the *Liberty* to chase those thieving Moobs and tackle 'em upon the open aether!'

'But, Jack, how can we?' I complained, hurrying behind him with the others as he started running back across the harbour towards the *Liberty*'s berth. 'If we go aboard the *Sophronia* those Moobs will leap upon us and take control of our thoughts!'

Myrtle, agreeing with me for once, said, 'I for one do not relish the prospect of being a mindless slave for evermore, let alone a mindless slave who wears a gentleman's top hat with a bathing costume!'

Jack stopped and turned and stared at her. I thought for a moment that he had finally seen sense and realised what a ghastly blister she was, such was the look of dawning revelation that broke across his features. But he said, 'You're right, Myrtle,' and then, turning to the Threls in their disguise, 'How much wool do you fellows have about you?'

Mrs Grinder's head vanished inside her poke bonnet and a great deal of muttering came from within her black bombazine bosom as her various portions debated among themselves. Then her head reappeared and said, 'About four balls each, we reckon, plus Corporal Boke's swiped a couple of lovely jumpers we can unpick.'

'That should be enough!' cried Jack.

'Enough for what?' asked Delphine's Moob, and I should dearly have loved to hear Jack's answer, but he was already haring away through the fog towards the *Liberty*, and calling out for the rest of us not to dally.

We parted from Mrs Spinnaker at the foot of the *Liberty*'s gangplank, where the dockhands, still quite overwhelmed at finding the Cockney Nightingale in their midst, vowed to take her post-haste to the Governor. Ten minutes more found us soaring into the aether once again.

I had been afraid that even ten minutes would give the *Sophronia* time enough to escape, but the approaches to Modesty and Decorum are treacherous, and there is really only one channel between the various asteroidal shoals and reefs. It is marked out with buoys, whose gas lamps gleam in the dark like a road of lights, and far ahead of us along that road we could see the *Sophronia*'s stern-lanterns twinkling as she sped towards open space.

Not that I had very much time to keep a look-out. Myrtle and I were forced to work hard, jumping to obey Jack's orders whenever he needed something done. For the Threls who had helped him work the ship before were now all busy, sitting cross-legged in a circle in mid-air and knitting for all they were worth. Honestly, to see the way their needles flashed, you would think they could have finished their World Cosy long ago, and knitted nice scarves and mufflers for half the other worlds as well.

And all around us, quite drowning out the clickety-click of the speeding needles, the *Liberty*'s engines sang their strange song, and the old ship's timbers creaked and grumbled as she drove swiftly onward through the aether. But not swiftly enough! Jack left me at the helm and scrambled aloft with his perspective-glass, returning a few moments later with a worried look upon his face. 'We need more power,' he confided. 'The *Sophronia* will be out in open aether soon, and riding the Golden Roads, and if we can't follow her there, we're lost.'

He shouted down the speaking tube for the Moob, and after a few moments more it popped up the wedding chamber companionway on top of Delphine's head.

'I'm sorry, Jack,' it said, through Delphine's mouth. 'I cannot go faster. I have done my best, but perhaps I did not learn Alchemy as well from Will Melville's thoughts as I believed. Perhaps there is something he kept hidden from me, or something that he himself did not know.'

Jack pondered upon this, setting one hand against the *Liberty*'s timbers to gauge the vibrations from the alembic. 'We were going faster before,' he said, 'when Myrtle was running things down there.'

My sister looked thoroughly pleased with herself, and then suddenly alarmed, as she realised the meaning behind Jack's words. 'Oh, Jack,' she declared, 'you must not expect me to let that thing squat upon my head again! I have already told you that I think it most improper!'

'You think *everything* most improper,' Jack told her. 'But

the fact is, there was some truth in what Delphine said, wasn't there? You've got a talent for Alchemy that Delphine ain't, and the Moob used it somehow. Between you, you'll get enough speed out of this poor old tub that we'll catch up with the *Sophronia* in no time.' He pushed himself away from the helm and flew to where Myrtle was floating, taking both her hands in his. 'Please, Myrtle. For me.'

I could tell that Myrtle was moved by his plaintive yet manly appeal, for she turned an entertaining colour and her spectacles grew misty. 'Oh, Jack,' she said. 'Oh, oh, *very well*. But I must insist that the Moob turns itself into some more ladylike item of apparel.'

The Moob on Delphine's head bowed, and then seemed to melt and spread, becoming a sort of wide-brimmed sun-hat, then a smoking cap, and at last turning itself into a very

passable bonnet, decorated with black flowers. It left Delphine (who tottered sideways with a most comical expression of perplexity as her thoughts became her own once more) and sailed through the air to settle upon Myrtle's head. 'Oh!' said Myrtle, and then Moobishness overcame her and her eyes turned blank and glassy.*

'Do her no harm, you hear me?' Jack told the Moob-bonnet.

'I will not,' it replied through Myrtle's lips, and she turned about and swam deftly to the companionway, and down it into the wedding chamber.

'Whatever is going on?' asked Delphine, one hand to her brow, staring about in confusion. 'Where are we? What is Myrtle doing? Why are you all knitting?'

'Part of the plan, Miss Beauregard,' replied Sergeant Tartuffe, not even troubling to glance at her. 'Now keep quiet, if you would; you'll make us drop a stitch.'

'What plan?' demanded Delphine angrily. 'Whose plan? Sergeant, put down those knitting needles and take up your gun! You are a soldier of France!'

'*My* plan,' said Jack Havock, fixing her with his coldest stare. 'I'm captain of this ship now, and the Threls have agreed to take my orders till the menace of the Moobs is dealt with. And you'll do as I say, too, or be confined.'

I clutched the cutlass Jack had issued me back on

* By which I mean, of course, *even more* blank and glassy than usual.

Modesty and tried to look as though I wouldn't mind using it should Delphine prove argumentative. But Delphine seemed to know when she was beaten, and she asked for nothing more than a quick account of what had happened. I told her about the goings-on at Starcross, and the Shaper engine which Sir Launcelot had caused to be set up beneath his hotel, and I am pleased to say that she looked quite green as she realised that there had been a far greater prize than her wormy old *Liberty*, and that it had been right under her nose all this time!

Then, while Jack recounted the things which had just occurred at Modesty, I crept down the companionway and peeked into the wedding chamber. I was rewarded with the surprising sight of Myrtle mixing powders and potions and stuffing them inside the alembic as confidently as any alchemist.

Hearing me, she looked up from her work, and said, 'Your friend Jack was right. Myrtle's mind is so much more attuned to the currents of the aether and the laws of Alchemy than the other young lady's. Finding the right proportions and ingredients is as easy as pie when I am sat upon her head.'

I was not sure quite how to respond. I am well-used to

hearing Myrtle talk through her hat, but it was somewhat unsettling to hear a hat talking through her. I mumbled some pleasantry, and went back above, where the Threls' knitting flapped like woolly flags all across the cabin.

'How's it coming?' Jack demanded.

'Nearly out of wool,' said Sergeant Tartuffe regretfully, holding up the loose scarf-like garment he had knitted. 'The colours ain't very nice, and I should have liked to put in a spot of cable-stitch, or some pom-poms to liven it up . . .'

'It will serve its purpose something admirable,' said Jack, and, without waiting for the Threl to 'cast-off', he took the item and wrapped it around and around his own head to form a huge woolly turban, which he used the knitting needles to pin in place. A decorative flap or panel hung from the back of the garment, and tied about his neck.

'I should like to see the Moob that can control my mind through all this,' he vowed, and the rest of us began to fashion turbans of our own.

Chapter Nineteen

IN WHICH BATTLE IS JOINED AND DARING RESCUES
ATTEMPTED!

yrtle does have her uses. No sooner had the *Sophronia* began to make that speckled golden bow-wave that signifies she has slipped into the alchemical realm and is travelling faster than light, than golden curlicues and fronds began to trail past the *Liberty*'s portholes too, and we all cheered, realising that my sister and the Moob had taken us on to the Golden Roads.

The *Sophronia,* indeed, was travelling slower than she might have. Either the Moob that crouched on Ssilissa's head was newer to the arts of Alchemy than ours, or else the lizard-girl was struggling weakly against its influence, or maybe her spines just got in its way, but our old ship was easily able to draw near. The Threls, who all looked like woolly mushrooms with those knitted turbans wound about their heads, started to heave open gunports and poke their carbines out, but Jack stopped them.

'No shooting yet,' he ordered. 'That will just alert the Moobs to us. I doubt they've even seen us, the dull-witted hats. We'll take 'em by surprise.'

In one of the ship's lockers we had found ropes and grappling hooks, and we carried them out on to the star deck as the *Liberty* soared closer and closer to the *Sophronia.* The Moobs aboard the *Sophronia* had noticed what we were about by then. Gunports opened all along her flank, and her space cannon spat smoke and flame and sent balls singing through the aether to smash through the *Liberty*'s hull. Huge jagged splinters, twice as tall as me, went flip-fluttering into space. A few of the Threls fired back, but the popping of their carbines sounded awfully tinny and toy-like compared with the full-throated roar of the *Sophronia*'s guns. Jack

stopped them, anyway.

'Hold your fire! That is my ship, and those are my friends. I want none of them harmed! It is their hats we must defeat, and we shall fight them hand-to-hand!'

At his command we whirled the grappling hooks about our heads and let them fly. Mine missed on the first attempt, but I retrieved it and tried again, and the second time it lodged tight between two of the *Sophronia*'s exhaust-trumpets. I gave a whoop of triumph, and looked round to see whether any of the Threls had managed to do as I had. But at that instant a ball from one of the *Sophronia*'s stern-chasers ploughed into the *Liberty*'s flank just below where I was standing. The decking beneath my feet erupted into a storm of tumbling planks and shards, and I found myself soaring upward, clinging for dear to life to that rope, with the power of the *Sophronia*'s engines dragging me through the void. And looking down at the *Liberty*, to see whether my friends were all right, I found that she had fallen far behind, and as I watched she seemed to blink out of existence altogether!

I guessed what had happened. That last shot must have done some damage to the alembic – and perhaps, I feared, to Myrtle too – and the *Liberty*'s chemical wedding had failed. She had fallen from the Golden Roads, and left me alone, a helpless drogue, trailing after the speeding *Sophronia*!

Of all the sticky situations I had ever found myself in, this, I thought, was the stickiest. But there was no use in moping. Exerting all my strength, and praying that the Moobs aboard the *Sophronia* might not have noticed me, I began to haul myself hand over hand along that rope. Closer and closer I drew to the space-barnacled hull of the old ship, and to the spray of brass trumpets in which my grappling hook had lodged. Once, web-bound among the reefs of Saturn, I had crept down one of those trumpets to hide from the white spiders, and I wondered hopefully if I might climb up one now and enter the *Sophronia* that way. But Ssil had the alembic going at full blast, and from every trumpet-mouth waste gases and spent particles streamed out into the aether. I doubted that I could swim against such tides, and even if I could, I should certainly be poisoned or roasted before I reached the safety of the wedding chamber.

I reached the grappling hook, firmly wedged where the trumpets' roots vanished through the *Sophronia*'s planking. I looked to left and right, I looked both up and down, but never a sign did I see of any useful hatch or tumblehome through which a space-wrecked mariner might force entry. The only openings in that cliff face of unfriendly timber were the mullioned windows of the stern-gallery, which stretched high above me, surrounded by carved angels and gilt-painted gingerbread work. Could I reach it? I wondered. My sense of caution told me I could not. But every other sense that I possessed screamed at me to try, or be whirled off the *Sophronia*'s side by the wind of her passage, to burn in her exhaust-stream or be lost in the emptiness of space!

Tying the rope about my waist, I started to climb, my chilled fingers finding what handholds they could in the gaps between the timbers. I shut my eyes and told myself that this was no worse than bird's-nesting on the rooftops of Larklight, but it was. For if I had fallen off Larklight's roof I should have had nothing worse than a telling-off from Father and Mother, and a chilly wait for them to come and retrieve me in the solar punt. Whereas, if I were to fall from the *Sophronia*, not only would I be doomed, but the last hope of saving the British Empire from the dominion of the Moobs would perish with me . . .

Well, gentle reader, to cut a long story short, I made it. Scrambling up over the carved scroll that bore *Sophronia*'s name, I peered in through Jack's cabin window. And, having assured myself that no Moob lurked inside, I tugged and tugged upon my rope until the grappling hook came free, whereon I drew it up and used it to smash one of the panes, and to clear the daggers of broken glass from the frame, until I was able to squeeze through. Naturally, every object in the cabin – as well as all the air – felt a strong and sincere desire to fly out the same way I'd come in, but I seized a book which tumbled past me and used it to plug the hole I'd made.*

That done, I let myself float limply in mid-air, uttering a sigh of relief that my perils were over. But I could not escape the nagging sensation that, in fact, they were only beginning. For when I looked out of the windows I could see no sign of the *Liberty* resuming her pursuit, and it seemed to me that I was trapped, quite alone, aboard a vessel packed with hostile Moobs, and with my former friends whom they'd enslaved. How could I hope to take back the *Sophronia* single-handed, armed as I was with nothing but a grappling hook and a woolly hat?

As I drifted there, contemplating this knotty problem, I became aware of an alarming sound. Surely those could not be footsteps approaching without the cabin door? But they could, and they were; an instant later the door was

---

* The book was *How to Write Love Letters: A Guide for the Perplexed, by A Lady,* which seems an odd volume for a pirate and spy to keep aboard his ship. No doubt Jack had been using it to prop up a wobbly table.

wrenched open and my old friend Grindle peered in, blank-eyed and top-hatted. The Moob which controlled him must have heard me breaking in, and had brought him aft to investigate. I had no time to hide, and Grindle saw me at once.

'Moob!' he growled, and drew his cutlass, which is a particularly vicious-looking weapon, as sharp as a razor and as heavy as a cleaver.

'Mr Grindle!' I cried, hoping against hope that he might recognise me. But he did not, of course, and only some very hasty aerial gymnastics saved me from being sliced in two as the cutlass slammed down, making a quite horrid gash in Jack's chart-table.

'Avast, ye ——!' muttered Grindle, and many other dreadful curses. I do not know whether the Moob he wore had found those naughty words in his own brain, or had picked them up from Wild Will Melville's crew.

I swiped at his Moob with my grappling hook, but Mr G. ducked and the barbs whistled past an inch or more above its black crown. The effort of the blow carried me clear across the cabin and I crashed against the bulkhead, the grappling hook tumbling from my hand. I thought that my last moment had come, for I was cornered, winded and weaponless, and there was nothing to stop Grindle from spiking me with his cutlass. But the Moob which governed him seemed to have changed its mind. He sheathed the weapon, and, reaching into a pouch on his belt where usually he kept his tobacco, drew out a glistening, staring Moob!

'Help!' I cried, as the new Moob flared into hat-shape and flew at me. The Moob ignored my flailing hands and settled on my head ... and yet nothing happened. I

remained myself, and realised that Jack's plan was working and that the Moob's influence could not reach through the many layers of Threl-knit wool I wore about my brain!

Grindle, convinced that I was already a slave of the Moobs like himself, had turned away from me, swimming towards the cabin door. I pushed myself quickly away from the bulkhead, caught up with him as his hand reached for the door-knob, and punched him as hard as I could, right in the middle of his top hat. The Moob, taken by surprise, flew from his head, losing its hattishness as it flailed about with its little black hands, trying to arrest its careering flight across the cabin. Grindle stood staring at me.

'Art?' he cried. 'How did you come here? And whatever is happening? By ——! We're aboard the *Sophronia*! I remember nothing since we all settled down to sleep last night . . . Only some dream about a *hat* . . .'

As he spoke, his Moob recovered itself and came whirling back towards him, but I was ready for it. Plunging past him, I snatched it from the air, wrenched *How to Write Love Letters – A Guide for the Perplexed* away from the window and stuffed the writhing Moob out into space. All the while I could feel the Moob that sat upon my own head wriggling and fidgeting, as if it could not quite understand why I had not come under its control. Before it could work out the secret of the woolly hat I grabbed it and forced it out after its friend. For a moment the two Moobs turned over and over in the *Sophronia*'s wake, just like a pair of lost hats bowling along a windy promenade. Then they dropped into the fiery plume from the exhaust-trumpets, and were consumed with two brief, coppery-green flashes of fire.

I set Jack's book back over the shattered window, and offered up a grateful prayer of thanks. My Threl-bonnet had worked, I had triumphed over the Moobs, and most important, I was no longer alone. True, Mr Grindle was curled up in mid-air with his head in his hands, going, 'What . . . ? But . . . ? Ooh, my aching noddle!' but I knew what a chipper old space dog he was, and felt sure that, even if he were not feeling quite the thing, I could still ask for no better ally in the battle that lay before me.

Reaching into Mr G.'s pocket, I drew out his hip flask and pressed it into his hand. As I had hoped, a few swigs of First Mate Navy Rum soon proved most restorative.

'There isn't time to explain everything,' I told him briskly, 'but the rest of the crew are under the control of those hats too. They are called Moobs, and they have dastardly designs upon the British Empire. We must free the others from their influence and stop the *Sophronia*!'

Mr Grindle wiped his mouth on his cuff and stoppered the hip flask. 'Hats, is it?' he asked. 'I'll give 'em hats! Is it just you and me who have escaped their influence, Art, lad?'

'Yes, Mr Grindle,' I replied. 'But every hat we knock

from someone's head will mean another friend restored to fight beside us!'

'A good point!' said Grindle, grinning.

'But, Mr Grindle,' I added, 'there are a great many more hats concealed in boxes in the cargo hold. Whatever happens, we must not let them escape!'

'Aye aye, Art!' cried that honest goblin, and touched a knuckle to his forehead in salute, for all the world as if I was Jack Havock. I felt terribly proud of myself for having come this far, and then terribly afraid of the trials that yet lay ahead. But there was no time to dawdle – why, at any moment some other member of the Moobish crew might come aft to see what had befallen Mr Grindle – so we shook hands, Mr G. flung wide the door, and we scrambled together along the passageway that led into the main cabin.

Well, I shan't go into too much detail about the battle. Mr Wyatt's engraving captures the flavour pretty well, and you already know that we won, for if we'd hadn't the rest of this book would be full of nothing but little black handprints and the word *Moob*. I shall just mention in passing that there was a deal of shouting and hullooing and crying out of the sort of words that would have made Myrtle demand everyone wash out their mouths with soap and water, had

He whirled about the cabin like a dervish.

she been there to hear them. And a deal of blows and buffetings and jostlings, too.

Nipper knocked me clear across the cabin almost as soon as I entered the fray with one great swipe of his pincers, which sent me tumbling through so many somersaults that I did not know where I was or even who for a few moments (but I forgive him, of course, for he was still possessed by the Moobs when he did it, and not in his right mind, poor crab).

When I righted myself, though, Mr Grindle had already sliced Nipper's hat in half with a swipe of his cutlass; the two halves shrivelled up like dead leeches and floated from Nipper's shell, and the crab, who had perhaps been less deeply under Moobish control than Mr Grindle, grasped at once what was happening, and set about helping us.

Not that Mr Grindle seemed to need much help. I suppose it was the influence of all that rum. He whirled about the cabin like a dervish, hacking a Moob from Mr Spinnaker's head, kicking another from Squidley's midriff. Yarg, still controlled by his Moob, lashed out with his own electric tentacles and caught Grindle a glancing blow across the bottom, which sent the poor fellow hurtling high into the air, a trail of smoke pouring from his trouser-flaps; but in another instant Squidley had pinioned his twin and wrested his hat from him, roasting it till it popped in a fierce arc of tentacle-fire.

While all this was afoot I whistled to Nipper and indicated the big trapdoor in the cabin floor, which led down into the hold. Dragging a sheet of oiled space tarpaulin from a locker, and tools from another, we set about nailing it over that door. For I had remembered what the friendly Moob aboard the *Liberty* had told me of his people and their ways, and how they may spread themselves out thin if they so wish, and I was very concerned that the ones down below might tumble to what was happening and come oozing up through the cracks around the hatch to help their friends, and then where should we be?

By the time we were done the fight was over. Our friends were themselves again, and Grindle and the Tentacle Twins had gone through into the wedding chamber to deliver Ssil from her Moob and make her stop the ship; I could hear the alembic cooling, the song of the engines dropping in pitch as the *Sophronia* slowed. I looked about me. Slain Moobs lay everywhere, withering and crisping underfoot like dead leaves. We could hear the others crying out, 'Moob, moob, moob!' beneath the deck, and sometimes a tiny black hand would reach up through a gap in the planking and Nipper would jab it with his pincers.

'How did they all get in there?' cried Colonel Quivering, querulously. 'What is this old tub? Some smuggler's schooner, laden to the gunwales with those wretched hats, I'll warrant!'

'Colonel,' I said, feeling jolly bold what with just having rescued everyone from the Moobs and everything, 'this is the *Sophronia,* the best ship in British Space, and if she's over-full of Moobs at the moment, it's only because you brought them aboard.'

'But what shall we do with them?' asked Nipper.

'That's for Jack to say,' I told him, and then remembered – Jack!

I ran to the stern cabin, with most of the others at my heels. The *Sophronia* was drifting gently through the aether. Behind her, far astern, Modesty and Decorum and their neighbour-asteroids shone in the unending night like flakes of silver. But of the *Liberty* there was no sign.

'He'll catch up,' said Ssilissa hopefully, when I had explained how I came to be parted from Jack Havock. 'He's out there even now, ssspeeding after usss . . .'

'Jack wouldn't let disaster befall any ship that he had command of,' said Nipper loyally.

Mr Grindle said, 'Oh, I do hope that it weren't a shot from my cannon that wrecked her! Even if I were under the influence of a mesmeric hat when I fired it, I should never forgive myself . . .'

And all the while we watched the darkness astern, and hoped at any moment to see the *Liberty* appear out of it, but she never did. And although I tried to be hopeful, I could not help recalling those last few moments before I was dragged from the *Liberty*'s hull. If that final shot had really holed her wedding chamber, then she might easily have exploded and been reduced to nothing but a cloud of cartwheeling spars and splinters expanding slowly into the cold of space. Myrtle might be dead. Jack might be dead!

We went back into the main cabin, and sat drinking hot chocolate around the cabin stove and deciding what was to be done.

I had expected that Colonel Quivering would take charge of things, being such a military gent, but it was not to be; both he and Herbert Spinnaker were left feeling rather weak and dazed after their Moobs were removed. Perhaps it was because of all the hard work they had been forced to do while under Moobish influence, clambering about on speeding trains, etc. Or maybe, having stayed longer at Starcross than Nipper and Grindle, they had been exposed for longer to the Moobish munching of their brainwaves, and were on the brink of fading and withering as Wild Will Melville's Yankee pirates had! Perhaps, if we had not seized back the *Sophronia* when we did, there would have been nothing left of them to rescue but their empty clothes! That was a dreadful thought, and it made me understand what our next move must be.

'Jack left Mrs Spinnaker at Modesty,' I said. 'She will already have raised the alarm. So it seems to me that we ought to return to Starcross, where others need our help. If Mother and Mr Munkulus are under the influence of those Moobs much longer, they'll turn thin and grey as used-up dish-cloths, and vanish away at last.'

The Tentacle Twins twittered to each other, their crowns fluttering with auroras of pink and green light. Nipper said, 'But what about Jack? Shouldn't we stay here and scour the aether for some clue to what's become of him?'

The others all looked very solemn. We were all thinking of the vast immensities of space, and of what little chance we had of finding any fragment of the *Liberty* if she had been torn to pieces, and I was burdened in addition by the knowledge that I might have to break to Father and Mother the awful news of the loss of Myrtle.*

Then Ssil said, 'Art is right. Jack left me in charge when he went off to Starcrosss, and ssince he's not here and nor is Mr Munkulusss, I sssuppose I am sstill in charge. And what I think is, if Jack is alive, then he will pull through sssomehow and make that old *Liberty* fly again no matter where she is or how badly she's been sssmashed. And if he isn't alive . . .' (Here she paused, and turned a pale violet, and

---

* I remember being very troubled about breaking this same bad news during our earlier adventures, when I believed that Myrtle had been eaten up by the white spiders. Some time when I am at leisure I must work out a suitable form of words and write it down and keep it always in the pocket of my Norfolk jacket, so that at least I shall have one less worry the next time we are in mortal peril. I imagine something along these lines might do the trick: Dearest Mother/Father (delete where applicable); I am most awfully sorry to have to tell you that Myrtle has been eaten/blown up/squashed/lost in the inky blacknesses of the interplanetary void/other. But do not grieve, for she did not suffer/deserved it/has gone to a Better Place, etc., etc.

her voice grew high and squeaky – poor lizard, she was very much in love with Jack.) '. . . If he *isn't* alive, then he would not want usss to be wassting time combing the aether-ssseas for sscraps of flotssam. He would want usss to deal with the ressst of the Moobs. And the only perssson I can think of who might know how to do that is Art'ss mother, who is as good and wise as Jack. Ssso the ssooner we rescue her, the better for all of usss.'

'But how do we rescue her if Starcross is full of Moobs?' demanded Grindle.

'That is for Art to tell usss,' replied Ssil. 'He has fought againsst these creatures and outwitted them, while we have only been their ssslaves . . .' And she brushed ruefully at her head-spines, which were still bent slightly out of shape, having been so long confined inside a Moobish topper.

Chapter Twenty

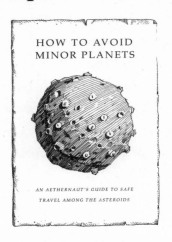

HOW TO AVOID
MINOR PLANETS

*AN AETHERNAUT'S GUIDE TO SAFE
TRAVEL AMONG THE ASTEROIDS*

In Which I Endeavour to Devise a Cunning Stratagem,
We Learn an Unexpected Fact about an Absent
Friend and Some Large, *Sophronia*-Shaped Dents Are
Almost Made upon Several of the Lesser-Known
Asteroids.

While Ssil busied herself in the wedding chamber, and Mr S. and Colonel Quivering were helped weakly into hammocks by the kindly Nipper, I wondered what to do with our cargo of boxed Moobs. Mr Grindle was all for opening the hold's outer hatches and venting them all into space, but that would hardly have been sporting. Anyway, I was pretty certain that mere exposure to the aether would do no harm to Moobs; they seemed as happy in that element as any Icthyomorph, and, since they were virtually immortal, they would sooner or later find their way to an inhabited world, there to begin causing mischief again. At least in the *Sophronia*'s hold we knew where they were, for it was well constructed, and now that we had sealed the inner hatch I felt confident the Moobs could not escape. So I decided to keep them under guard, and carry them back with us to Starcross. 'Once we have rescued Mother,' I explained, 'she can tell us what we must do with them.'

Grindle looked doubtfully at me. He still nursed a headache, poor fellow, and it was making it hard for him to look on the bright side of things. 'So how exactly is this rescue to be accomplished, young Art?' he enquired.

'I am working on that,' I assured him, and went up on to the star deck for a good, hard think.

We soared back through the asteroid belt as fast as ever we dared (although you may be sure that was still not *very* fast, with so many reefs and rocks and sharp, uncharted worldlets to beware of). We had little sleep, for Ssil kept us busy running up to the star deck and out along the bowsprit to keep a look-out, and ever and again the cry went up, 'World ho!' or 'Reef! Reef on the starboard bow!', and we would all have to hold on tight as the helmsmen swung the ship this way or that to avoid collision. Even then, there was many a treacherous shoal which went unnoticed in the dark, and sometimes a jagged rock would come scraping along the outside of the *Sophronia*'s hull. Once, when I did find time to catch some sleep, I was rudely awoken by the sound of saws and hammers, and sat up thinking I was back at Larklight, with Chippy Spry and his carpenters at work all round me – but no, it was just Grindle and the Tentacle Twins busy repairing a gash which some passing asteroid had opened in our bows.

Meanwhile I kept trying to devise a plan which would Frustrate and Confound the Moobs back at

Starcross. I have read ever so many accounts in the *Boys'*
Own Journal of famous battles where clever chaps like
Caesar, Wellington and Qrrmstruqx of Poo triumphed
against overwhelming odds, and I racked my brains for
some way in which I might follow their example, but the
only answer I could come to was, 'I wish Jack were here; *he*
would know what to do!'

Still, I refused to be downhearted. Do you remember
what I was saying earlier about how tiresome it is being used
as a hostage and bargaining counter all the time? Well, it
seemed to me that I now had a chance to show my
shipmates that I was far more than just a helpless child. I
was determined that I, Arthur Mumby, would lead them to
victory, with a plan as cunning as any Jack Havock had ever
dreamed up.

Yet I could not help running over and over in my mind a
sort of dismal arithmetic problem, to wit, that my army
consisted of me, two elderly gentlemen who were not
feeling quite the ticket, a grumpy goblin, two anemones, a
large crab and a blue lizard of the gentler sex. Whereas the
forces ranged against us might be infinite in number, for I
had no notion of how many Moobs might have poured
through the time-hole at Starcross since I left. Nor did I

know where they would be keeping the prisoners we sought to free.

'Why did they keep Mr Munkulus there?' I wondered, as I stood with Grindle on the star deck, keeping watch for unexpected worlds. 'If only they could have hung on to the colonel or Mr Spinnaker instead. Old Munkulus would have been much more use to us!'

'Well, I've been thinking about that, Art,' replied the old aethernaut. 'Oh, watch out below!' he bellowed, interrupting himself, and the *Sophronia* yawed to starboard to let an unknown blue planetoid slide past, on whose surface small mouse-like beings were leaning out of lidded craters to shake their woolly fists at us, demanding to know if we were blind, and whether we thought we owned the aether. As their indignant whistlings and hootings faded astern Grindle returned to the matter of Mr Munkulus.

'Thing is, young master Art,' he said, 'Mr Munkulus and me go a long way back, and I know things about him that maybe others don't. And when you told us about how those fiendish Moobs were breeding advertising spores to make people think of them as desirable items of headgear, well, I thought to myself, *that's* why they've kept poor old Munk penned up.'

'Why?' I asked. 'You mean that, because Mr Munkulus was an Ionian and Io is the centre of the Jovian ideospore business, those Moobs think he can help them with their devilish plans?'

'They don't have to think, do they?' said Grindle darkly. 'They have eaten of his thoughts and dreams, and know all about him. So they must know that when he was a young Ionian, fresh out of the chrysalis and still dizzy from his metamorphosis and easily led, our Mr Munkulus had a job with . . .' (and here the honest old aether dog lowered his voice, as if his friend's secret were too dreadful to speak aloud even in that great emptiness) '. . . with *an Advertising Agency!* He was chief spore-tweaker for Spondule and Quirm, one of the biggest firms on Io. But after a few years of it, breeding spores to persuade females that they were too fat or too thin, and that only Whilkin's Efficacious Liniment could make them beautiful, or convincing gentlemen that life without a set of Trumpeter's Steam-Powered Golf Clubs isn't worth living, well, he came to his senses and saw that *any* life would be more honourable than the life of an advertiser. So he ran away aboard an aether-ship, resolving never to breed another spore.'

'O dear Lord!' I cried.

'I thought you'd be shocked!' said Grindle, with the air of one whose tale of horror has gone down just as he hoped. But what had made me cry out so intemperately was actually a small world which had popped out of the darkness ahead with no warning at all. Rather a crumbly place it looked, but its inhabitants had livened it up by constructing a very pretty system of rings for it out of papier mâché and bits of silver paper. I'm afraid the *Sophronia* chipped a couple of the outer ones rather badly as she swerved to avoid the place, and soon afterwards Nipper came aloft with a rather sarcastic message from Ssilissa, who said she had thought we were keeping watch and she was *so* sorry for having interrupted our naps by nearly colliding with an asteroid.

After that we took our job of look-outs far more seriously, and I did not have time to quiz Mr Grindle any more about our friend's surprising past. But I kept thinking about Mr Munkulus's skill with ideospores, and wondering if that might somehow be made a part of the plan of battle which I was trying to construct . . .

And then, that afternoon, while I was in Jack's cabin sketching vague maps of Starcross on bits of paper and drawing arrows on them and rubbing them out, and sucking the end of my pencil, and arranging old mugs and jars of bloater paste to represent the forces at my command, and having them drift off and get lost as I was hunting for something to represent the Moobs, and actually feeling jolly glad I had all those things to think about because they left me hardly any room for thinking about how much I missed Mother, and Jack, and even Myrtle, well, it was *then* that Nipper scuttled in to announce that our journey was done, and that he'd just sighted Starcross, clear and true upon the larboard quarter!

'I've gathered everyone in the main cabin, Art,' he said excitedly. 'And they are all as keen as English mustard to learn your cunning plan!'

Moments later, I stood before my valiant little army, and Starcross hung outside the portholes. The asteroid looked just as we had left it. I had half expected to see it crawling with Moobs, but from space the hotel and its promenade

seemed unchanged, with the colourful flags fluttering on the pier and the elegant bright curve of the railway bridge sweeping down to Starcross Halt.

'Tell usss the plan, Art,' said Ssilissa, watching me with great respect. Nipper and the Tentacle Twins and even Mr Grindle looked just as eager to hear what cunning strategy I had devised. All of them had shielded their heads in readiness for our coming battle with the Moobs, and out of the shadows of the tarpaulin hats and blanket turbans they had fashioned their eyes gleamed expectantly at me. Even the Tentacle Twins, who had wrapped their stalks in makeshift metal cummerbunds, looked all agog. Of course; they were used to being led by a human boy! Jack Havock had been no older than I when he first led them all to freedom aboard this ship! Only Colonel Quivering and Mr Spinnaker looked sceptical as they waited for my instructions, but perhaps they were still simply feeling poorly.

I cleared my throat, and explained my plan of battle. There wasn't much of it, I'm afraid.

'We shall set down on the promenade just outside the entrance to the pier,' I announced. 'We shall all arm ourselves with as many swords and guns and cutlasses as we can carry, and as soon as the ship is landed we shall swarm out and charge into the hotel, where we shall wallop, pistol or poke every Moob we see.'

There was a sort of wondering silence for a second or two. Then Nipper said, 'Is that it?'

I gulped, and nodded. 'I always think it's best to favour the direct approach in these matters,' I said.

'It's a wonderful plan!' cried Nipper, and to my relief the others all seemed to agree, except for Colonel Quivering, who had doubtless been expecting me to propose Flanking

Manoeuvres and Softening Up The Enemy's Centre with our Light Horse.

'Worthy of Jack himself!' cried Grindle loyally, and Ssil put her blue arms around my neck and kissed me, which caused me to blush rather more than is proper in a military mastermind.

To cover my confusion I began arming myself from those handy tubs of cutlasses and boarding pikes which Jack and his friends keep dotted about the *Sophronia*'s cabin, in much the same spirit that Mother leaves out bowls of nuts and sweetmeats for visitors to Larklight over Christmastide. The others all followed my example, and before long we looked like the most fearsome *banditti* you can imagine, and I must say it boosted my confidence remarkably to have a few shooting irons stashed about my person. Nevertheless, I could not help wishing ardently that Jack were with us as Ssilissa set us moving towards our landfall.

Soft as thistledown, the *Sophronia* settled on the promenade. Nipper kicked open the main hatch, and we all went storming out through it. At first all was silence, but as we ran past the beach cafe we heard the squeak of wheels, and out of the shadows came rolling two striped booths, extending pointy hands and gleaming gun-barrels as they advanced. At once we all let fly with our kerflunderbusses* and multi-barrelled pistols, and a rattle of gunfire echoed from the front of the hotel. As the smoke cleared the two sinister sideshows collapsed, mere heaps of scrap, with smoke and sparks spewing from their riddled mechanisms.

'Huzzah!' I said.

Grindle prodded the nearest wreck with his boot. '*Hello, boys and sausages . . .*' it said creakily, its voice running down slowly into silence.

'Well,' said Nipper, 'unless those Moobs are all stone-deaf, they will know that we are here now.'

We reloaded our guns and hurried up the hotel steps, pausing at the top to check that our anti-Moob hats were in place and turbans tight-wrapped. Then, with pistol in one hand and sword in the other, and feeling every inch the bold adventurer, I kicked one of the doors open, Ssil shoved the other open with her tail, and our companions followed us inside in a rush of feet and pincers!

No Moobs came whirling down to try and steal our brains from us. Nothing stirred at all, except for a few

---

* Like a blunderbuss but much, much LOUDER.

hoverhogs busy snuffling up cake crumbs, and an auto-waiter which rolled to greet on us on well-oiled wheels and said, 'Welcome to Starcross, ladies and gentlemen. I take it you will be joining the other lady for tea?'

We lowered our weapons and looked at each other, flummoxed.

'*What* other lady?' asked Ssilissa.

'Mrs Mumby,' said the automaton patiently. 'She is expecting you.'

It spun about and wheeled away, and we followed it into the withdrawing room, expecting a trap. But there sat Mother, dressed quite neatly and properly in her good blue gown, taking tea with Professor Ferny and Mr Munkulus. And all about them, on tables and sofas and the carpeted floor, Moobs lay heaped about like well-stuffed black cushions. If you listened closely you could hear them murmuring, 'Moob, moob, moob,' in a most contented way.

'Hello, Mother,' I said.

'Hello, dears,' said Mother brightly, looking up and seeing us all standing stunned in the doorway.

'We're here to resscue you, Mrss Mumby,' said Ssilissa.

'Well, of course you are, dear,' said Mother. 'I was only saying to Professor Ferny and dear Mr Munkulus that you

would certainly come back to rescue us.'

I was not sure what to say next. It is disconcerting for a fellow to come bursting into a resort hotel, armed to the eye-teeth and expecting to do battle with a pitiless foe, only to find that the pitiless foe is asleep all over the floor and he is expected to take tea instead. I gulped once or twice, and said, 'Mother, I'm afraid Myrtle is lost!'

'Oh dear, again?' said Mother, with a look of concern which deepened as I explained about the *Liberty* and its fate. But when I had finished she said, 'Never mind; I am sure she and Jack will turn up. I may no longer have all the powers of a Shaper, but I am certain that I should *know* if anything terrible had befallen them. Now do pull up some chairs, all of you; you must be famished. I believe there is a plate of ginger shortbread somewhere . . .'

As if in a dream we did as she bid us, pushing the un-protesting Moobs aside with our feet and gathering around the table. Colonel Quivering congratulated Professor Ferny on his swift recovery, and the intellectual shrub replied that it was nothing – that thanks to Mother's quick thinking he had been removed from the poisoned mulch before very much damage had been done, and that a night in a bowl of restorative plant food had done wonders. Mr Munkulus, meanwhile, asked his shipmates what had been happening to them, and gave us joy of our escape from the Moobs, and shared our concern at the fate of Jack and Myrtle. He looked most embarrassed at having been a part of the Moobish plot himself, and still more embarrassed when we asked him what the Moobs had kept him behind at Starcross for.

'Oh, they had me assisting Professor Ferny,' he rumbled. 'Doing this and that, you know . . .'

'Your friend Munkulus is far, far too modest,' rustled Professor Ferny. 'Those spores which he bred for the Moobs are a work of art! He had even *me* yearning after one of Titfer's Top-Notch Toppers!'

'But, Mother!' I cried out at last, quite unable to contain my curiosity a moment longer. 'What about the Moobs? What have you done to them? How did you escape?'

'Oh,' said Mother calmly, holding out teacups for the mechanical teapots to fill, and also filling two shallow bowls for Yarg and Squidley to dip their feeding-tentacles in. 'I did nothing at all. The Moobs eat thoughts, you know – indeed, I can see you know that, from those items you have so cleverly wrapped around your heads. Thoughts, and memories, and dreams. Well, I have a great many thoughts, and four and a half billion years of memories, and so the Moobs who so rudely clambered upon me were very quickly full, and fell asleep, whereupon their friends set about snacking on *their* dreams. That enabled me to regain control over myself once more, and close the passage into Futurity which they had had me open. I believe that all the Moobs in this era are currently napping.'

'And when will they awaken?' asked Mr Spinnaker nervously, looking about at the dozing Moobs who clustered on every pouf and windowsill.

'Oh, not for a few more hours, I expect,' said Mother. 'And by that time we shall have them home. I am planning to carry this hotel into the distant future where these creatures dwell, and put an end to all this silliness. Poor Moobs! It is such a miserable era that they inhabit. I wish I could do something to help them so that they will no longer feel the need to come barging into other people's bits of history and spoil their holidays.'

Like so many things my mother says, this left me speechless. Still, I was very glad that she was herself again, and that she knew a way to put things straight. I believe we all felt the same, for everyone around that table relaxed, and some of us went so far as to remove our headgear, which was growing itchy in the cosy warmth of Starcross.

We drained our teacups and ate up the ginger shortbread. Then, with Mother leading the way, we went down again into the cavern beneath the hotel. Moobs were piled in every corner and heaped up in masses on the metal stairs. We tried our best not to tread upon them, but it was impossible not to dislodge a few; they rolled down with wet wobbling sounds like those new rubber hot-water bottles, and mumbled softly in their sleep, 'Moob, moob . . .'

At the bottom of the stairs Sir Launcelot Sprigg sat upon a wooden chair – indeed, he had been tied to it, and gagged with a napkin from the dining room. He looked most displeased at being treated thus, but of course Mother could not trust him to run around free, and anyway, it served him right.

As for the great machine, Larklight's old engine, it had changed while we had been gone. I could not imagine how Mother had found time to make so many alterations, to string so many lengths of cable and duct about it like Christmas paper-chains, and add so many dials and switches to its mahogany control desk. When I asked her about it she said, 'Oh, I simply made time.'*

The old machine, it seemed, was now ready to do all that Sir Launcelot Sprigg had wanted, and more; it would move through space, and also through the Fourth Dimension. No wonder that he looked so furious, fastened to that chair in a corner and forced to watch this miracle of science take shape, knowing that it would never be his to command!

---

* It seems that she had found a way to keep Starcross *hovering* in the Fourth Dimension, so that while less than a day had passed in the world outside, more than a week had gone by in Starcross, giving her plenty of time to tinker.

'There,' said Mother, and she patted the flank of her machine as if it were some faithful old dog. 'She is good for one last journey, I believe. All we need do is pull this lever, and turn that handle, and tweak that – well, I do not believe there is a word for one of *those* in any Earthly language, but we shall tweak it just the same, and this hotel will be transported in an instant to that far-off future where Moobs eke out their cheerless existences.'

And as she was saying all this she *did* pull that lever, and turn that handle, and tweak the final what-do-you-call-it, and the old engine began to sing and churn and spin and shift in and out of various dimensions, while the rest of us clung to any solid thing that we could find, for the waves of giddiness we felt when Starcross whisked us back through a hundred million years to ancient Mars were as nothing to those which swept over us now, as the hotel went careering into the unknown vistas of Futurity!

On and on that dizzy, falling feeling went, until we began to grow used to it, and were able to uncover our eyes and let go of the things we had clung to when it started and walk about. Yet still a certain lingering unease remained. Perhaps it was a sort of disappointment at being cheated of our famous battle, but I think all of us who had been aboard the

Sophronia felt the same nagging worry: that things were moving a little too swiftly and smoothly, and that somehow All Was Not Well.

It was Grindle who finally put his finger on it. He raised a hand. Something about my mother always makes him very polite and school-boyish, and although he had something that he was itching to say, he kept it bottled up until she smiled at him and said, 'Yes, Mr Grindle?'

'Thing is,' Grindle said, 'and pardon me for speaking out of line, yer ladyship, but as soon as we land in the time of the Moobs, aren't hundreds and millions of them going to come a-swarming in on us, all bent on eating up our thoughts?'

Mother turned to look at him. Her vast mind was busy with far deeper questions, and so her gaze was mild at first. 'Mm?' she said. Then what Grindle had just asked seemed to sink in; her grey eyes widened; she put a hand to her bosom.

'Oh crikey!' she said.

Chapter Twenty-One

We Arrive in the Depths of Futurity and Find Them
Chilly and a Trifle Dark.

The trouble with having a mother who is so very old
and so very wise is that it is easy to start thinking
that she knows everything and is always right. But
like any of us, Mother can forget little details sometimes,
and that was exactly what had happened. Or perhaps she
was still a bit confused after her time as a mind slave of the
Moobs. At any rate, it seemed she had been so busy

reconfiguring her old machine to carry us into their future age that she not spared much thought to what would actually happen when we got there.

'We mussst put our hatss back on,' said Ssilissa. 'That will protect usss.'

But would it? I could see that Mother doubted it. A few Moobs might be foiled by wool and blankets and the like, but if we came under attack by many millions of them, it could not be long before their small black hands would find a way through our defences, and we would perish in Futurity as their slaves!

'Mother, stop the machine!' I cried.

'I would rather not,' she replied. 'We are travelling through unknown reaches of Time. Who knows what civilisations now rule the worlds of the Sun, or what mischief we might cause if we suddenly appear among them? No, we must exert our minds and think of some sure way to keep ourselves safe when we reach the Moobs' era. The journey will take another hour or so, I believe.'

I exerted my mind. And sure enough, I found a plan there! 'Huzzah!' I cried. 'Mother! Why not have Mr Munkulus design an advertising spore that will convince those Moobs what a good idea it would be *not* to sit on our heads and eat our brainwaves up?'

Mother looked thoughtfully at me, and the more she thought, the more convinced she seemed to be that my idea was a good one. 'Well done, Art!' she said. 'But why stop at just dissuading the Moobs from sitting on us? That is hardly kind. What we need is a spore that will *inspire* them a little. Something to stop them moping about in their chilly future age, and start enjoying it and making the best of things.'

'But breeding a complex ideospore like that would take months, or even years,' Mr Munkulus protested.

'Then we shall *make* months and years!' said Mother. 'I shall divert a portion of the machine's power into a sort of time-greenhouse, where we shall be able make time pass as quickly as we like and breed whatever ideospores we need!'

And so that is what we did.

Mr Munkulus and Professor Ferny hurried into that secondary cave which opened off of the main cavern, and there busied themselves with tweezers and test tubes of dormant ideospores. Every few minutes one or other of them would emerge with an earth-filled tray in which some tweaked spore lay waiting, and Mother, having tinkered with curious silvery bits and bobs in an open panel on the side of her machine, directed a bluish ray upon it, which made strange Ionian puffballs swell abruptly from the soil, and burst, and be replaced with more – whole generations of spores going through the cycles of life and death in about as long as it takes me to blink. And then our brainy botanists

would carefully carry the results away, and seal themselves and Mother back in their laboratory to peer at the resulting spores through microscopes and magnifying glasses, and drop them into flasks of different coloured chemicals, and watch how they reacted. And after a lot of discussion and the shaking of heads (or leaves, in Ferny's case), Mother would come out and say, 'It is not quite ready yet, I fear,' and the whole process would start again.

And all the while, Starcross went plummeting into the future, century after century, millennia after millennia . . .

It is all very clever, this spore-breeding business, but I don't believe it will ever catch on in a big way as a spectator sport. After watching for ten minutes or so, the rest of us wandered off to find something to eat, and to check on the Moobs, who were still sleeping peacefully. A strange light hung over the pier and the dry beach, and glimmered in the *Sophronia*'s rigging. Nipper and Ssil and I went out on to the steps and looked up at the sky above the promenade. It had become a swirl of light, painted with the smeared tracks of a million stars that whirled about us. The Milky Way spun above the *Sophronia*'s upperworks like an immense wheel, endlessly circling. But as we stood watching it, too awed to speak, I began to notice that the light was dimming, and that

the shadows we cast upon the hotel steps were not so dark. We watched the whirling stars grow red and dull, and one by one, at last, go out.

'What's happening?' asked Nipper.

'We're drawing near the end,' said Ssil. 'We are passsing through the autumn of the Universsse, and into winter.'

'The end of all things,' I whispered. 'The end of all hope . . .'

'Oh, there is always hope, Art,' said Mother, opening the door and stepping out to join us. With her came all the others, led by Munkulus and Grindle, who carried between them a tray containing what looked like many grey-green cannonballs, moulded out of moss and dust.

'Are dose de spores?' I asked.

'Of course,' said Mother. 'There is no need to hold your nose in that dramatic manner, Art; they will have no effect upon the human brain.'

'Oh! But they will work on Moobs?'

'I certainly hope so! Come, let us carry them aboard Jack's ship; it will be so much easier to distribute them from there. I believe we have just enough time . . .'

How cold it had become there upon the steps of Starcross! Now only a few stars were left, and most of them were dim and red, like embers glowing in a heap of black ashes. We hurried together aboard the *Sophronia,* where I helped Mr Munkulus load a spore-ball into each of the old ship's space cannon. I wondered if we should drop one ball into the hold, so that we could make sure it worked by observing the effects upon the captive Moobs there. But Mother said, 'No, Art; after all, it might not work, and then think how depressed we should all feel, for there is no time to make more, and we are almost at our journey's end.'

My dizziness returned, and I guessed that we were slowing. I went carefully to a porthole and looked out. Above us, the sky was faintly washed with the dim red glow of the last, dying suns. But clouds of utter blackness lay across that sky: great, complicated, raggedy-edged clouds bigger than worlds, which seemed to swirl and billow in an unseen wind. And in those blacknesses, as I watched, countless tiny firefly lights began appearing, bobbing and winking as they spread over the abandoned vaults of Heaven.

'New stars!' said Nipper, who is a hopeful sort of crab. 'New stars are growing!'

'No, they ain't,' said Grindle.

In the infinite emptiness which lay all about us, the cold bright eyes of countless Moobs were turning hungrily on Starcross.

Mother clapped her hands. 'Jolly good!' she said. 'We're here! It *is* rather cheerless, isn't it? No wonder those naughty Moobs are so keen to come and live upon our nice, warm Nineteenth-Century heads.'

And now those clouds of darkness swirled up like thunderheads, billowing, spreading, growing ever larger.

'Mother!' I cried, for I realised of a sudden that I was watching vast aether-borne flocks of Moobs swirling towards Starcross, drawn, no doubt, by the tantalising scent of our thoughts and memories and dreams . . .

'Don't worry,' Mother said merrily. 'Mr Munkulus, would you take us aloft, please?'

'All hands to the guns!' roared Mr Munkulus, running up to the helm. We all rushed to obey him. Ports creaked open, gun carriages rumbled, tackle creaked and ramrods rattled as the cannon were run out. And nimble Ssil was already in her wedding chamber, stoking the alembic, so that the decks beneath us trembled and the flapping of the aether-wings sent drifts of the ash of dead suns whirling across the promenades of Starcross.

'They are almost upon us!' cried Mr Spinnaker, peeking out of a porthole. And from outside we could hear a sound like a distant storm; a mumbling, confused, many-throated roaring of 'Mooob! Moooob! Mooob!'

The *Sophronia* rose precipitately from the promenade, giving me the feeling that my stomach had been left behind. At once, with a soft pitter-puttering, the Moobs began to rain against her hull. Tiny hands reached in through gaps in her timbers. I saw a Moob curl in through an open gunport and settle itself on Mr Grindle's head, only to be wrenched off again by Squidley. Other Moobs swirled through the cabin, struggling to find a way to our thoughts through tarpaulin hats and woolly turbans.

Then Grindle and the other gun captains tugged their lanyards, and the cannon went off with a crash that made the whole ship shudder.

Of course those balls, being only made of compressed ideospores, did not fly out like cannonballs in a battle. As each gun fired the shock of the explosion blasted the ball it held back into spores, which flew from its muzzle in an expanding cloud. Spores spread among the close-pressed bodies of the Moobs, who surrounded the *Sophronia* like clouds of animalculae about a whale. For a moment, a grey-green mist enwrapped them all, and some blew back through the gunports to dim the lanterns in the cabin.

A few Moobs which had got aboard earlier and had been circling frantically, looking for a head to land upon, now ceased their movements and hung thoughtfully in mid-air, their small hands twitching faintly as the ideospores went to work upon their Moobish brains. And the gun crews reloaded with fresh spores, and ran out their guns to fire again . . .

I went to where Mother stood beside a porthole. Beyond the glass, strange gyres and currents were sweeping through the legions of the Moobs. Eyes shone and hands wavered, but at least they showed no more sign of wishing to overwhelm us.

'What is happening to them, Mother?' I asked. 'What are the spores doing?'

Mother smiled. 'Their heads are filling with ideas, dear.'

'But are there really enough spores to affect them all?'

'Oh no, but those whom the spores do not reach will eat up the thoughts of those they do, and so the ideas will spread among them.'

'It is as if you are giving them all an education!' I cried. 'I say, could you not have Mr Munkulus knock up an ideospore which would fill my head with an understanding of long division and Latin grammar?'

'No, Art, dear; that would be cheating.'

The Moobs formed fancy knots and twirls and mandalas. Some, who had not yet tasted of the new spores, came zooming in as if to steal our thoughts from us, but were distracted by those who had, and became docile, too.

'They have no more need to eat up other people's thoughts and dreams,' said Mother. 'They are having thoughts and dreams of their own now, thanks to Art's topping plan.'

You may imagine how I swelled with pride at such praise! I should have liked to hear her say more upon the subject, but she was still delightedly watching those happy Moobs and, after a moment, she went on, 'Some of them are dreaming up stories, or pieces of music. Some are beginning to ponder upon ways of making the dying stars last longer. A few are planning journeys of discovery and exploration, far out among the cinders of the island galaxies. One or two are wondering whether there might be other universes into which they may find their way . . .'

It all seemed rather a lot for a simple advertising spore to have achieved. I could not help wondering whether Mother had perhaps used this method before, during her colourful past, as a way to light the flame of consciousness among the brute ancestors of other races. Had she, long ago, alighted beside some hairy primitive on the pre-historic Earth and blown into his face a few spores of similar design? But no; surely *that* would have been cheating . . . wouldn't it?

Before I could ask her, she pushed herself away from the porthole and sailed through the cabin, seizing a marlin spike on her way. Landing beside the hatchway which Nipper and I had earlier nailed shut, she quickly prised it open with the spike, bent nails pirouetting into the air all around her as she worked. And as the hatch came open, out came sliding all the Moobs we'd trapped there; changed Moobs now; amiable Moobs, their small heads stuffed with wonderful ideas by the spores which had showered down upon them through gaps in the *Sophronia*'s planking. To see the way they rolled and tumbled and somersaulted in mid-air almost made me wish that Mr Munkulus's spores *did* affect the human brain, so that I could understand the wild thoughts they'd seeded in those happy Moobs.

The cannon fire had ceased. My shipmates all stood by their silent guns, watching that black rainbow of Moobs arch up from the opened hold and out of a handy porthole which Yarg and Squidley threw open for them near the prow. And as they swept from the ship to join the Moob-tides which swirled all about us, Mr Munkulus turned the ship, and Ssilissa cooked up some element in her alembic that made a rosy glow come from her exhaust-trumpets, and steered her slow enough among those dancing garlands of Moobs that she did no harm to them. Five minutes more, and we were settling safely on to the promenade at Starcross.

'And now,' said Mother, 'we must find Myrtle, and dear Jack.'

Back in the hotel, she asked the kitchen automata to toast us some muffins and scramble us some eggs, for it is hungry work, all this plunging through the Veils of Time. Professor

Ferny excused himself, and went to stand a while in a pot of fortifying compost in the greenhouse. Colonel Quivering and Mr Munkulus hurried off to see if the larders of Starcross contained any First Mate Navy Rum, and the rest of us returned to the cavern, where Sir Launcelot was still bound to his chair. (I noticed that Yarg and Squidley each gave him a surreptitious kick as they passed, but I felt a little sorry for him. After all, he had missed all the fun.)

'Should we untie him, Mother?' I asked. 'He must be getting most awfully stiff.'

'Just leave him a little longer, dear,' said Mother, going to her machine, pulling levers, turning switches. 'As soon as we are back in our own time . . .'

That dizzy, spinning sensation that I had come to know so well swept over me again as Starcross commenced its voyage back across the centuries. I knew that outside, the sky would be starting to fill with stars again, the great Catherine Wheel of the Milky Way turning once more above the rooftops of the hotel. Deciding to take a look, I turned towards the stairs – and saw that Sir Launcelot was gone!

'But he was there a moment ago!' said Mother, vexed, when I drew this to her attention.

'Well, he is not there now,' was all that I could say. Nor

was he. His chair was there, and the cords which had bound him lay draped about it like cold spaghetti, but the man himself had slipped away while we were busy watching Mother work her miracles at the control bench. At the top of the iron stairs, the door into the hotel hung half open.

Nipper's eye-stalks drooped in shame. 'It is my fault,' he confessed. 'I did not like to see him bound up so tightly, so I just loosened the knots a tad to preserve him from the pins-and-needles . . .'

'And he has repaid your kindness by sneaking off,' said Mother, patting the good crab's shell.

'We must find him!' I said. 'Who knows what mischief he may be planning?'

Mother looked doubtful. 'Very well, Art,' she said, 'but do be careful . . .'

I ran back upstairs with Nipper and Ssil and the Twins. Mother stayed behind, for she dared not leave the Shaper machine unattended when it was operating. Mr Spinnaker stayed with her in case Sir Launcelot should return.

I suppose Sir Launcelot had had plenty of time to think while we were busy dealing with the Moobs, and he had realised that as soon as we returned to the year 1851 he would be handed over to the authorities, who would probably hang him for a traitor. At any rate, he must have decided to make a dash for the railway station, in the hope that he might leave Starcross as soon as Mother restored it to our own time. He was haring across the lobby when we sighted him, blundering into potted palms and side-tables as he struggled against the giddying sensations of our Chronic journey.

'Stop!' I shouted, stumbling a little myself.

Sir Launcelot glanced back at me, and threw himself at the glass front doors, which opened before him so that he went tumbling down the steps.

'What's afoot?' cried Colonel Quivering, appearing from the direction of the wine cellars clutching several bottles of fine vintage port.

'It's Sir Launcelot!' I explained.

'He's essscaping!' added Ssil.

All together we rushed out on to the steps. Sir Launcelot's tumble had done him no harm, and he sat on the promenade with the contents of his coat pockets scattered all about him, looking up at the stars. I looked up, too. The whirl of the Milky Way was slowing, and I realised with a start that our journey was ending – though why the return trip was so much faster than the outward one, I cannot say. The familiar stars and asteroids hung above Starcross's bone-dry beaches again, and with one last wave of dizziness we were back in 1851.

'Now then, Sprigg,' said Colonel Quivering, taking charge. 'You come with us!'

Sir Launcelot stood up shakily, looking jolly cross that his escape attempt had failed. But as he was about to start back up the steps to us, we all became aware of a strange sound coming from the sky above the railway terminus. A star moved there, and grew bigger, and was not a star at all, but a glitter of starlight on space-frosted planking and ancient iron. With a whoosh, a rush, a rising rumble the ship soared over us, circling the hotel once before crashing down upon

the promenade not far from where the *Sophronia* lay. She
landed with such a wallop that whole sections of her
battered hull were burst asunder, and all of us who
stood watching ducked and shielded our faces from
a shower of splintered planks and rusty nails
which came raining down upon the steps and on
the striped canopy above the hotel entrance.

When the sound of falling debris had faded
and we dared to look again, the ancient ship lay
still, careened over on her larboard gunports in
a pall of alchemical steams. Shattered though
she was, there was no mistaking her.

'It's the *Liberty*!' I shouted. 'It's
Jack! Huzzah!'

We all went
running down
the steps, as
from holes and
hatches in the
Liberty's hull her crew
came scrambling. Sir
Launcelot stood looking
most pitifully perplexed as

we dashed past him to greet our friends. For there was Jack, limping on his injured leg, but looking otherwise unharmed, and reaching back to lend a hand to Myrtle, who looked perfectly appalling, of course, in the ruins of her patent Nereid, but whom I felt jolly pleased to see anyway. Can you imagine the relief we felt as we realised that the *Liberty* had not been destroyed after all by that shot from Grindle's gun, and that far from being lost upon the aether Jack and Myrtle had managed somehow to steer her here to find us?

And yet, as we drew close, I could not help noticing that Jack and Myrtle wore worried and preoccupied expressions, and that even our friendly Moob, which fluttered in the air above my sister like a black banner, seemed ill at ease and kept writhing its little hands together in a most troubled way. And as we came closer still, and Myrtle called out my name and ran to embrace me, I saw the reason for their unhappiness. For those Threls, whose services I had purchased for Britain with the promise of wool, had clearly switched sides again after I was dragged from the *Liberty*'s hull, and now had their toy-like carbines pointed at Jack and Myrtle, and at the rest of us!

And last to emerge from the old ship, looking quite radiant in the moment of her triumph, and armed with two revolvers, was Delphine Beauregard!

Chapter Twenty-Two

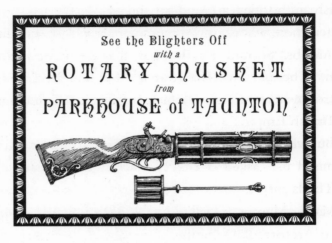

See the Blighters Off
with a
ROTARY MUSKET
from
PARKHOUSE of TAUNTON

IN WHICH WE CONFRONT AN ADVERSARY EVERY BIT AS
BEASTLY AS THE MOOBS, THOUGH SOMEWHAT LESS LIKE
A HAT.

I shall say this for the French; they do not give up easily. When that broadside from the *Sophronia* sent the *Liberty* tumbling, Jack Havock had been stunned by a flying splinter, and Delphine had seen her chance. Leaping to the helm, she steadied the stricken ship, and helped Myrtle and the Moob to repair the damaged wedding chamber. Then she addressed her Threls, pointing out that since there was now no hope of catching up with the *Sophronia*, and the British authorities at Modesty had been alerted to the danger, there was no more cause for them to worry about the Moobs. 'So return with me to Starcross,' she had told them. 'There, I shall insist that Mrs Mumby gives me control over her machine, which I shall use to utterly undo the British Empire!'

'But what about all that nice wool young Master Mumby promised us?' asked one of the Threls suspiciously.

'Master Mumby is lost in space,' retorted Delphine, 'and his promise perished with him. Not that the promise of an Englishman is worth much anyway.* Join with me again and I shall see to it that you have all the wool you need. Not only will France give you

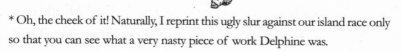

---

* Oh, the cheek of it! Naturally, I reprint this ugly slur against our island race only so that you can see what a very nasty piece of work Delphine was.

flocks of sheep – infinitely superior breeds to the threadbare British varieties, incidentally – but I shall use the Starcross machine to go back in time, and establish those flocks on pre-historic Threlfall. Think how your history will be altered then! What a fine, thick World Cosy will warm the toes of all Threls! What a fortune your woollen stuffs will make for you, and how widely your knitting skills will be praised among all the worlds of the Sun!'

Well, you can hardly blame the poor Threls, I suppose, for letting themselves be swayed by such an offer. By the time Jack regained consciousness the *Liberty* was back under Delphine's command, and Myrtle and her Moob were driving her towards Starcross as fast as her battered engines would carry her.*

'And now we are here!' said Delphine brightly, jumping from the *Liberty*'s hatchway and marching towards the hotel, her Threllish hirelings at her heel, herding the rest of us ahead of them like sheep. 'I was alarmed when we first arrived, for I could see no sign of the hotel, the pier or

---

* Poor Myrtle could do nothing else for fear that Delphine would harm Jack, and she had spent so long with the Moob upon her head that she looked quite pale when she arrived at Starcross. As for the Moob, it had grown somewhat Prim, and had taken to flinching whenever the Threls used colourful language.

anything, but then it popped back into being . . . You have been visiting the past again, I take it?'

'We have been in the future,' I said, 'where we sorted out all our difficulties with the Moobs.'

'Excellent!' cried Delphine. 'I had wondered what we should do about those creatures. Now I shall not have to worry. Nothing stands between me and the machine!'

'Mother does,' I objected. 'She will never let you control it, any more than she would let Sir Launcelot.'

Sir Launcelot, who had been gathered up by the Threls along with all the rest of us, snorted dismissively. 'The Mumby woman would do anything to protect her brats,' he told Delphine. 'And you have both of them!'

So there I was, back to being a hostage or bargaining chip again, after all! Delphine smiled at the nefarious knight and said, 'Thank you, Sir Sprigg. May I take it that you are on my side in this matter?'

'I'm against the Mumby woman and that black hooligan Havock and all their unearthly pets and hangers-on, if that's what you mean,' huffed Sir Launcelot.

'Not quite,' said Delphine, 'but I think we may be able to form a useful alliance . . .' And she signalled for one of the Threls to pass the beastly fellow a gun before they herded us all back through the hotel and down into the boiler room.

'Good Lord!' cried Mr Spinnaker, looking up at us all as we trooped down the iron stairs. He reached out to tug at the sleeve of Mother, who was busy at the control desk with her back to us.

'Silence!' shouted Delphine. 'This hotel is now under the control of the French Empire!' And she had her Threls thrust us all into the middle of the cavern, and stand watch over us with their carbines.

'Hello, Delphine,' said Mother, turning from her work. 'Oh, Myrtle, Jack; I am so pleased to see you well!'

'You may save your pleasantries for later,' snapped the young

Frenchwoman. 'I understand that you have just conveyed this hotel into the distant future, and restored her safely to the present. So I don't imagine it will cause you too much trouble to take us on another little journey. I wish to be conveyed to the year 1801.'

'Why?' asked several of us, but I could guess. 1801 – the year that Wild Will Melville first launched his USSS *Liberty* to prey on innocent British shipping! I could imagine the plot that had formed itself in Delphine's beastly brain. She meant to travel back so that she could join forces with her Yankee grandfather. Starcross would become his base; the *Sophronia* would be added to his rebel navy, and perhaps, with Mother's time engine at his disposal, he would finally achieve what he had set out to all those years ago: the overthrow of the British Empire!

'You absolute . . .' I started to say, but I could not think of any term of abuse one may properly hurl at a young lady, so I stopped.*

'I imagine there may be all sorts of complications and paradoxes involved in meeting one's own grandfather,' said

---

* I discovered later that Messrs Gargany and Stringg also publish a wall chart called *101 Terms of Abuse Which May Properly Be Hurled at Young Ladies*. How I wish that I had had a copy about me!

Mother cautiously.

Delphine paused a moment to consider this. Jack saw his chance. He knew those Threls well enough to understand that, for all their talk of favouring France, they were good fellows really and would hesitate to shoot him. So he flung himself at Delphine, reaching out to wrest the pistol from her hand. And he would have done it, too, except that his injured leg slowed him, and that he had forgotten Sir Launcelot.

Maybe it was by some strange influence of Mother's time engine, or maybe it was just my own impression, but everything seemed to happen with an awful slowness. I saw Delphine turn as Jack hurtled towards her; I saw Sir Launcelot grin as he swung his pistol at Jack, and the way that it jumped in his fat fist when he pulled the trigger. I saw the muzzle spew smoke and sparks and smouldery lumps of wadding. And I saw Jack arrested in mid-leap; bowled backwards, head over heels like a woeful acrobat, with a red buttonhole of blood blooming on his jacket!

He crashed to the floor. Myrtle swooned. Ssilissa ran to him, crying, 'Jack! Jack!' Delphine shouted for Sir Launcelot to hold his fire, and stood trembling, with her own pistol still in her hand and her Threls all scowling and tut-tutting and pointing their carbines from one to another of us, as if to assure their mistress that they would certainly have shot Jack down themselves had not Sir Launcelot Sprigg beaten them to it.

'Ow,' said Jack Havock, lying helpless on the floor while Ssil tore his shirt open and tried to staunch the blood that flowed so redly from the wound beneath his collar bone. Poor Jack – he had already been a snack for a pre-historic sand clam, and now he had been shot as well! I suppose that type of thing is all in a day's work for a bold young adventurer, but it still seemed awfully bad luck.

'Silence!' cried Delphine again. 'Now do as I say, Mrs Mumby, or I shall destroy a few more of your pets!'

Mother, with a look of infinite sadness, turned back to her machine, made a few last adjustments, then stepped away. 'The time engine is set to return to 1801,' she said. 'But I will not be the one who takes you there. It can only lead you into danger and disaster, and if you wish that upon yourself, Delphine, then it must be by your own hand.' She pointed to one of the levers on the machine.

'What sort of danger?' asked Sir Launcelot warily. 'What sort of disaster, eh? It's a trick, Miss Beauregard! You can't trust her, you know! She ain't human!'

'It's a trick, all right,' said Delphine, with a sneer. 'She hopes to scare us with these prophecies of doom, and stop me from doing what I came here for!'

She ran to the machine, and Sir Launcelot went with her, probably hoping that he might trick her himself and gain control of it at last. Delphine smiled as her slender hand grasped the lever which would launch her on to the Seas of Time again. 'Into Posterity!' she cried.

She pulled the lever, and once more that awful dizziness swept over us. And yet it felt different somehow. There was no sense this time of motion; nothing but a fan or cone of bluish light which spilled from some high nubbin of the old machine and illuminated Delphine and Sir Launcelot where they stood at the controls. I saw them exchange surprised glances, and make as if to step out of that shaft of brightness, but the light was changing, hardening, growing silvery and opaque, until it hid them from us, like a cone of mercury, or the bell of some enormous trumpet placed mouth downwards on the floor.

'Mother! What is happening to them?' Myrtle cried.

Mother was helping Ssil to bandage Jack's wound. In the light of that silvery apparition her face looked old and chilly as some ancient statue's. She said, 'I made a minor alteration to the machine. I believe it is what vulgar people would call "a booby trap". It is working splendidly, don't you think?'

'But what is it *doing* to them?' cried Colonel Quivering.

The surface of the

silver cone swirled with stormy patterns, and began to grow transparent again. It took on a reddish tinge, then, no longer a cone, just a shaft of light, fading quickly, withdrawing into whatever secret projector had created it. Where Delphine and Sir Launcelot had stood, only their clothes remained: Delphine's dress, blue-black as space, with the necklace of amber beads about its collar, and Sir Launcelot's evening suit, with yellowish sweat stains visible inside the stiff round of his empty collar. The villains' weapons clattered to the floor, and the clothes crumpled on top of them with crisp, starchy, settling sounds.

'Oh Lord!' murmured Mr Spinnaker.

'Sssss!' exclaimed Ssil.

'Long live the Queen!' declared the Threls, sensing which way the wind was blowing and hastily changing sides again.

'Moob!' said the Moob.

'Mother!' I gasped. I was deeply shocked at her cold-bloodedness, for I felt certain that Delphine and her accomplice were no more, and that Mother in her infinite power had crushed them as carelessly as you or I might crush an ant. 'You have vaporised them!' I declared.

'Oh, Art, what nonsense!' she replied, tying Jack's bandages. 'As if I would do such a thing! Go and help them, while I look to Jack and your sister.'

I went cautiously towards those heaps of clothes, and Nipper and Grindle came with me. The heaps stirred faintly as we drew near. A strange noise came from within the collapsed tent of Delphine's dress. Sir Launcelot's tail coat moved clumsily across the floor. Something was alive inside those garments, and we all drew back, recalling tales of witches who turned their enemies into toads . . .

And then another little sound came from Delphine's dress, and Ssil, standing behind us, said suddenly, 'Oh, you sssillies!' She pushed us aside and stooped over the dress, and pulled out from within it a tiny, pink, blue-eyed, perfectly human baby girl, which lay in her arms, waving its chubby hands and feet about in the jolliest manner and gurgling up at Ssil's blue face. And Mr Munkulus pulled open Sir Launcelot's shirt (sending studs flying everywhere in his haste) and fetched out a boy baby, just as tiny, who seemed to think his four strong arms a most excellent cradle, and who, after blowing a few bubbles and saying, 'Boogle woggle wiggle,' fell fast asleep.

Myrtle sneezed loudly, which was a result of Mother having raised her up, and waved a pinch of Mr Grindle's snuff under her nose. Her eyes opened. 'Oh!' she said. 'Babies! Where did they come from?'

'We ain't entirely sure,' Mr Grindle confessed.

'They are Delphine Beauregard and Sir Launcelot Sprigg,' Mother said. 'Or rather, they will be. They would insist on being beastly, so rather than setting the machine as Miss Beauregard demanded, I set the time-greenhouse mechanism we used upon the ideospores, only reversing it and taking Delphine and Sir Launcelot back to the age of six months, give or take a day.'

'Aren't they sssweet?' said Ssil, and the Threls gathered round to tickle the babies' feet and say, 'Oo's got pwetty little toesy-woeses, then? Eh?' before remembering where they were, and doing their best to look like fearsome space mercenaries again.

'And Jack?' asked Myrtle anxiously. 'Can we place Jack in this machine, Mother, and let it revert him to a time before that horrid person shot him?'

Mother shook her head. 'Jack's wound will heal well enough in the natural way, given the proper care. Time reversion is a somewhat dangerous procedure. We would not wish to turn Jack into a baby, would we? Or to send him back so far that he vanished altogether?'

'No,' we all said; we would none of us want such a terrible thing, not even Jack, who had a nasty hole in him and would bear the scar of it for ever. Mother gave Nipper strict instructions on how he was to be cared for, placing great emphasis upon cleanliness, and then re-revived Myrtle, who had insisted that *she* should be the one who nursed Jack back to health, but promptly fainted again when she saw all the blood.

Then, returning for one last time to her machine, Mother made a few more adjustments to its controls. 'Stand well back, everybody, please,' she warned us.

We all did as she asked, Nipper carrying Jack with great solicitude, Ssil and Mr Munkulus cradling the sleeping infants. That dizziness came over us all again, so that I had to lean on Nipper for support. Mother hurried over to join us, and we stood and watched as the old Shaper machine performed its uncanny dances.

And then it vanished. One moment it was there, humming and singing and glowing and shifting as gamely as ever a mysterious engine of extraterrestrial design can, and the next it simply wasn't. There was a mild thunderclap, as air rushed in to fill the empty space it had left in the middle of the boiler room. The lace cuffs of Delphine's abandoned dress fluttered in a momentary breeze.

'Where has it gone?' asked Myrtle.

'It is still travelling, back and back through time, to a hundred-million-year-old beach on Mars.'

'And what will it do when it gets there?' I wondered.

'It will destroy itself,' said Mother. 'All Sir Launcelot's tinkerings have left it most unstable, so it was an easy thing to induce a runaway alchemical reaction. It will destroy itself, and the section of Mars on which it stands will be blasted into fragments which will fly far, far out into the aether until one of them becomes part of the asteroid belt. An object known as –'

'– Starcross!' I said.

'Quite so. And with the machine gone, those rifts and frayings in Time's fabric which have troubled this portion of space should all cease.'

I frowned. 'But, Mother,' I observed, 'if the machine is destroyed in the year 100,000,000 BC on Mars, how can it ever have been here? Or at Larklight, in our own time? Will it mean that all our adventures never happened?'

Mother frowned, as if she hadn't thought of that. Myrtle said, '*Some* people are too clever by half.' Jack groaned faintly as he shifted in Nipper's claws and his wound pained him.

'Come,' said Mother, leading the way upstairs. 'I do not usually approve of intoxicating fluids, but I believe poor Jack would benefit from a good, stiff brandy. And we must mash up some bread and milk for Delphine and Sir Launcelot.'

On a lonely stretch of Martian beach, ever so many centuries before the birth of Christ, a number of ugly, transparent animals were squabbling over the carcass of a giant land starfish, which had been lately exploded by a maritime distress flare. A sudden vibration made them pause, tasting the air with their horrible feelers. They had no

eyes, and so could not see the curious old machine which had appeared quite suddenly a little further along the curve of the bay. They had no ears, so could not hear the sound that came from within those massive galleries of ducts and whirligigs: *Tick* . . .

Tick . . .

Tick . . .

Tick . . .

The explosion, according to learned gents who wander the Red Planet in sennet hats and gaiters, studying rocks and fossil sand clams, tore a crater the size of several asteroids in Mars's flank, and ripped a swathe of the planet's atmosphere out into the aether, so ending the age of the great starfish in a most dreadful cataclysm.

But Mother says the great starfish were on their way out anyway and would never have amounted to very much. *She* says the explosion merely cleared the way for other forms of life to thrive and flourish, including some which would grow eventually into the Martians we know today. *She* says 'tis an ill wind that blows nobody any good.

And, let's face it, she should know.

Chapter the Last

A few days later we were sitting outside the beach cafe on Starcross promenade, well wrapped up against the chills of space, watching the starlight play upon the *Sophronia*'s rigging and upon the hulk of the USSS *Liberty*. Our friend the Moob had just settled for a spell on Mother's head, and was using her voice to explain that it was not unhappy at being left behind when the other Moobs returned to their own time, as it had conceived an affection for the modern era and looked forward to exploring it more thoroughly. And Mr Spinnaker was suggesting that it might like to accompany himself and Mrs S. on their forthcoming tour of the music halls of Mercury, for it had occurred to him that if it did not mind disguising itself as a top hat again they might work up together quite a nice act in the Conjuring and Mind-Reading line.

'Listen!' said Mr Grindle suddenly, pricking up his ears. 'A train! A train!'

It took a few seconds more till we could hear it, but he was right. With a long *Whoo-Whooooo!* a train came thundering across the heavens and swept down the long incline to Starcross Halt. Not just any old train, either, but an armoured train of the British Space Grenadiers, its engine sheathed in a steel cowl like the helmet of a mediaeval knight, its steel-cased carriages fairly bristling with guns and phlogiston agitators, and the Union flag fluttering from its guard's van.

It screeched into the station amid spreading clouds of steam, and out from hatches all along its length came pouring brave British soldiers, stomping along in their fighting machines, or perched on the saddles of mechanised cannon. They surged towards us in a veritable tide of shining gun-metal and scarlet cotton drill, and when they had quite surrounded the tables where we sat their ranks opened and a large figure wearing a fanciful military costume of her own design burst through, crying, 'Oh, my dears! We are so 'appy to find you safe and well, and not a top 'at in sight!'

'Your ordeal is over!' announced a splendid major, appearing behind Mrs Spinnaker, mounted on a roan thoroughbred. 'Now, where are those accursed Moobs?'

'How sweetly kind of you to come!' said Mother. 'And so well turned out! But I'm afraid you are too late.'

'Eh?' said the splendid major, looking on in alarm as the Moob slipped from her head and arranged itself around her shoulders as a stole. 'Well, it's no simple matter to prepare an armoured space train; there are orders to write, requisition forms to be sent in, dockets and suchlike . . .'

'Major,' said Colonel Quivering, his brisk military tones

causing the splendid fellow to spring to attention and salute. 'There is not a single Moob in Starcross, with the exception of that fellow wrapped around Mrs Mumby, who is a friend of ours and has done great service to the Empire. All other Moobs live many millions of centuries from now, and they are very happy there.'

'Oh,' said the major, looking crestfallen. 'Oh. Well. Better give the place a look-over, just in case ... Come along, chaps!'

He set off towards the hotel, with his troops behind him, moving with a speed and discipline which did credit to the British Army.

Mrs Spinnaker had been busy meanwhile enjoying a most touching reunion with Mr Spinnaker, but she extricated herself at last and sat down to ask us all, 'So what's been happening? The tide's out, I see.'

'I'm afraid the tide's gone out for good,' said Mother. 'Starcross no longer jumps to and fro in time.'

'That'll be bad for the hotel business,' observed Mrs Spinnaker. 'Pity, for it's a nice old place. What do you say we make old Sir Launcelot an offer for it, 'Erbert, my angel?'

'I say that's a capital idea, Rosie, my petal,' replied her husband. 'It'll make a pleasant sort of weekend-home, for when we're not performing.'

'I'm afraid Sir Launcelot is not here to accept your offer,' said Mother. 'He has Mysteriously Vanished, along with Miss Beauregard. It is rather a tragedy, but at least neither of them left any family behind to mourn them. Indeed, I suspect they were both widely disliked, and will not be missed at all.'

She was about to say more, but at that moment a wail from the far side of the table drew Mrs Spinnaker's attention to Mr Munkulus, who was cradling a baby in each pair of arms.

'Oh, what perfect angels!' she cried, clapping her hands together. 'Ain't they perfect angels, 'Erbert?' (And Mr Spinnaker muttered, yes, indeed, they were very charming little monkeys.)

'There's some as might call 'em angelic,' said Mr Grindle wearily, 'but there's others as have been kept up nights listening to their bellyaching and complaining, and wonders as whether they won't turn out just as bad this time around as last.'

'Oh, what a dreadful thing to sssay!' Ssil chided him. 'I'm quite sure that with a proper upbringing, in a loving home . . .'

'That's it exactly,' said Grindle, beating his hand upon the table for emphasis. 'A home's what they need. An old aether-ship like the *Sophronia*'s no place for babies.'

Yarg and Squidley, very tired of having their tentacles tugged by tiny hands, whistled their agreement.

'They are orphans, you see,' said Nipper, looking nervously at our guests.

'Foundlings,' Mr Munkulus agreed.

'Oh!' cried Mrs Spinnaker. 'Oh, 'Erbert, don't you think . . . ? Might we – ? Mayn't we – ?'

'What Mrs Spinnaker is trying to express,' said her husband gruffly, 'is that if these infants are in need of a home, then we should be very honoured, and indeed chuffed, was they to come and live with us. For despite Rosie's triumphs upon the stage, it has long been a source of regret to us that we have no children of our own.'

'That sounds a most sensible idea,' said Mother, helping to support the infants as Mr Munkulus, looking somewhat relieved, handed them into the care of their new foster parents. 'I am sure you will make a much better job of bringing them up than their own families did – I mean, would have done.'

'What are their names?' asked Mrs S., looking with a

most rapt expression from one tiny, gurgling face to the other.

'Delphine and Sir L—' Nipper started to say, but the Tentacle Twins wrapped their arms about his shell and muffled the rest.

'Their names?' said Mother thoughtfully. 'Their names, of course, are Modesty and Decorum.'

And while all this is discussed, and the conversation turns to cribs and perambulators and nannies, and the contrite Threls present the proud new parents with the tiny booties and bonnets which they have been knitting by way of practice as they wait for the *Sophronia*'s captain to be well enough to carry them back to Threlfall, where they may get on with their World Cosy; while all this is happening, Jack Havock is sitting with my sister on the sand below the promenade, at a point where, one hundred million years ago, the sea might have lapped in gentle waves.

'Jack,' asks Myrtle, carefully, for fear the faintest hint of boldness might make his wounds begin to hurt again, 'you never did tell me, when we were on Mars and aboard the *Liberty*, why you did not answer my letters?'

Jack looks awkwardly away across the dried-out sea, towards the knoll which was an island once (where some of the Threls are helping Professor Ferny to dig up two trees, and carry them back towards the waiting train, with the intellectual shrub hurrying beside them, calling out, 'Take care! Mind their roots! I am quite certain that I can effect a cure, if only we can get them safely to my laboratory at Kew!'). And then he says, 'Thing is, Myrtle, we're not meant for each other, are we, me and you?'

'It is "you and I", Jack, dear. But I cannot see what makes you say so. Surely you know that I . . . that I . . .'

'What I can see,' says Jack, 'is that you're a young lady. A pretty, clever, elegant young lady. And a rough old aether-ship, cruising on Her Majesty's service out in the nether end of nowhere, ain't the place for you.'

'There is Another, isn't there?' declares Myrtle, commencing to sniffle piteously. 'Some other young woman has claimed your heart; someone ever so much more brave and dashing than I. Oh, I cannot hate you for it, Jack, dearest. I wish you joy. Though I do hope she has only the conventional number of heads and arms and so forth . . .'

'Hush, hush, hush,' Jack has been saying with no effect at all throughout the main part of this speech. Now he reaches out and sets a finger to Myrtle's lips, which makes her stop talking so abruptly that she gets hiccups. 'It just ain't the life for you, that's all,' he says. 'You're not suited to being chased by monsters and eaten by clams and shot up by secret agents, and if you were, why, you wouldn't be my Myrtle any more.'

For a moment, misery and anger struggle for control of Myrtle's phiz, and then, as usual, anger wins. She springs to her feet, throwing up a storm of pale sand which falls but slowly in the gentle atmosphere down here upon the beach.

'I declare, Jack Havock,' she declares, stamping her foot, 'I'll show you! Mama has been asking me what I should like to study. Very well; I shall study Alchemy. The Moob said I had a talent for it, didn't he? I shall become the best lady alchemist there is, and when I know all about it I shall come and find you out in the nether end of nowhere, and *then* we shall see who is suited for whom . . .'

At which point I cannot help but let out a stifled snort of laughter, and Myrtle realises that I have overheard all this, concealed under the wheels of a nearby bathing machine.

Things might have gone badly for your hero, for she really was in a most terrible bate when she realised I had listened to all her tender talk with Jack. But the Luck of the Mumby's was on my side, and just as she was dragging me out from under the machine by my stockings, and threatening me with all sorts of torments,* another whistle sounded, and we looked up to see a second train pulling in to Starcross Halt. It was a small passenger train, which must have been shunted into a siding further up the line to let that armoured affair come tearing through, and had now resumed its journey. We all ran back on to the promenade and watched as a number of gentlefolk emerged, who had doubtless expected a seaside holiday at Mr Titfer's hotel,

---

* You would imagine that Myrtle would think it unladylike to be forever kicking, punching and boxing the ears of a mere innocent child, e.g. me. But she says that being beastly to one's younger brother is a genteel sport in which ladies are quite able to participate, like grouse-shooting, or riding to hounds.

and looked most put out to find plenty of side but no sea
whatsoever.

And among them, looking his usual amiable and
bewildered self, with a shrimping net over one shoulder and
a wide straw hat upon his head . . .

'Father!' I cried.

'Father!' cried Myrtle.

'Edward!' cried Mother.

And we ran to him, and he to us, the Mumbys reunited.

'Are you all quite safe?' he asked, as soon as he was able.
'In Modesty they said that dangerous hats may be on the

loose at Starcross. Did they mean "bats", perhaps? Or "gnats"? And wherever is the sea?'

'I'm afraid the asteroid belt will never now be numbered among the truly first-class resorts for sea bathing,' said Mother. 'I think that we should take the next train back and spend the rest of our holiday on Ganymede. I imagine the great sea lilies are just coming into flower there, and we might take a day excursion into the cloud-tops of Jupiter, so that I may introduce you to my old friend Thunderhead.'

She took his arm, and together they turned towards the cafe, with me and Myrtle following.

'But first,' she said, 'I think we should all benefit very much from a nice cup of tea.'

FINIS

*Sober them up and lock them in a suite of rooms for a few weeks
with pens, ink, paper and a good supply of biscuits.*

TWO GENTLEMEN OF DEVONSHIRE

Who are these ragged figures lurching out of the fog that swirls eternally across this dreadful Moor? Their eyes are wide, their hair unkempt, their gait unsteady and their demeanour barely human. Why, 'tis MR REEVE and MR WYATT and they have been to the PUB again. But sober them up and lock them in a suite of rooms for a few weeks with pens, ink, paper and a good supply of biscuits, and they will turn out the neatest illustrated tale of adventure you could ask for.

Mr Reeve is the author of the *Mortal Engines* quartet and *Here Lies Arthur*, as well as the illustrator of many children's books and co-writer of a musical, *The Ministry of Biscuits*.

Mr Wyatt leads a double life as a daring intelligence agent for Her Majesty, and is generally to be found swinging from bamboo bridges in the depths of the Sumatran jungle, or engaging in gondola chases through the canals of Venice. But this has not stopped him from becoming one of the leading illustrators of his generation, and his work has graced the books of Professor Tolkein, Mr Pratchett, Mrs MacCaughrean and many others.

ACKNOWLEDGEMENTS

And where would Mr Reeve and Mr Wyatt be without the guidance and inspiration of their three lovely editrices, Miss Fountain, Miss Szirtes and Mrs Brathwaite? In the soup, that is where, and being pelted with croutons by retired schoolteachers, outraged at their slack grammar and listless cross-hatching.

That lovely ditty 'Dearest Margaret, You Are Danish and Your Dog's Not Very Well' is an ACTUAL SONG and was written by Mr Nick Riddle ('The Cheeky Chappie from Chippenham').

Have you read my first Heroic account of our
Truly Remarkable space adventures?

Hardback edition

Paperback edition

A Rousing Tale
of Dauntless Pluck
in the Farthest
Reaches of Space

It was just another normal morning in space when disaster
struck. My sister Myrtle (who is quite irritating, as girls
generally are) and I faced the most awful peril, and we
hadn't even had breakfast.

A Mr Webster was coming to visit. Visitors to our house were
rare and so a frenzy of preparation ensued, but it was entirely
the wrong sort of preparation, as we discovered when we
opened the door. This is the story of what happened next, and
our Dreadful and Terrifying adventure to save each other
and the known Universe.

And coming soon: MOTH STORM – in which I relate my latest
and most Exceptionally Perilous experiences . . .

A Selection of the Charming Reviews My First Sensational Adventure, *LARKLIGHT*, Received from Some Notable Houses of Journalism – A.M.

'Inspired space adventure.'
SUNDAY TIMES, TOP 5 BOOKS OF THE YEAR

'*Larkkight* is completely engrossing, miss-your-tube-station excellent. The first in a new series by the writer of the popular *Mortal Engines* quartet, it is a brilliantly witty quest set in outer space that will get children turning pages at the speed of light.'
TELEGRAPH

'The rollicking, devil-may-care attitude of the book is an absolute delight. This book will provide enjoyment for all ages, and I long for more from Reeve's pen.'
LITERARY REVIEW

'Reeve's mechanical fantasy world is every bit as enthralling as in his *Mortal Engines*, and Wyatt's illustrations add to the fascination.'
INDEPENDENT

'Satisfying, enjoyable and engaging. Mr Reeve has done it again.'
MR PHILIP ARDAGH, GUARDIAN

'It keeps you gripped all the way through.'
SUNDAY EXPRESS

'Fantasy and history are most entertainingly combined in this ingenious and inventive story of Victorian space travel, "decorated throughout" by David Wyatt.'
THE IRISH TIMES, CHILDREN'S BOOKS OF THE YEAR

'Elegantly contructed, a frothy confection of fanciful imagery and fantastical footnotes.'
GUARDIAN

'*Larklight* is a glorious space adventure set in 1851. Forget what history tells you, and enjoy this laugh-out-loud, old-style page-turner which is coupled with David Wyatt's fantastic illustrations.'
FUNDAY TIMES

'It's a fully illustrated book – pictures by David Wyatt – that harks back to the adventure stories I remember reading as a child. Any fan of fantasy or science will love it.'
MR CHARLIE HIGSON, *MAIL ON SUNDAY*

'Remarkable . . . Out of this world.'
SUNDAY TIMES

'Truly original.'
PUBLISHING NEWS, STARRED CHOICE

'An exhilarating space novel.'
FIRST NEWS

'It's hard to pin down Philip Reeve's prodigious imagination in just a few words. It's Monty Python meets Dan Dare meets *Diary of a Nobody*, and it rattles along, cheekily tangling historical figures in Reeve's brilliant fictional web.'
SUNDAY HERALD

'Imaginative and great fun to read this is a splendidly produced book, complete with end papers advertising Victorian artefacts.'
CAROUSEL magazine